"You can't arrest me, sir," she told him, unmoving. "I didn't break any laws."

"Intent is reason enough for me to take you in for questioning."

She tossed her head and the moonlight shimmered from dark hair, turning her skin to palest ivory, even as her eyes glittered with the reflection of starlight. "Hard up for a woman?" she asked softly.

"Now that you mention it," he returned quietly, "I am…a little."

"There's no *little* about it," she countered, "Either you're on the prowl for a handy female, or you're not." Her chin lifted, a challenge he'd not thought to hear spewing from her lips.

"If you touch me, I swear I'll kill you, Mr. Lawman. You can toss me in your jail cell if you like, but you better have a damn good reason for doing it."

She was either a very brave woman or totally without good sense…!

* * *

Texas Lawman
Harlequin Historical #736—January 2005

Acclaim for Carolyn Davidson's recent titles

The Marriage Agreement
"Davidson uses her considerable skills to fashion a
plausible, first-class marriage-of-convenience romance."
—*Romantic Times*

Texas Gold
"Davidson delivers a story fraught with sexual tension."
—*Romantic Times*

A Marriage by Chance
"This deftly written novel about loss and recovery
is a skillful handling of the traditional Western,
with the added elements of family conflict
and a moving love story."
—*Romantic Times*

The Tender Stranger
"Davidson wonderfully captures gentleness in
the midst of heart-wrenching challenges, portraying
the extraordinary possibilities that exist within
ordinary marital love."
—*Publishers Weekly*

CAROLYN DAVIDSON

TEXAS
Lawman

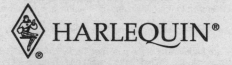
HARLEQUIN®

TORONTO • NEW YORK • LONDON
AMSTERDAM • PARIS • SYDNEY • HAMBURG
STOCKHOLM • ATHENS • TOKYO • MILAN • MADRID
PRAGUE • WARSAW • BUDAPEST • AUCKLAND

ISBN 0-373-29336-4

TEXAS LAWMAN

Copyright © 2005 by Carolyn Davidson

Please address questions and book requests to:
Harlequin Reader Service
U.S.: 3010 Walden Ave., P.O. Box 1325, Buffalo, NY 14269
Canadian: P.O. Box 609, Fort Erie, Ont. L2A 5X3

To Erin and Bob Bittner, two of the lawmen of this day and age, who also happen to be very near and dear to my heart—this book is dedicated. May you find happiness together as you begin your walk through life as man and wife, and may God's face shine upon you in all the years to come.

And to Mr. Ed, manager and husband of the year—every year—who loves me.

Chapter One

Benning, Texas
April 10, 1901

He drew his gun and lifted it before him, sighting down the barrel to where his prey stood beneath a tree, in a gladed area on the northern side of town. Revealed in the moonlight by a stray break in the clouds overhead, the figure was unmoving, a pale shirt and dark trousers fitting the slender form like a glove.

The flow of dark hair gave away her gender. That, and the narrow waist that was belted snugly, emphasizing the rounded hips that filled a pair of trousers almost to bursting.

"I can see your badge. Go ahead and shoot, Sheriff," she said quietly, the sound carrying to where he stood. "Shall I step forward and give you a better target?"

Brace Caulfield lowered his gun. *"Damn."* The single word was uttered in disgust—the vehemence aimed at himself as he stuffed his weapon into the holster that was tied to his thigh. "Walk over here, lady," he said harshly. "You pret' near got yourself shot just now."

The woman obeyed slowly. Perhaps, he decided, to prove to him that it was her choice alone that prompted her movements. Stepping carefully over the hillocks in the clearing, glancing down at where she walked, she approached him and then halted, not quite within his reach.

"Who are you?" His voice was strong, the tones strident, for the mere seconds during which he'd sighted her down the length of his gun barrel had shaken his composure. Never had his weapon been aimed at a woman, and his anger rose against the female who had caused him to do so.

"You don't need to know," she said quietly. "I won't be here any longer than it takes to round up my horse and climb on."

"What were you doing in town scouting out the back door of the hotel?" he asked.

He'd seen her there first—just a glimpse of a man, he'd thought—wearing a light-colored shirt. Now he recognized that the pale fabric held the lush curves of a woman's bosom. A woman full grown. Not the youthful creature he'd thought her to be when he'd taken her measure for the second time, just moments since.

"Nothing illegal," she answered. "I was looking for someone."

"Most folks use the front door," he said bluntly. "You have a problem with that?"

"The man I was watching for didn't want to be seen. I knew if he left the hotel it would be from the rear entrance."

He propped his hand against his hip, just above the gun that weighed heavily against his leg. His eyes narrowed as he listened to her explanation, and his tone was rasping as he spoke. "You were looking for a man."

It was a statement of fact and she merely shrugged, not prone, it seemed, to offer any more information than she already had.

"Who?" he asked, his voice quieter now, the sound somehow more threatening.

"I'm not sure you need to know that," she said. "If you're going to shoot me, go ahead. Otherwise, you have no reason to stop me from mounting my horse and leaving town."

"You left your animal behind when you ran off," he pointed out, one long finger tipping his hat back a bit. And then that finger pointed to his right, where lights glowed from a string of establishments along the street that centered town. "He's tied to a hitching rail in front of the general store."

She bit at her lip, looking in the direction he pointed. "Who did that?"

"My deputy. I figured you'd be back to get the mare, and Jamie's keeping an eye out, waiting for you to show up."

She turned abruptly and stalked away. "Well, I wouldn't want to disappoint him, would I?"

He kept pace with her, allowing her to stride in front of him, wondering why he hadn't recognized immediately that the slender form he'd followed between buildings and behind the newspaper office, almost to the woods, was not a man at all. He was certainly having no problem now sorting out the difference between her womanly form and that of a male.

She walked down the sidewalk beside the dark stores, past the saloon where music and loud voices carried over and under the swinging doors to clash in a raucous symphony of sound. The general store was dark, the proprietor gone for the night, and in front of his establishment stood a mare, saddled and ready to ride.

"Did you find the man?" Brace asked the woman as she stepped down to release her mare from the hitching rail.

She turned to face him, reins in her hand. "No. If I had, you'd have heard a gunshot, Sheriff. I'd have killed him." With a quick move she was in the saddle, and Brace took a long stride toward her, reaching for her reins.

"Whoa, lady. You can't make a statement like that and then just ride away."

"You can't arrest me, sir," she told him, unmoving, as if she would not put her mare's mouth in jeopardy by fighting for the reins he held. "I didn't break any laws."

"Intent is reason enough for me to take you in for questioning."

She tossed her head, and the moonlight shimmered from dark hair, turning her skin to palest ivory, even as her eyes glittered with the reflection of starlight. "Hard up for a woman?" she asked softly.

"Now that you mention it," he returned quietly, "I am…a little."

"There's no *little* about it," she countered. "Either you're on the prowl for a handy female, or you're not." Her chin rose, and a challenge he'd not thought to hear spewed from her lips. "If you touch me, I swear I'll kill you, Mr. Lawman. You can toss me in your jail cell if you like, but you'd better have a damn good reason for doing it."

Her eyes were wide and unblinking as she faced him down, and he felt unbidden admiration for the courage she displayed. She was either a very brave woman or totally without good sense, defying a lawman with the ability to put her in a cell and throw away the key. Not that he was likely to do such a thing, but the temptation was there.

For if he placed her in custody, he'd have a chance to find out something about her—he'd have a day or so, perhaps, to dig deep into her reasons for being in Benning, Texas.

"I can't allow a woman to go riding off alone in the dark without someone to look after her," he said bluntly. "Unless you're willing to tell me who you are and what's going on here, I can't let you leave. Your gentleman friend may very well be watching us even now, just waiting for a chance to snatch you up."

She laughed, a bitter sound, and shook her head. "He won't be coming near me. He doesn't know I'm here. I've been following him for the past two weeks, and when I saw him ride into Benning this morning I followed. He left his horse at the livery stable and went into the hotel before noon. I've been watching ever since."

"I didn't see you," Brace said. "And I pretty much know everything that goes on in this town."

"If I don't want to be seen, I can always find a hole to crawl into," she told him. "I'm not afraid to be on my own, and I don't want to take a chance on Les—" She inhaled sharply.

"Is that his name?" Brace asked. "Les?" He frowned consideringly. "Hmm, doesn't ring a bell with me. A stranger in town, you say?"

She glared at him, obviously angry with herself for giving away even that small bit of information. Her lips thinned, as if she would deny another word passage between them, and he shrugged as if he were baffled by her silence.

He reached up, gripping her elbow, catching her off balance. She jerked back, but to no avail. Brace Caulfield was a tall man, strong and well muscled, and a woman, no matter how tough she pretended to be, stood little chance of escaping his hold.

"You want to get down off that mare by yourself," he asked, "or shall I help you?"

"Damn you," she snarled. "I haven't done anything wrong."

"Maybe not," he said agreeably. "But I have a feeling that you'll be safer with me than riding out of town at this time of night." His grip on her arm tightened a bit and she shot him a look of pure venom, her face illuminated by the full moon that played hide-and-seek with drifting clouds overhead.

With ease she slid from her saddle and stood before him. "Now are you satisfied?" she asked.

"Not by a long shot, lady," he murmured, and then watched as his deputy joined them in the middle of the street.

"I figured when I saw you trailin' her you didn't need me standin' guard over that mare," Jamie said, his attention fully on the female who stood between the two men.

"Well, you can come in handy right now," Brace told him, handing him the reins and nodding toward the livery stable just down the street from the jailhouse.

The deputy led the mare away, and the woman watched as her horse disappeared inside the open door of the livery. "Come on inside," Brace told her, then watched as the woman reluctantly crossed the threshold into the small office.

"Sit down," he said, leading her to a chair and applying a bit of pressure to insure she obeyed his order. He reached to the lantern that hung over his desk and, scratching a match against his rear pocket, he lit the lamp, his eyes narrowing against the glare. Then, leaning against the edge of the desk, he removed his hat, placing it behind him in an automatic gesture. "Now talk," he told her. "Your name first, if you please."

She set her jaw stubbornly, and her glare was filled with defiance. "Sarah Murphy," she said flatly. "Now can I leave?"

"Why are you on this fella's trail, Miss Murphy?" Brace asked quietly, ignoring her query. She was mute, her lips tightly pressed together, and he watched her patiently, knowing that he could outlast any woman in the world when it came to remaining silent.

Her shoulders slumped a bit, but with a visible effort she lifted her head, meeting his gaze head-on. "He's a monster, of the very worst kind."

"What did he do?" Brace asked, careful not to raise his voice. Gentle probing might work best with a wary woman, he thought.

Sarah's face became a mask of despair as he watched, and the words she spoke seemed to come from some bitter well within her. "He was married to my sister. They had a child, a boy. And then Sierra died and her *beloved* husband took off with the child."

"What happened to your sister?"

His worst fears were confirmed as Sarah Murphy lifted a bleak gaze in his direction, and her words verified his thoughts.

"She was strangled, just over two months ago. By a stranger, according to Les. Someone who broke in to the house and attacked Sierra."

"And you don't believe that?" Brace asked quietly, prepared for the shake of her head, the scornful line of her lips as she denied his query.

"He'd threatened her before. When Les drinks he's a demon, mean and hateful. Even sober, he's got a cruel streak a mile wide."

"Why didn't the law stop him?" It seemed like a logical question to Brace, knowing how his own office would react to a woman's death.

"A woman like my sister doesn't get a lot of consideration in a town like Big Rapids, Missouri," Sarah said. "I'd think you'd know that in many places women are at the bottom of the list, and the town we lived in isn't much different. She was just an ordinary female who made some wrong choices in life." Her mouth twisted in distaste. "The first of which was marrying Lester Clark."

"So you followed him to Benning, Texas." Even to his own ears, his voice sounded unbelieving. "Why on earth would he leave Missouri and come to a place like Benning, Texas?"

"I think his people are from the west side of the state. Other than that, I have no idea. I just followed him." She looked down for a moment, and Brace wondered if she was fighting tears. Her shoulders hunched a bit, then straightened with obvious effort, and she lifted her chin and met his eyes with a gaze that glittered. "Les has my nephew. I want Stephen back."

Brace considered that idea, recognizing her impassioned plea as that of a woman allowing her emotions to take the reins. "If this man has the child with him, I'd say he has a perfect right to him. Being his father gives him that, legally."

"Even if that man killed my sister?" Her voice was

choked with tears as she spoke the question, and he hesitated to reply, knowing she would resent his answer.

"You have no proof of that, do you?" Before she could respond, he held up a hand and continued. "If the law thought there was any chance of such a thing, they'd have been on his trail faster'n you could—well, pretty damn quick," he said, altering his reply for female company.

"Men always believe other men." She spit the words at him and he heard the unspoken message. She'd been shunted aside, given short shrift by the lawmen in question. And perhaps with good reason. Then again, she seemed like an intelligent female. Maybe there was more to this than was visible on the surface.

"And you have no idea why he came here?" Brace asked.

She shook her head, and once more her hair shifted with the movement, seeming almost alive, with waves falling upon her shoulders and back. Enough to distract a man, Brace decided, unable to conceal the admiring glance he turned upon her. She was young, not looking to be more than twenty—too young for a man like him to be considering.

Her eyes were in shadow and he bent toward her, lifting her chin a bit, the better to see the blue depths. With a sharp movement she twisted her head, effectively removing his hand from her skin. He allowed it without an argument. He'd seen the moment of panic she'd attempted to hide, noted the automatic withdrawal from his touch.

Straightening slowly, he watched her, willing her to shift in the chair, waiting for the long moments of silence to have an effect. And waited in vain.

Sarah Murphy would no doubt make a good hunter,

possessing the ability to remain still and in one position for however long it might take for a deer to leave its hiding place and meander across her path. Brace could almost envision such a scene, and then he smiled at his fanciful thoughts.

"You think this is humorous?" she asked. "You're enjoying keeping me here?" Her chin tilted again, this time at her own volition, and her gaze touched his with a stony glare. "If Les is leaving town while you stand there leaning on your desk, it won't make much of a difference. I'll still find him, no matter where he goes."

Brace shook his head. "Not tonight, you won't." He reached behind him, opened the desk drawer and removed a ring of keys. They jangled at his touch, and he palmed them, then stood erect. "You need to use the necessary before I put you in a cell?" he asked politely. "There's one out back."

He watched the blush climb her cheeks, painting her throat and then suffusing her face with color. "You're determined not to leave me any self-respect, aren't you?" Her jaw clenched, and again her hair caught the light as she tossed her head defiantly.

"I'd think you'd rather use the outdoor facility than the slop pail in your cell," he said reasonably. "Up to you."

"What's the charge against me?" she asked, obviously reluctant to accompany him to a cell.

"Vagrancy, for now," he told her. "I'll decide in the morning if I need to jail you for threatening to murder a man. All depends on how the night goes."

"How the night goes? What is that supposed to mean?" Her face lost its rosy hue quickly as she responded to his statement. Then she rose with care, as if her legs required a bit of coaxing in order to hold her upright. "Lead the way, Sheriff," she said.

"First, let's see if you're wearing a weapon," he said mildly. "If you were planning on shooting a man, chances are you have access to a gun." He cast a measuring glance at her and couldn't resist a smile. "Can't see where you're hidin' it, though. Those pants fit you like a glove."

"Are you going to search me?" she asked. "Shall I empty my pockets?"

"Are you armed?" he returned, taking one long step, looking down at her from closer range.

She shook her head. "No. I have a gun in my saddlebag." And then she shrugged. "Unless you count the knife in my pocket, I'm not much of a threat to you."

"Let's have the knife," he said, holding out his hand.

She slid slender fingers into her side pocket and withdrew a small penknife, placing it onto his palm with a slap. "There you are. Did you feel threatened?"

"Any weapon is dangerous if its user is intent on causing bodily harm," he answered quietly. "This little knife could do a lot of damage."

"Well, all it's been used for up until now is cutting branches to use for bedding and for a spit over my fire."

Brace slid it into his pocket. "For tonight, it'll be safe with me," he told her. "Now, have you decided about the trip out back?"

"I suppose you're coming along." Her words were a statement of fact, he decided, and he answered in like form.

"You'd better believe it, ma'am."

He lifted a hand toward the back door of the jail, and she led the way past two empty cells and then opened the door to the outside. The darkness was almost solid before them, the moon hidden behind a cloud, the stars barely seen. The faint outline of a small building gave notice of her destination, and Sarah walked toward it.

"Do I get to go in alone?" she asked, her hand on the latch.

"Now, Miss Sarah, you should know better than to ask that. I'm not a man given to looking where I've not been invited. I'll just wait right here."

She pulled the door closed behind her and he grinned into the darkness. Damn, she was a handful. He'd give much to keep her around for a while, but overnight was probably as far as he could go without causing an uproar, should the ladies in town hear of it. Turning his back on the outhouse, he folded his arms across his chest and waited.

Standing with her hand on the latch wasn't getting her anywhere, Sarah decided. The knowledge that the lawman waited outside, just six feet away, was daunting, the presence of a jail cell with her name on it even more so. She'd never been in jail. Indeed, had never had a run-in with the law in any way, shape or form. Unless she counted the sheriff who'd checked out Sierra's death and uttered bland words of sympathy.

The door opened silently, but the sheriff turned to face her without hesitation. His face was a blurred shadow in the night, the shine of the silver star on his shirt allowing her to spot his form before her. Walking beside him, she headed for the jailhouse and reached for the door. The light from the lawman's office cast a gleam before her and she stepped inside the hallway and waited for him.

"I'll get you a bucket of water and a towel," he

offered, gripping her elbow and crossing to the first cell.
Using the largest key on his ring, he opened the door
and swung it wide, ushering her inside.

Without protest she obeyed his unspoken order and
stepped into the small cubicle. Just large enough for a
simple cot, a chair and the aforementioned slop pail in
one corner, it was barren of any comforts, and she
scanned the bed she would use for the night.

"I'll get a blanket and see if I can scout up a pillow
for you," the sheriff said.

"Don't you have many prisoners, Sheriff?" she
asked. "I'd think these lovely rooms would come complete with furnishings."

"Nope. Benning is a pretty quiet town. Not much
doing usually."

"No wonder you were so thrilled with finding a law-
breaker like me on the premises," she said caustically.
The cot beckoned, and she made a deliberate effort to
appear nonchalant as she walked across the cell and sat
down.

He stood in the open door of her accommodations
and slid one hand into his pocket. "I'll be right back
with all the comforts of home," he told her, then closed
the metal portal with a clang and walked toward his
office.

Sarah watched him go, finally allowing her trembling
hands permission to entwine in her lap. Her breath was
rasping in her lungs, and she felt a deluge of tears
threatening. Not for the world would she succumb to
their flow until the dratted lawman was far, far away,
she decided. No doubt he'd settle her for the night and
then go on home, where he probably had a nice comfortable bed.

And then in less than five minutes she discovered how wrong she was.

"My name's Brace Caulfield," the lawman told her as he approached with one arm full of blanket and pillow, a white towel balanced atop the pile. His other hand held a bucket of water, and he deposited it on the floor while he unlocked the cell.

Ungraciously she sat on the bunk while he carried his bundle inside and placed the bedding on the chair, then lowered the bucket to the floor at the foot of her cot. Only her good upbringing forced her to utter a grudging thanks for his efforts, and she was answered with a brief nod.

From his back pocket he withdrew a candle and several matches and in less than a minute had lit the taper, then allowed the wax to drip onto the floor. The candle was set in place, and its glow illuminated the cell around her, providing comfort she hadn't expected. She hoped it would last at least until she went to sleep, although that might be a long time from now.

"I'll be in my office all night," he told her. "If you need anything, just call out."

"You're not going home?" she asked disbelievingly. Surely the man had a home to call his own.

"Not with a female in my jail," he told her forcefully. "There's not much chance of danger to you, but I don't think it's wise to ask for trouble. That saloon down the street is full of fellas who'd give their eyeteeth for a chance to touch your pretty face."

"I doubt they know I'm here," she protested, unwilling to face the thought of him in the next room.

"Well, we're not gonna give them a chance to come looking, are we?" Locking the door with a quick twist of the key, he stuffed the ring into his pocket and watched her for a moment through the bars. "You're safe, Miss Murphy. If you're thinking I'm gonna come in here and bother you, don't give it another thought. My mama raised me to be a gentleman."

And somehow Sarah knew he spoke the truth. In the light of her candle, his eyes were dark and shadowed, yet compelling, as if he looked into her very depths and knew the fears she held within her.

The candle indeed lasted, longer than she'd expected, and her gaze focused on it for long minutes as she coaxed her body to relax on the hard cot. It still burned as her eyes finally shut.

She awoke in the dark, aware of another presence nearby, and sat up with a start.

"It's all right, Sarah. It's me, Sheriff Caulfield." The voice came from outside her cell, and as she focused on its source she was able to see the tall, shadowed figure of the man who spoke.

"Is something wrong?" she asked, her voice husky with sleep.

"No. Just making sure you're all right. Do you want another candle?"

It would not be wise to give in to her natural inclination, she decided, and refused his offer. Inviting the man into her cell was the last thing she wanted to do in the middle of the night, given her trembling hands and fearful thoughts. He was too inviting, his calm, sure voice offering security and safekeeping. And she needed every bit of independence she could muster for the days ahead.

"No, I'm fine," she told him, with a fine disregard for the truth, then placed her head back on the thin pillow and closed her eyes, choosing to live with the lie she'd spoken.

Chapter Two

Sleeping on a chair guaranteed a miserable night. Brace had realized it before midnight, and by three in the morning he was ready to occupy the cell next door to his prisoner. The fact that she would likely rouse and be wary of his presence a few feet from where she lay kept him seated before his desk. His head finally sought the hard surface and he dozed fitfully, opening his eyes when the rising sun appeared in the window.

Yawning and stretching, he made his way to the cell where Sarah slept, curled on her side, the blanket drawn up over her shoulder, the miserable pillow tucked and rolled beneath her neck. At least she'd had a flat surface upon which to spend the night. Hard and barren of a mattress it might be, but he'd warrant the cot was a sight more comfortable than the chair he'd occupied.

His key rattled in the lock and the young woman's eyes blinked, then opened fully, and she peered at him blankly for a moment. Then recognition kicked in and she pulled the blanket over her head. "Go away." It wasn't even a polite request.

He ignored the words with a grin as he stepped into the cell. "Thought you might want to take a walk," he suggested, as if it were an option. Either she went now or in an hour or so. And unless he missed his guess, she was going to be mighty uncomfortable if she had to sit on that cot until he returned with her breakfast.

"A walk?" The blanket flew off and she swung her legs over the side, sitting upright and shaking her head as if to clear it. A yawn required covering her mouth with one hand, and then she eyed him boldly. "And where is this walk going to take me? To the gallows?" she asked sweetly. "Or haven't you had time to get them built yet?"

"You've got a smart mouth for a woman dependent on my good nature," Brace said softly. He turned from her and stepped through the cell door.

"Wait." The single word halted his progress, and he glanced at her idly over his shoulder.

"What for? You all of a sudden decide to be polite?"

She sighed and rose, staggering a bit as she took a single step toward him. An involuntary sound passed her lips and he frowned as she gritted her teeth and shuffled her way to the door where he stood.

"What's wrong?" he asked. "You don't like the accommodations?"

"Not much. The ground was softer, I think. At least I had a little grass under me."

"Where was that?" Brace asked.

She shook her head. "Couldn't say. Somewhere the other side of town. Under a tree, next to a creek."

"Wallin's Creek, probably," he surmised. "About four miles down the train tracks and a little to the south."

"That sounds about right." She halted in the cell doorway and looked at the back door. "That door unlocked?"

Brace shook his head. "Nope. I'll have to open it for you." Easing past her, he brushed against her shoulder and she flinched from the contact. "Sorry," he said lightly. "Didn't mean to push you."

She recovered quickly. "You didn't. Just caught me off balance." Her eyes were bright blue, he noted again, just before she lowered the lids, hiding her expression from his sight. Dark hair hung in a tumble of waves and curls over her shoulders and down her back. His gaze was drawn by the sight. He'd thought he preferred golden hair, but with a slow grin he revised his opinion.

In seconds he'd unlocked the door and opened it, waving her through. "Go ahead," he invited, and then watched as she walked past him and down the short path to the outhouse. She was easy enough to look at, he decided, taking full advantage of the view of her rounded bottom, outlined nicely by the pants she wore. He leaned against the doorjamb and waited patiently until she reappeared.

"I'll get you some warm water if you want to wash up while I'm gone," he told her as she walked past him again, heading for the open cell door.

"I'd appreciate it," she said politely. And then ruined the nicely spoken words with a glare from those brilliant eyes. "How long will it take for you to decide I'm not a threat to your community, Sheriff?"

"You in a hurry to go someplace?" He locked the cell door and stepped away from the bars.

"You know damn well I am," she said bitterly. "You're holding me without a valid reason, and you know it. Either charge me with a crime or let me go."

"All right," he said agreeably. "I'll think of something while I go find you some breakfast."

She settled on the edge of the cot and leaned her chin

on her fist. "Don't forget the warm water. I'd like to scrub the smell of your jailhouse off my skin."

"Your skin smelled pretty clean to me," he told her. "I took special note of it."

Her glare would have melted wax, he thought, and smiled to himself as he strolled back into his office. A bucket from the closet clutched in one hand, he left the jailhouse and walked across the street to the hotel. The alley led to the kitchen door and he pushed it open and inhaled the scent of breakfast.

"You got some warm water I can use?" he asked.

Bess Casey looked up from the griddle where six round pancakes were browning and waved a hand at the reservoir attached to the side of the cookstove. "You know where it is. Same place it was last time you needed some for washin' up."

"It's not for me," he said. "I've got a prisoner over at the jail. I'll need some breakfast right quick, too. And about four cups of coffee."

"Bad night?" Bess asked with a questioning look. "You look a sight, mister."

"Sleepin' on a chair'll do that to you," he agreed.

"I suspect you've got a perfectly good bedroom in that house of yours," she told him. "Why didn't you use it?"

"My prisoner is a female," he said, that explanation enough to make Bess nod her head.

"Good enough reason," she said. "Does the lady want coffee, too?"

"I'll find out," Brace said, dipping water into his bucket. "I'll take this to her and be right back."

"You'll have to wait a bit. Got four orders for breakfast lined up already," Bess told him. "I'll put more bacon on right away."

He nodded and left the kitchen, the scent of hot coffee wafting behind him. If he'd brought his mug along he could have taken a cupful with him.

The storekeeper was out front, sweeping the sidewalk as if his very life depended on the cleanliness of the wide boards. "Mornin', Sheriff Caulfield."

Brace nodded a greeting. Mr. Metcalfe was not one of his favorite people, but he'd at least be civil. The flagpole in front of the newly built post office was still empty, but even as Brace glanced that way Titus Liberty came out the door with the spanking new flag in his arms. "Morning, Sheriff," the gentleman said smartly. "You're up early."

"So are you, Titus," he said.

"Almost time for the morning train. Got to meet it and pick up the mail." Having graduated from a corner of the general store to a building constructed by the government for his use, Titus was proud of his position. "You expectin' anything in the mail?" he asked Brace.

"Doubt it." And if he was, he'd have to spend an hour deciphering it. Reading was a problem. He'd about decided to contact the new schoolteacher and see if she'd be willing to take up his lessons where the last volunteer had left off. His lips formed a straight line as he thought of the woman he'd had in his sights and spent more than a year yearning for. Faith was gone, and with her his hopes for a home and family of his own.

Honesty made him recognize that she'd never been his, but he'd had dreams. His pace had slowed crossing the road, and now he turned the handle on his office door and stepped inside. Dust motes floated in the sunlight and he left the door open, allowing the warmth to invade the interior of the building.

"Here's your water," he said, keeping an eye out as he approached the cell. Sarah sat on the cot, right where he'd left her, and he placed the bucket on the floor while he opened the cell door. Setting it inside, he nodded at her. "Breakfast will be here in ten minutes or so. I'm going back right now for coffee. You want some?"

She nodded and rose to walk toward him. "Thanks for the warm water," she said, a bit grudgingly, he thought. The woman was obviously unable to ignore the manners she'd been taught in her lifetime, and he smiled his acknowledgment of her words.

"My pack was tied on behind my saddle," she told him. "Can I have it?"

"What's in it?" he asked, then added as an afterthought, "Besides the gun." *Doggone.* He'd forgotten the dratted thing last night, so besotted with the female in front of him he'd neglected his duty as a lawman.

"A change of clothes," she told him. "Clean stockings and a few other items."

He nodded. "I'll get it for you, right after breakfast. Maybe Jamie will be here by then and he can walk over to the livery stable."

Her eyes were shadowed as she met his gaze. "How long are you going to keep me here?" she asked. "My nephew is probably being carted off to the next town while we're standing here talking. I know this isn't important to you, but that child is my reason for living right now."

Brace backed from the cell and locked the door. "I'll check at the hotel and see if the fella's still there," he told her.

She nodded, and he thought he caught sight of the glitter of tears as she bent her head. It bothered him, touched him at his very core. Maybe because she was a woman alone—and yet it was more than that. Sarah Murphy was vulnerable, even given her possession of a gun and the small knife she carried. She was a woman—capable perhaps, but nevertheless a female, alone in a situation that threatened that essence of womanhood she possessed.

In less than an hour Brace had fed his prisoner and verified that the man she sought had checked out of the hotel, and was even now leaving town. A muscular fellow, tall and broad of shoulder, he stood in the doorway of the livery stable. Beside him was a child, a boy of about seven, Brace decided. Dark haired and slender almost to the point of being skinny, the boy shifted restlessly beside his father, and Brace could not help but stroll to where Lester Clark waited impatiently for his mount to be saddled.

"Mornin', stranger," Brace said mildly. "Anything I can help you with?"

A dark glance from beneath lowered brows was his reply, and then as if he'd caught sight of Brace's badge, the man shook his head. "Just trying to get an early start. Once I get my horse I'll be out of your way."

"You headin' west?" Brace asked. "The road is a pretty straight shot from here, but you'll run into some rough spots. We're kinda isolated here."

"I'll make it," the man answered, his speech clipped and concise.

"Pa?" The boy looked at his father appealingly. "You said we was gonna look for Aunt Sarah. Is this where she is?"

The glare was a demand for silence and the boy appeared to shrivel before Brace's eyes as he bent his head and considered the dirt at his feet. "I just wondered," the child murmured, and was delivered a sound, open-handed blow to his shoulder for his trouble.

The narrow shoulders hunched, and a stifled sob reached Brace's hearing. It was the opening he'd hoped for and he bent, one knee on the ground as he crouched beside the child. "You lookin' for your aunt?" he asked quietly. And then with a quick glance at the child's father, he continued. "Maybe I can help you find her."

Better that this encounter take place within his jurisdiction, he decided, than on the road to Wichita Falls. If Sarah Murphy confronted this man on her own, she might not come out the winner. In fact, her chances of such a thing happening were next to nothing.

"We don't need any help," the stranger said. "The boy doesn't know what he's talking about."

"But, Pa—" An upraised hand formed a fist and the boy was silent.

"I wouldn't do that if I were you," Brace said flatly.

"He's my kid. I'll do as I please." The force of his anger reddened the man's complexion, and his eyes shot darts of flaring rage in Brace's direction.

"Not in my town, you won't," Brace told him, rising, one hand resting on the butt of his gun. He knew he presented an intimidating picture, dressed in black as was his usual custom, standing even taller and broader than the man who faced him.

"I'm leaving, Sheriff," the stranger said, reaching for his horse's reins as the mount was led toward him.

"That'll be fifty cents," Amos Montgomery said, his gaze moving quickly from one to the other of the men before him. And then he caught Brace's eye. "Problems, Sheriff?"

Amos Montgomery was stalwart, muscular and had a body that reflected his line of work. Being a blacksmith seemed to go right along with running the livery stable, and Amos did both with strength and purpose. Now he allied himself with Brace in a manner that could not be mistaken.

"No, I don't think so," Brace said easily. "This young'un and I are going to pay a visit to the hotel and find us something to eat."

"He's my son," Lester Clark said harshly. "You have no right to haul him away like this."

"I have every right. This is *my* town," Brace said, aware that he was infringing on parental rights, and found that he was uncaring as to Lester Clark's rights, as a parent or a citizen. The man rubbed him the wrong way. Abuse of a child was about as low as a man could go. And unless Brace missed his guess, the man's motives were not as pure as they might be. He certainly wasn't showing any degree of love for the little boy right now, anyway.

The child's small hand crept into Brace's palm and nestled there, his fingers trembling as if they sought refuge. Looking upward, the lad bit his lip and then glanced with a sideways look at his father. Donning his lawman's scowl, Brace looked at Lester Clark, daring the man to defy his edict.

"It may be your town," the man said, "but as a citizen I have rights. Mainly as it pertains to my boy."

"Well," Brace said, his words slowing into a drawl, "let's just let the doc take a look at your boy, Mr. Clark, and see if he finds any traces of abuse."

"I can treat him any way I want to," Lester blustered. "He belongs to me."

"Last time I heard, it was against the law to own another human being," Brace said in that same soft, low voice. "You can own a horse or a dog, but there's no way you can put your brand on a child."

"Where's the judge in this godforsaken town?" Lester asked harshly.

Brace smiled, a feral grin that he'd been told turned him from a nice, decent gentleman into a wolfish creature who could scare the britches off the devil himself. He stood taller, his hand once more touching the butt of his gun. From beneath the brim of his black hat he cast a scornful glance at the man before him.

"The judge comes into town every two months or so," Brace said. "He should be here in a couple of weeks. Would you like to wait for him in one of my cells?"

That the second cell was currently holding a young woman was information Lester Clark needn't know, Brace thought. Especially since she'd just as soon shoot the man as look at him. And for a moment he wondered which of the two was the more dangerous.

"You're not locking me up, mister," Lester snarled. "I haven't done anything illegal."

"Well, don't ruin your record now," Brace told him. "I'm takin' this boy to see the doc, and from there we'll find something to eat at the hotel."

"I'm real hungry," the boy said softly, as if he feared his father might overhear his words. He was about as close to Brace's leg as he could get without climbing it. The urge to snatch the child up and into his arms was almost irresistible, but Brace settled for bending to the boy, brushing a big hand over the lad's dark hair and squeezing gently at his narrow shoulder.

"Come along, son," he said, holding tight to the small hand that was now fisted around his index finger. With a glance over his shoulder at Amos, he sent a silent message, and the blacksmith apparently had no difficulty in deciphering it.

"I'll keep an eye on things," he said curtly.

Lester Clark stood in the middle of the road and watched Brace's departure, and the venom of the glare he cast upon the man and child was almost palpable, Brace noted. The boy trotted along without complaint, and Brace looked down at him as they neared the jailhouse.

"I got somebody inside you might like to see," he said. "Want to make a quick stop?" And without waiting for a reply, he crossed the threshold of his office. Jamie sat at the desk, his boots propped on its surface, his hat sliding down over his eyes as he dozed.

"You want to bring Miss Murphy out here?" Brace asked quietly, and then had a hard time restraining his smile as his deputy jerked to attention. His boots hit the floor and he was upright in seconds.

"Yes, sir, I can do that," he said, glancing down at the boy who held Brace's hand as if it were a lifeline. Snatching up the keys from the desk drawer, he hastened through the door, and in moments Brace heard the rattle of the lock, and then the squeak of the cell door opening.

"What's going on?" Sarah Murphy's voice held a puzzled note, and then she was there in the doorway, and the child beside him shivered and uttered his aunt's name with a pleading sound.

"Aunt Sarah?" Poised beside Brace, the boy tugged his hand free and launched himself at his aunt with a cry of anguish. "Aunt Sarah," he repeated, and as she bent to receive him, he reached her and clung to her. His legs circled her waist and his arms wrapped around her neck, his small face buried against her throat.

"Let me take him," Brace offered quickly. "He's too heavy for you."

Sarah shot him a look that might have made a lesser man tremble. "Don't touch him. It's me he needs."

Brace pushed his chair toward her instead, waving a hand at the wooden seat. Sarah settled there, rocking the child and crooning words of comfort against his dark head. For a long moment the two men were silent, then Jamie turned away, as though his emotions were caught up in the drama before him.

"Stephen. Oh, Stephen, I've been looking for you," Sarah said quietly, pulling back from the boy's grip to look into his eyes. "Are you all right?" She held him away from her, scanning his small form, her gaze snagged by a bruise on his forearm. "What happened here?" she asked.

"Nothin'," Stephen said, as if the purple abrasion were of little account. And it probably *was* hardly noticeable to the lad, Brace decided, now that his aunt held him close. "Everything's all right now, Aunt Sarah. I knew you'd find me."

She looked up at Brace, her eyes filming with tears. "Thank you," she whispered. "I owe you." And then she looked toward the doorway and beyond it to the road. "Where's his father?"

"Over at the livery stable, trying to figure out what his options are," Brace said. "I offered him a bed here, but he wasn't of a mind to accept. I suspect he's gonna stay at the hotel for a while, unless he gives up and heads on down the road. But I wouldn't count on that, ma'am."

"He won't get this child from me," she said fiercely, her grip on Stephen tightening. "I'll do whatever I have to in order to keep him safe."

"Well," Brace began, his mind working as he reached for her and eased her from the chair, "let's go over to the hotel first off and feed this young man some breakfast."

"It's closer to dinnertime, isn't it?" Sarah asked, her confusion apparent.

"Yeah, I suspect it will be by the time we make a stop at the doctor's office, but this boy hasn't had anything to eat today, unless I miss my guess."

She looked down at Stephen, whose gaze traveled from one adult to the other in a bid to keep up with the conversation. "Haven't you eaten this morning?" she asked.

He shook his head. "No, ma'am. Pa said we was in a hurry."

"I'll just bet he did," she muttered. Her face dark with anger, she lowered Stephen to the floor before her and he stood where she'd placed him, apparently willing to do whatever she bid him. "Let's go," she said, gripping his hand and walking to the doorway. "Lead the way, Sheriff."

"This isn't anything permanent, ma'am," Brace told Sarah. They sat at the small table, watching Stephen devour a plateful of pancakes and eggs, and Brace felt more than a twinge of anger at the man who'd neglected the boy to such an extent.

"I'll not give him up," Sarah said firmly. She clasped her hands before her on the white tablecloth and her chin jutted forward as if she had drawn a line in the sand and dared him to step over it. "Lester is not getting his hands on him again."

"He's his son," Brace said quietly. "I broke the law by taking Stephen today, if you really want to know the truth. I can keep him at arm's length till the judge comes to town in a couple of weeks, but I doubt you'll have a leg to stand on once we go to court and present your case.''

Sarah leaned over the table. ''I don't care what it takes, Lawman, I won't give him up again. Did you pay attention to what the doctor uncovered in his office? Didn't you see the bruises he wears?''

''Yeah, I saw them,'' Brace said agreeably. ''But the fact remains that Stephen's place is with his parent. That's legal and binding, no matter what you and I think about it.'' He leaned back in his chair and shot a grin at the boy, whose wary gaze was once more following the adult conversation that concerned his future.

''Isn't there any way? Legally, I mean?''

''You're a nice lady, Sarah, but you're a woman alone. No matter how bad the boy wants to be with you, you won't be considered a good risk, not stacked up against a father's claim, anyway. In fact, you're gonna have a tough time finding a place to stay while we wait for the judge. You aren't going to be safe here, not with your brother-in-law running around town.''

''If I leave, he'll never find us,'' she said quietly. ''We can skin out of here after dark, and by morning he won't have a trail to follow.''

Brace sighed and shook his head regretfully. ''Sorry, ma'am, but I can't let you do that. You're gonna have to stick around till the judge shows up. I can't let you run off.''

''You can't stop me,'' she said harshly.

''Yeah, I can,'' he said. ''If I have to I can stick you back in a cell and take the boy home with me. That way I'll know where the both of you are.''

''No.'' The word was accompanied by a violent

shake of her head. "Anything but that," she whispered. "Don't take him away from me."

"I'm not leavin' you, Aunt Sarah," Stephen said stoutly, thrusting his chin forward in a fashion much like that of his aunt.

"Well, we can try something else," Brace said, leaning back in his chair. "You could both come home with me. I've got a couple of extra bedrooms I never use. As a matter of fact, I rarely even use any part of the damn house. I spend a lot of nights here at my desk, or, on occasion, at the hotel instead of going all the way home."

"Why?" she asked, confusion alive in her face. "Why don't you stay in your house?"

"It's lonely there," he said simply. "And sometimes I need to be handy in case there's trouble at one of the saloons." His smile was sheepish and he knew it. "It's no fun to rattle around in an empty house."

"Will there be a problem if we stay there?" she asked. "Will you be in trouble with anybody in town if you let us move in?"

He shook his head. "I don't see why. It's my house, bought and paid for with hard cash. I'd think I can pretty much do whatever I want to with it, including inviting company to stay if I want to."

"I don't want to damage your reputation," Sarah said softly.

"More likely that I'll damage yours," he answered with a slow grin. And for the first time he wondered what had possessed him to make such an offer. The woman was about as appealing as any he'd ever met. Dressed in her pants and shirt, she drew every eye, especially those of the men who'd had a hard time keeping their gazes from her as she walked from the jailhouse to the hotel. She was slender, but rounded in all the right places, and he'd probably do well to park her somewhere other than his front bedroom.

But the offer had been made, and Brace Caulfield wasn't a man to back down once he'd made a decision. "I picked up your pack from the livery stable. I kept the gun, just in case you planned on using it." He watched her closely, noting the wary expression she wore. "You'll be safe with me," he told her, and as he watched, she nodded slowly.

"I suspect I will. I found that out last night."

"About last night," he began, and halted when she held up a hand to silence him.

"Let's not talk about it," she said, glancing at Stephen. "You were within your rights, and the way things have worked out, I'm not going to complain."

"All right." And wasn't that an easy resolution to the issue. He'd thought he'd have to mend fences, but apparently Miss Sarah Murphy wasn't a woman to hold a grudge.

All in all, this might be an interesting proposition.

Chapter Three

It rose two stories high, the roof sloped and gabled, the windows abundant, their surfaces gleaming in the sunlight. All in all, it was a place that appealed to her, and Sarah found herself slowing her pace as she walked from the buggy toward the wide front porch. It was barren of furnishings, but the cool, shaded area looked to be ideal for a swing, perhaps a rocking chair, or even just a bench beside the door.

She could imagine whiling away the hours of eventide here, watching the sun set and the first stars appear in the night sky. The notion was fanciful, and she moved it aside for the more practical questions that begged to be answered.

"Why did you buy a place so large?"

Sheriff Caulfield looked a bit uncomfortable, she thought, but gamely met her challenge. "I'd thought to find a wife and settle down here, maybe have a family."

"What changed your mind?" She'd seldom ever been so intrusive, but there was a sense of sadness about the man that spoke to her. Perhaps he'd been disappointed in love, or had lost his beloved to death. Sarah looked up at him, her gaze seeking to look beyond his casual manner. "You needn't answer," she said hastily as his mouth tightened. "I was rude to press for details."

"No." He shook his head. "Not rude, Miss Murphy, just being a woman, I suspect." His smile appeared then, and she welcomed its return. "I found that my job took more time at first than I'd planned, and then I decided that the choices in Benning were pretty scanty."

"Surely in a place this size there are available women," she said, her tone unbelieving. "Or are you too fussy?" She'd murmured the query beneath her breath, smiling to brighten the mood a bit.

"Maybe," he answered. "I'm of the opinion that marriage is a contract that shouldn't be entered into lightly. And unless a man has the time to invest in a marriage, he hasn't the right to expect a woman to haul more than her share of the load."

Sarah stepped up onto the porch and crossed to the wide front door. "I doubt you'd be selfish," she said bluntly. "You seem the sort of man to play fair, no matter what the occasion." She looked up at the fanlight over the door. "A woman chose that."

He followed her gaze. "What makes you say that?"

"The colors, the design. It's absolutely worthless, except for the beauty of its reflection inside the house." She met his gaze. "It's not of much real use, but it's a touch of unexpected beauty."

He reached past her to open the heavy door, and she noted the lack of a key in his hand. "I take it you don't lock your doors."

"Haven't found any need to," he said. "Although, with you staying here, I may have to make some adjustments to my routine."

"Not unless it's common knowledge that I'm here," she answered. "I don't think we'll be in any danger, do you?"

His eyes narrowed as he looked down at her. "I wouldn't want to bet on it. Your brother-in-law is not a happy man right now." He stood back and ushered her into the wide foyer, touching Stephen's shoulder as the boy passed in front of him. The child flinched noticeably at the lawman's touch, and Sarah's mouth firmed as she tightened her grip on the small hand she held securely.

Brace followed her inside and then leaned against the door. "What do you think?" he asked. Spoken casually, the words held a touch of pride. His dark eyes softened as he scanned their surroundings: the table against the wall, the bench beside it, the staircase that climbed to the second floor. On either side were doorways and open arches, and Sarah yearned to explore the rooms beyond her vision.

"You have a housekeeper?" she asked, noting the clean floors, the gleaming wood of the banister and the lack of dust in the corners.

"Someone comes in once a week. Looks like she was here yesterday, doesn't it?"

Sarah turned to face him. "Just how often *do* you come home?"

He fidgeted a bit, she thought, and then his smile appeared, curving one side of his mouth as if he were unused to such a display of good humor. "Couple of times a week, I suppose," he answered. "There's not much here to keep me comin' back, Miss Murphy. It's got furniture, but without folks living in it, a house feels pretty empty, don't you think?"

She nodded toward the nearest archway. "May I explore?'' she asked, unwilling to step beyond good manners, though her instincts were crying out to look into the room that beckoned her. Something about this house, this man, drew her. He'd offered a haven for Stephen and herself, and though she'd accepted tentatively, the first glimpse of his home had decided her.

I've come home. The thought was almost frightening, and she trembled as he nodded his permission. At her side, Stephen clung to her hand, and together they crossed the threshold into the parlor. It was well furnished, warm and welcoming, unlike many formal rooms. A fireplace stood against the outside wall, apparently unused for some time, its hearth swept clean of ashes. Light curtains allowed the sunlight to cascade across the carpet, where the colors glowed in a rich display.

"It's lovely," she whispered, turning in a slow circle, Stephen clutching her fingers and following her lead.

"Come see the library," Brace said, issuing the invitation in a measured tone. Instinctively she recognized that the room he was about to show her was important to him, and she followed his lead across the foyer to a matching room on the opposite side of the house.

Two walls were lined with bookshelves, and the third boasted a bay window with a wide, cushioned seat that begged a reader to curl there with her favorite book. A desk stood against the fourth wall, and furnishings that promised comfort were grouped before a fireplace.

"What do you think?" he asked again, watching her closely, as if her opinion was of great importance to him.

"It's wonderful," she said. She lifted one hand to include the shelves of books. "Have you read all of them?"

She thought his eyes darkened as he shook his head abruptly. "No. I don't seem to find the time," he answered. Yet a look of intense longing made her wonder that he didn't spend his evenings here, that he didn't utilize this room that was of such obvious importance to him.

He led the way back to the hallway and then toward the kitchen. "The dining room is next," he said, pointing at another wide archway, beyond which sat a gleaming table, surrounded by eight chairs. A glass-fronted buffet against the outside wall caught her eye, and she noted the gleam of china and silver behind the upper doors.

"Do you use it?" she asked, and was not surprised at his abrupt movement of denial.

"No. I don't entertain."

"What a waste," she told him, unaware of the yearning quality that imbued her words. They walked on, and she could barely resist a final look at the gleaming perfection of the room. Then she found her pleasure in its beauty almost eclipsed by the warmth of the kitchen into which he led her.

Windows hung with checked curtains and possessing wide sills caught her eye, and she murmured beneath her breath at the sight of pots of flowers in dire need of watering. *That's a man for you,* she thought. With a sigh she stepped before the sink and pumped water into a handy pitcher. From there she headed toward the abused plants, pouring refreshment into the dry dirt they inhabited.

"I'm not real good at that sort of thing," he said, humor lacing the words. "I think sometimes I should just give up on having anything that needs care. The woman who lived here was real big on flowers and such things, and I promised her I'd take care of them.''

Sarah shot an amused look in his direction. ''She'd have done better to take them with her.''

''Couldn't,'' Brace said bluntly. ''She got on a train and headed east to be with her children. Wasn't any way she could haul along half the garden with her.''

Sarah looked around the sunny room, finding small touches that appealed to her feminine side, such as it was. She'd long since given up the idea that she'd ever be the sort of woman to wear silk finery. But that didn't stop her from admiring the suggestions of a woman's hand in putting together this house.

''Can you cook?'' Brace asked, and she laughed.

''I've been told I'm pretty good at it. I'd say I can find my way around a kitchen about as well as you'd expect.''

''To tell the truth, Miss Murphy, I have no idea what to expect from you. You haven't come anywhere near my first impression, that's for sure.''

She turned to him. ''And what was that?''

He looked down at Stephen, and his smile was tender, she thought. ''I didn't take you for a woman who'd be so besotted by my house,'' he said. ''I had a notion you were trying not to be any more girlish than you could help.'' He slid a hand into his pocket and leaned against the doorjamb. ''In fact, I was pretty certain you were—'' He grinned suddenly, halting as if he hesitated to speak his mind. ''Well, now. Let's just say I was wrong about a couple of things. And probably right about a couple of others.''

''Oh?'' A glance down at Stephen, who was following the conversation with interest, silenced her then. He had enough upset in his young life. He didn't need to hear a lawman dissecting her character this morning.

"To get back to the question, ma'am," he said politely. "Can you cook? Or maybe I need to ask instead, are you willing to put together a meal?"

She looked around the room. "Out of what?"

"The pantry has a good assortment of food. Nothing fresh, but maybe you could turn out some jars or cans, enough for you and the boy to get along with for the rest of the day."

"What about you?" she asked. "Or don't you plan on staying long?"

"I'm going to leave for a while, but I'll be back. I think some fresh milk and a loaf of bread might be a good idea. If I'd been thinking, I'd have stopped at the general store."

"I think you were in a hurry," she told him, recalling their rushed exit from the hotel, the buggy he'd hired at the livery stable and his casual yet thorough search of their surroundings as they'd made their way here to his home. His horse had been tied to the rear of the vehicle, and she hadn't questioned his motives.

"I'd rather not have been followed," he admitted. "You're just half a mile from town here, but there's a lot of trees and some pretty heavy brush along the road."

"We're not starving," she said, recalling the food Stephen had put away in the hotel restaurant. "I think we can hold off until you come back."

"I have something to show you," he said, casting a furtive glance at the boy, who had yet to move from her side. And then he crouched in front of the lad. "Do you think you could take a look upstairs and maybe find the bedroom you'd like to sleep in while you're here?'' he asked.

''Yes, sir,'' Stephen answered, as if used to obeying without quibbling. He released Sarah's hand, a bit reluctantly but without argument, and went from the kitchen to the wide staircase. She took a single step toward the doorway to watch him as he made his way up the stairs, and then she turned back to Brace.

''What is it?'' she asked.

''There's a gun in the pantry,'' he told her. ''I'm assuming you know how to handle a shotgun.''

She nodded. ''I'd appreciate it if you'd give me back my handgun, though.''

As if he made a momentous decision, he looked at her for a moment, then nodded slowly. ''All right, but if push comes to shove, if there's any trouble, you'll be better off with a long gun. Scattershot will do the trick if someone gets close to the house.'' He slipped her pistol from his waistband and turned it in his hand, then placed it in her palm, his other hand beneath hers.

And then he covered it for a moment, capturing her fingers in his clasp. ''Be careful, Sarah.''

He'd gotten himself into a pickle. Not only had he hauled a woman into his house, but he'd taken a child from his legal father and hidden that child. Brace rode slowly back to town, the mare and buggy stored in his shed until he decided his next move. His black mount made short work of the half mile he traveled, and in moments the general store was before him.

His office door stood open, Jamie propped there watching him. Brace lifted a hand in greeting and Jamie pushed away from the wall. ''Hey, Brace,'' he said in greeting. Hands stuffed in his pockets, he rocked back and forth on his heels. "You had company a while ago."

"Lester Clark?" He wasn't surprised, just thankful that Sarah and the boy were safe for now.

"He's madder'n hell. Said you stole his kid." Jamie shifted uncomfortably. "Was it legal? Takin' the boy, I mean?"

Brace tried his best to look patient. "Now, what do you think, Deputy?" And then he answered his own query. "Hell, no, it wasn't legal. Just the right thing to do. The boy is wearing bruises from one end to the other."

"What are you gonna do about it?" Jamie asked, squinting for a moment, then pulling the brim of his hat down.

"Keep Stephen and his aunt out of sight for a couple of days. At least until the judge comes into town."

Jamie's lips twisted in a knowing grin. "I'll bet you'll be staying out at your place for the next few nights, won't you?"

Brace's jaw firmed, and he noted the involuntary response Jamie could not disguise, his grin fading as he sensed Brace's anger. "Didn't mean anything by that," he said quickly. "I suspect you'll be out there keepin' an eye on those two."

"You're right there," Brace told him harshly. "And no one had better find out that's where they are."

"Not from me," Jamie said hastily. "I'll just hold the fort here, unless there's some reason or another to hustle on out there and notify you."

"About the worst that generally happens on a Friday or Saturday night is a fight at one of the saloons," Brace told him. "You can handle that."

"You takin' off for the rest of the day?" Jamie

asked. "I figured you might, in order to get your guests settled in out at your place." He grinned widely. "About the first time you've let anybody walk through that front door, ain't it?"

Brace shot him a look designed to quell his curiosity, but to no avail.

Jamie was intent on poking into the subject. "Never could figure out why you wanted such a big place, anyway," he said lazily. "Seems like you'd rattle around in that house all by yourself."

"I don't spend a lot of time there," Brace admitted. "But one of these days—" His words were cut off by a shout from the front door of the hotel. Bart Simms was on the porch, waving a piece of paper in one hand, his fist making emphatic movements in the air.

"You'd better get yourself back in here, mister. You're gonna pay this bill, or I'll know the reason why."

"Trouble," Jamie said in an undertone, standing erect and patting his gun with a proprietary touch. "I'll handle it, Sheriff. Go on along and tend to your business."

Brace shook his head and reached out a restraining hand as Jamie would have stepped into the street. "Hold it."

They watched as Lester Clark turned and dropped his bag at his feet, then glared at the hotel owner. "I paid in advance," he said, and then, for good measure, stalked back to where Bart stood and snatched the paper from his hand. "This isn't worth squat," he shouted.

"Well, I may want to argue that," Brace said, pitching his voice to carry across the street. He strolled to where the two men stood, and Bart cast him a thankful look. But Brace's attention was focused on the other man. "You're just bound and determined to occupy one of my cells, aren't you, mister?" he asked.

"You can't arrest me," Lester shouted. "You've already stolen my boy from me and hidden him away somewhere. All I want to do is get my hands on him, and we'll be out of your hair."

"You're not going anywhere until you pay your account at the hotel," Brace told him, folding his arms across his chest, a pose he knew caused the few troublemakers in town to think twice before they crossed him.

"I paid in advance," Lester said stubbornly.

Brace smiled. "Well, we can solve the whole problem, then. All you have to do is show me the receipt."

Lester blustered for a moment. "I didn't keep it. Didn't think I'd find a bunch of crooks in Benning." His sneer was eloquent. "Course, when the local sheriff himself is beyond the law, that's about what you'd expect."

"Either pay your bill or gather your gear and head across the street to the jailhouse," Brace told him firmly. And then he waited, his full attention on the angry man before him. In less than a minute Lester dug into his pocket and withdrew a handful of money, sorted through the coins and chose two to give Bart Simms.

"Thanks, Sheriff," Bart said, glaring in impotent fury at his erstwhile tenant. "You know damn well we don't charge in advance for our rooms."

"I'm aware of that," Brace said, watching closely as Lester picked up his bag and headed toward the livery stable. "I think I'll just follow along and see what our friend is planning."

"Where'd that young'un go to?" Bart asked in an undertone. "Like I told my missus, he was a pitiful sight to behold."

"That he was," Brace agreed. "Don't worry about him. He's safe and sound." *Sleeping in one of my bedrooms tonight.* Two of them had beds available, and he hoped to heaven that the boy hadn't laid claim to the big double bed Brace used on occasion. He'd already wondered about letting Sarah Murphy have it, and decided that might not be the best idea.

Where he would put the woman he hadn't the faintest idea, but the deed was done. He'd invited her to stay, and he'd best be thinking about providing her with a bed. Of her own.

"Good. I was hoping you'd remember the milk," Sarah told him when he entered the kitchen bearing a full jug from his nearest neighbor. His bundles were deposited on the round kitchen table quickly—a loaf of bread from the neighbor's wife and a dozen eggs from her white leghorn hens. A small crock held a round of butter, and Brace looked down at his offerings with satisfaction.

"I brought some coffee from the general store, too," he said. "You know how to make it?"

"I suspect I can try," Sarah said, amusement in every syllable. She brought a blue speckled bowl from the pantry and filled it with the eggs, then unwrapped the loaf of bread, lifting it to sniff with appreciation. "This is wonderful," she said. "I'll have some supper ready in no time flat."

He settled at the table, watching as she moved around his kitchen. It was strangely satisfying, he thought, to have a woman here. For a year or so he'd believed this might never come to pass. Silently he cautioned himself not to get too excited about Sarah Murphy's presence in his kitchen. She'd probably not be sticking around for long. She had things to do, and he was merely offering his hospitality until her life was in order.

"I can't thank you enough for taking us in," Sarah said, turning from the stove to face him. "Stephen found a litter of kittens in the shed, and he's out there playing with them. I hope you don't mind."

"No. Old Tabby manages to keep our rodent population under control with her offspring," he said easily. "I've got the only feed barrels hereabouts that aren't on the menu for those pesky mice."

"There're mice out there?" Sarah asked, her eyes flitting to the back door and beyond it to the large shed. "They won't bite, will they?"

Brace laughed. "I can't believe a woman like you would be afraid of a mouse."

Her chin rose a bit and her eyes flashed a dark message in his direction. "I'm not *afraid* of them. I just don't like them."

"They're a fact of life, Sarah. If you have a farm, you have mice. If you have a cat like Tabby, you can keep them pretty much under control."

"You don't have them in the house, do you?" she asked, darting a glance toward the pantry.

He couldn't believe her. His amusement spilled over into laughter again. "A woman who managed to follow a rascal like Lester Clark across the country, toting a gun and keeping track of her prey for who knows how long, shouldn't blink an eye at whopping a mouse with a broom," he said cheerfully.

"I'd rather shoot Lester," she said sharply. "And where is he, anyway? Has he left town yet, or are we going to be hidden here till kingdom come?"

"Till it's safe," he said firmly.

"It's not going to be safe for you, once the folks

hereabouts realize I'm parked in your house," she said bluntly. "Don't you know what sort of stories people will start spreading? You're asking for trouble, mister."

"You'd rather be in jail?" he asked mildly.

"Of course not. I'd rather be bundling up my nephew and heading back home."

"And what happens if Lester Clark chases you down?" he asked. "He's bigger than you are, sweetheart. He carries a bigger gun. And I don't think he's a very nice fella."

"Well, that's the understatement of the year," she said quickly. "I know all about Lester. He's not going to shoot me."

"And how do you know that?" Brace asked.

"He has other plans for me."

Brace was silent, his mind reckoning the truth of her words, and finding them to be logical. "What's his problem?"

Sarah turned toward the stove and stirred the contents of a kettle. Her movements were vigorous, her back stiff and straight, and he'd warrant her cheeks were flushed. Either with anger or embarrassment. Maybe both.

"You ready to eat?" she asked. And then, without waiting for his answer, she dished up into a bowl the meal she'd concocted from his supplies and carried it to the table.

"What's that?" Brace asked, peering into the savory mixture.

"Beef stew," she answered. "You didn't have any decent flour, so I couldn't make biscuits. It's a good thing you brought bread home." She reached into the kitchen cupboard, brought forth three smaller bowls and placed them on the table, then looked at him.

"Would you mind calling Stephen in? He's inside the shed. I told him not to venture outside."

Brace rose, ambled to the back door and stepped out onto the porch. "Stephen," he called, pitching his voice to carry the fifty feet or so to the outbuilding. He was rewarded by the sight of a grinning child, a kitten cuddled in each arm as he stood in the open doorway. The look of pleasure on the boy's face made this whole mess worth it all, Brace decided.

"Come on in, son," he said. "Your aunt has supper ready for us."

"I think we need to talk," Brace said, aware that this conversation was overdue. "I want to know just what your plans are, Sarah. And don't tell me you're ready to trot back where you came from when you know damn well that your brother-in-law will be hot on your trail the minute you leave town."

"I thought you said he took his horse and left." She hesitated, then offered her opinion. "Probably heading for his family's place west of here."

"And you really think that's the end of it?" Brace asked. "He didn't bring the boy this far just so he could walk away and forget the whole thing. Though it doesn't make sense to me that he'd let you find him so easily. He could have lost you if he'd had a mind to, don't you think?"

She nodded. Reluctantly, he thought without surprise. "It isn't Stephen he really wants," she said quietly. "It's me."

"That's about what I figured." He leaned back in his chair and watched as Sarah's cheeks turned pink. She lowered her eyelids, as if she could not face his scrutiny, and she seemed to concentrate on the design in the oilcloth. Her index finger traced a yellow flower, and then she found an errant crumb from supper and brushed it to the floor.

"My sister was also my twin," she said after the silence had stretched to several minutes. "Lester wanted to marry me eight years ago, but I wouldn't accept his proposal. I was too young, just sixteen, and deathly afraid of him, to tell the truth. He has a violent temper." She looked up at him then. "I already told you that, didn't I?"

He nodded encouragingly and waited for the rest of the story, aware already that the ending would not be to his liking. "You told me," he said. "The same time you told me he'd killed your sister."

"Sierra was timid," she said. And then her smile twisted her lips in a grimace. "We weren't much alike. Not like two peas in a pod, as my mama used to say." She sighed. "We looked alike, but I use my right hand and Sierra used her left. It was the one way my father could tell us apart sometimes, except for when I lost my temper."

And that was something Brace could well imagine. Sarah was a spitfire. His thoughts spun, snagged by one statement she'd made. "Could Lester Clark tell you apart?" he asked. "Or was it you he really wanted, but had to settle for your sister?"

"You're a pretty smart fella for a lawman," Sarah said with a wry glance in his direction. "I think you're way ahead of me."

"I'm assuming you figured Lester out first thing, Sarah. So why didn't you warn your sister about him? She was sixteen, too—far too young for marriage."

"She wouldn't listen. He can be charming when he wants to be, and Sierra was easy to fool. She could have had any number of men if she hadn't been so besotted with Lester.'' Sarah shook her head, and her eyes lost their brilliance. ''She was sorry from the first day she married him. I don't know why she stuck it out for so long, except that she got pregnant right away.''

''Was that reason enough?'' Brace asked bluntly. ''Couldn't she have gone home?''

Sarah shook her head. ''Not in a town like we lived in. My mother is the head of the garden group and my father is a town councilman. Walking away from her marriage was not an option. Besides, by then Lester had stolen money from my father's company and the bank was after him. My folks felt disgraced by the whole thing.''

''I'd say it was more of a disgrace to have to plan her funeral,'' Brace noted.

Sarah's eyes rose to meet his. ''You're right. They *knew*. No matter that they pretended to go along with Lester's story about someone lying in wait for Sierra, my parents knew what really happened. Lester probably didn't mean to kill her. My parents didn't want that sort of scandal to taint their reputations. They'd covered up her injuries for years.'' She paused and shrugged. ''I know they mourned her terribly, and I suspect they felt guilty. They tried to make amends by taking Stephen into our home. They were good to him, and between us, we took care of him until the day Lester made off with him.''

''I sure as hell hope they went to court to make Lester pay for what he did, not only stealing from your father, but his part in your sister's death,'' Brace muttered darkly. ''And now Lester is after you. The man must be demented.''

Her sidelong glance held a touch of macabre humor,

he thought, as did the words she spoke. "To want me? Thanks a whole lot." How she could still scrape up that small amount of humor in her situation gave him a glimpse into her mind. She was a woman of courage, and given a fair chance could have held her own against a man of Lester's ilk.

She was also considerably older than he'd guessed at first. Twenty-four, if he'd figured right, if it had been eight years since Lester's proposal. She was old enough to know her mind. And that made her more eligible as a woman in his eyes, a thought he set aside for future consideration.

The situation she faced at this point reeked of danger and duplicity. Her safe haven right now was here, with him, Brace decided. And he'd see to it she and the boy came to no harm. Although where that would leave him, once this thing was resolved, was a question he'd rather not consider right now.

Suddenly the thought of Sarah Murphy walking away and leaving him alone again held no appeal whatsoever.

Chapter Four

The beef stew was excellent, and Brace's expectations were lifted by the flavor of fresh, homemade food. He'd do well to keep Sarah on here, and would no doubt be assured of regular meals.

"You can cook," he said quietly, the words a firm statement. He watched as Stephen left the table and trotted out the back door toward the shed. It seemed the lure of kittens was strong. The child disappeared inside the small building, and Brace's brief fear was relieved when Stephen reappeared moments later with two kittens in hand. He sat in the yard and frolicked with the tiny animals, his laughter bringing Sarah to attention.

"He hasn't sounded so happy in a long time," she said quietly. "Thank you, Sheriff. I really appreciate what you've done for us. I just hope you don't get in hot water over this."

"I'm not worried," Brace replied. "I'd rather put my job on the line than see a child abused. There's always another job around the corner if I need to start looking."

Sarah smiled. The man would never have to go out scouring for work. He was prime material, a masculine sort who seemed cut out for the career he'd chosen.

Lawman. He fit the title to a T. Tall and strong, with principles and moral standards. Compared to him, Lester appeared less than worthless.

"I doubt they'll be out combing the woods for a new man to take your place anytime soon," she told him. "They'd be foolish people if they let you loose."

"I'm not worried for today, anyway," he repeated. "And if you keep on cooking this way, I'll have a hard time turning you loose myself, Miss Murphy."

She met his dark eyes and smiled. "Sarah," she said, correcting him mildly.

"Sarah." He repeated her name slowly, as if he savored it on his tongue, and she felt a blush stain her cheeks. His eyes were piercing as he took her measure. "You'll do, Sarah Murphy." And then the sound of Stephen at the back door caught their attention.

"Aunt Sarah?" He called her name fretfully, and his small face pressed against the screen mesh of the door. "Are you still here? You're not going away, are you?"

"I'm here, Stephen," she answered quickly. "Now, why don't you come on inside and get your bedroom settled before dark?"

"Yes, ma'am," he said readily. "I saw the one right at the top of the stairs, and I like it just fine."

"The first room is a storage area," Brace said quickly. "It has just a narrow slit of a window and no furniture to speak of. I've used it for odds and ends."

"I like it just fine, sir," Stephen said. "There's a bunch of soldiers there in a box and some little, bitty wooden animals. I'd like to sleep there if it's all right."

Brace smiled, thinking of the menagerie of carved animals he'd stashed on a shelf in the room, and then again as he considered the collection of tin soldiers he'd played with as a child. "If that's what you want, it's all right with me, son," he said. "I'll bring down a bed from the attic for you. I think there's a decent mattress up there."

"Thank you," Sarah said quietly. "Not having a big window won't bother him at all, I'd venture to say. He'd be fearful of someone..."

"I understand." And he did. The child was vulnerable, afraid of the man who had fathered him but treated him as a possession in order to gain what he really wanted.

Sarah. The thought of Lester's hands on Sarah's flesh made Brace's hackles rise.

He turned to her now and watched as she wiped the last of the bowls and set it on the shelf. "How about picking out a room for yourself?" he asked, and smiled as she nodded her agreement. "Let's go on up before the sun sets, so you can see what you're getting into."

"I already checked things out," she said softly. "I went up to see the space Stephen chose for his own. He dragged me up for a look-see, and I glanced into the other rooms while I was there."

"All right. Let's take your things up, then, and you can set your belongings to rights," Brace suggested. Without awaiting her agreement, he rose and walked to the hallway, searching out the worn canvas pack she'd brought with her. The woman traveled light—he'd give her that much. "Is this it?" he asked. "Did you leave anything at the hotel?"

"No. I snatched up just what I thought I'd need for a couple of days when I left home. I guess I didn't realize how long this trip would be."

"We can get you more at the general store if need be," Brace said, trudging up the stairs, thinking he'd like to dress her in silk and soft lace. The errant thought scampered through his mind, and he relegated it to the compartment labeled "Forbidden." It would not do to frighten the woman with his interest. And yet, as he turned from the doorway of his spare room to face her, he was lost in the vision of feminine grace she exuded. Soft and womanly, yet young and untried. For he'd warrant she had not known a man, had not succumbed to passion.

"I'm fine," she said. "I don't require much in the line of clothing. Not so long as you have a scrub board and a clothesline handy."

"Come on in, Sarah," he said, walking ahead of her into the small bedroom. A narrow bed drew her eyes and she glanced at him. "It's a bed designed for one person," he told her. "I won't be changing the rules on you. Just thought I'd better let you know. I'm not a man to take advantage of a woman." And wasn't that a shame, he thought. He'd rarely been so taken with a female—only once before, in fact. And the difference between them was in his favor—this one was available.

He watched as Sarah unpacked her clothing, noting the scant number of items she carried to the dresser: several pieces of underclothing and a full-bodied white nightgown. Two dresses were stuffed into the bag, plus another pair of britches and what looked like a boy's flannel shirt. As alluring as the britches she wore had proved to be, he wondered what she would look like in one of the dresses and then shook his head.

"What?" she asked sharply.

"Just thinking," he told her, walking to where she stood by the bed. The case was empty now and he took it from her. "I'll put this in the attic, Sarah. You won't be needing it for some time."

"You mean to keep me here?"

"Do you have a better place to go?" His voice had hardened as he spoke, and she stepped back from him, releasing the makeshift luggage into his grasp.

"You know I don't," she admitted. "I just hate to owe anyone anything."

"Keep cooking like you did today, and you won't be in debt to me even a little bit," he told her. He bent and touched his lips to her forehead, then felt shame wash through him as she jolted, moving away from the bed.

"Sorry, Sarah. I didn't mean to scare you off. You just smell so good and look so pretty, I couldn't resist. I won't be bothering you."

"Oh, you're no bother, Sheriff. And you haven't scared me off. I'm just not used to a man's touch on me."

Now, what he was supposed to make of that was a conundrum, Brace decided. The lady might have run off in a fit of panic had he kissed her as his body was prompting him to do. He lifted a hand and brushed it against her cheek. She stood silently, shivering a little, as if she readied herself for flight. Her eyes held questions he was not ready to answer, he decided. Yet for this moment he found it difficult to resist the woman.

Bending just a bit, he allowed his mouth to touch hers, brushing their lips together in a chaste kiss that would have satisfied even his own mama, who had forever told him how to treat a lady. And Sarah Murphy was a lady, if ever one existed. "I'll just take this upstairs," he said quietly. "I hope you'll be happy here, and safe, Sarah. Mostly safe, I guess. But if you found a little comfort in staying with me, I'd sure appreciate your ideas on the subject."

She looked up at him—a considerable distance, since

Brace stood well over six feet tall. "I like you," she said simply. "You would have made a hit with my mother and father. I just wish there had been men like you around the place when I was considering marriage, long ago before I was old enough to know better."

"Have you given up on the idea?" he asked. "You're too young to spend the rest of your life alone, sweetheart. Surely the right man will come along one day."

A strange look of yearning touched her features and she looked aside. "Perhaps."

The luggage was quickly stowed in the attic and a mattress was carried to the storage room for Stephen. Brace stood at the top of the staircase, looking down into the library. From his vantage point he could see just a few feet inside the door, but he heard Sarah's low tones distinctly, almost as if she spoke to herself, naming books and then rustling the pages as she apparently took them from the shelves and looked through them.

He went down quietly, unwilling to disturb her, and took a stance in the wide doorway. She was curled in the window seat, her legs tucked beneath her, glancing through the pages of a leather-bound volume he'd often yearned to read. Only the fact that the woman who'd taken on the task of teaching him that particular skill had left, returning east to Boston, kept him from his dream.

"Enjoying it?" he asked softly, and then walked to the desk and lit the lamp there. "I'll bet you can see better with a little light on the subject," he teased, and was rewarded by her upward glance as she smiled in his direction.

"I've never seen so many wonderful books in one place in my life," she said, holding the volume against her breasts. Brace thought for a moment that Charles Dickens was a lucky fellow, for she held one of that author's works. And then he banished the thought as unworthy. Yet the urge to set her book aside, lift her from the window seat and surround Sarah with his arms in order to hold her against his yearning body was almost more than he could resist.

The man's thoughts were easy enough to read, Sarah thought. He'd stayed away from her, but his hands had been stuffed into his pockets, as though he must keep them in line, away from the woman before him. The memory of his lips touching hers, of his hand brushing the skin of her cheek, was clear in her mind. And so, for long seconds she wondered how his arms would feel, strong against her, circling her waist, drawing her against his long, dark-clad body.

The book she held lay now in her lap and she looked down at it, tracing the gold letters on its cover with one fingertip. "Have you read this?" she asked.

She thought his answer was reluctant. "No, not yet." And then he admitted to a lack in himself she would not have believed, had another person stated it as fact. "I don't read well," he said. "In fact, up until a couple of years ago, I was without any reading skills at all. A friend helped me, and I can handle whatever comes along in my job, and even some of the newspaper. But I'm afraid that Dickens is still out of my class."

"He's not difficult to understand," she said. "I'd be happy to help you, if you like. Or else I could read to you and you'd have a chance to enjoy some of his work that way. Stephen loves to have me—" She halted her words in midthought and blushed.

Very becomingly, Brace thought. "I'd like to hear you read, Sarah," he said. "When you sit down with

Stephen, if I'm here, I'd like to listen in.'' Her smile of response made him bold. ''And if you feel up to the challenge, I'd like to sit at the kitchen table with you during the evenings and have you work on my—''

''I'd be pleased to help you, Brace.''

Well, he thought, smiling as he looked down to where she sat, he'd come a long way. From ''Sheriff'' to ''Brace'' was quite a step for one day. ''And I'd appreciate the effort on your part,'' he told her.

''Aunt Sarah?'' Stephen's voice echoed through the hallway, and Sarah leaped from the window seat.

''I'm here,'' she called out. ''In the library, Stephen.'' And then in a softer tone, ''Are you all right?''

He skidded to a halt before the warmly lit room, and his eyes sought her out. ''What'cha doin'?'' he asked, and then stepped forward, almost hurling himself into her arms. ''The kittens were hungry, Aunt Sarah, and their mama was busy washing them, so I shut the door of the shed and came inside. I woulda fed the tabby cat, but I didn't know what the sheriff wanted her to have.''

''There's food for her in the kitchen,'' Brace offered. ''We can wait till morning, or else I'll go out and leave a dish of milk for her tonight.''

''I think she's hungry,'' Stephen said. ''Washing all those babies is hard work.''

''It won't be long before they can wash themselves,'' Sarah said wisely. ''But for now their mother is happy to do it. I do think she could use a dish of milk, though.'' Her eyes cut to Brace, and he understood the silent query.

''Let's go, Stephen. I'll pour the milk and you can offer it to her. I'll bet she likes you better than me, anyway.''

Stephen shook his head. ''Naw. She just likes it because I was petting her and talking to her. She's still your cat." He reached for Brace's hand, and his small fingers clutched at the longer, more capable digits he touched. "Come on, sir. I'll help you with her. She's not afraid of me."

Brace smiled at the boy, relishing the feel of small fingers pressed against his palm. Children were trusting little souls. Too bad this one had found abuse in such unexpected places. Stephen should have been safe, secure in his father's love. Instead he'd been used as a pawn by a man whose selfish passions had driven him to draw Sarah into his reach. He looked at her now, noting the possessive look, the loving tenderness in her eyes as she watched the boy. She was a staunch champion, this Sarah Murphy.

The house was settled down, the candles blown out, the lamps darkened. Brace stretched out in his bed, pulling the sheet from the bottom to better accommodate his length, and yawned widely as he considered the woman who slept across the hallway.

She'd escorted Stephen to the storage room he'd chosen, had carefully inspected the bits and pieces of Brace's own childhood that had so caught Stephen's interest, and then had settled on the side of the narrow bed to listen while the boy squeezed his eyes shut and folded his hands.

A long litany of words and phrases had followed, a petition to the Almighty, a bedtime prayer that seemed to be a regular item in Stephen's life. But, for probably the first time, a new name was added to the list the boy recited as he named his family, one by one calling their names.

"And bless the sheriff," he'd said solemnly. "Thank

you for this nice room and the nice house he lives in, and for the food he let us eat for supper.''

Brace remembered the small, scrunched-up face, the smile that had been blinding in its brilliance as blue eyes opened and Stephen looked up at his aunt. ''I think that's everybody,'' he'd said, and then reached his arms to hug her and lifted himself from the pillow to plant a loud kiss against her cheek. Sarah had blown out the candle and headed for the door before Stephen called out, his words not for Sarah, but for the man who watched from the hallway.

''Good night, sir.''

''Good night, Stephen.'' He thought now he'd give a whole lot to claim the child as his own. It would be a pleasure to listen to the boy, to watch him at play and to know that he was a permanent fixture in his life. He should have married before this, perhaps had a child of his own to love and protect. And yet, as he'd told Sarah, there hadn't been anyone, except for Faith Hudson. And she'd gone where her heart led her. He could not fault her for it, but his chest tightened a bit as he thought of the woman he'd loved.

Now another woman had come along. And if he was half as smart as his mama had always said he was, he'd snatch her up and make her a permanent part of his life. And how would Miss Sarah Murphy feel about that? His mouth twitched as he thought of her, remembering her trim figure, her long hair finally let loose at bedtime, when she'd bent low over Stephen, allowing its length to surround her face and then fall to her bosom as she sat up on the edge of the bed.

He'd give a whole lot to haul her into his own bed right now, he decided. But that wasn't the route Sarah would be willing to take. Perhaps he could woo her, win her over gradually. And on that thought he closed his eyes and listened to the sounds coming from the room across the hall, where the object of his meandering thoughts was settling in for the night.

The door was quietly opened, and then the candle was extinguished as he heard her bedsprings give way beneath her slight weight. "Good night, Sarah," he called softly, and was pleased by her answering words.

"Good night, Brace." Then after a moment's silence, her whispered words filtered through the dark. "Thank you."

A week passed uneventfully. The days took on a rhythm of their own. Sarah cooked breakfast early and called Brace and Stephen when it was ready. Reluctantly Brace took his leave shortly after he'd finished the meal, heading for the middle of town and the office he kept there. It was a worry, leaving Sarah alone in the big house, but there was no help for it. He couldn't very well take her to work with him, and there'd be talk aplenty if he stayed home with her. Besides, there was Stephen to consider. Brace's first task was to drop the boy off at the small schoolhouse at the edge of town.

The boy was under strict orders to remain inside until Brace arrived to pick him up later in the day. It made a shorter workday for Brace, but he knew instinctively that there would be no complaint from the townspeople. They'd gotten their money's worth from him, and he could pretty well do as he pleased.

What he was pleased to do, he found, was to go home to Sarah. She was usually wrapped in a large apron, working in his kitchen when he arrived. Flushed and bright eyed, she seemed happy to see him, and those short minutes of greeting and her hurried instructions to make himself ready for supper began his evenings on a high note.

They sat in the library some evenings, Sarah reading aloud to Stephen, with Brace an eager listener. Other nights, once Stephen was in bed, they sat at the kitchen table and Sarah patiently tutored Brace with some of the simpler books he owned. The reading was coming easier these days, he realized.

"Why didn't you learn to read in school?" Sarah asked gently as she shifted the current book to lay it in front of him. Folding her hands before her on the table, she watched him from eyes that were warm and soft in the lamplight.

"I just couldn't seem to put the letters together. The teacher in our school was impatient with me. Told me I was just lazy. But there was never another child who wanted to read for himself more than I did. I felt left out and lonely. My sister read everything in sight, and my mother simply shook her head at my stumbling efforts."

"How cruel." Sarah, it seemed, was not partial to Brace's mother at this moment. "I can't imagine not getting help of some kind for a child with a special need." She eyed him thoughtfully. "It's strange that none of your other skills were affected. You're eloquent and present a picture of intelligence. No one would ever guess that you have a problem of any sort."

"I don't tell folks," he said shortly. "Just one other person knows. Except for Jamie, my deputy, and he only suspects. I ask him to read the posters for me and the mail that comes in. But I can handle most of it."

"It's not shameful, you know." Sarah's voice was stern and Brace looked up at her, for a moment ignoring the words on the page before him.

"Maybe not," he said. "But I felt ashamed. My whole life was tainted by it. Until I met a woman, Faith Hudson, and she began to tutor me."

"Were you in love with her?" Sarah asked quietly with a wistful note in her voice.

"I could have been. But she was married and ended up going back east to her husband." He reached out one big hand to Sarah, clasping her fingers in his. "To tell the truth, Sarah, I'm almost glad she's gone. I've just begun to realize that she wasn't the woman for me."

Sarah was quiet, her eyes scanning his face, then her gaze dropped to where their hands were joined in an easy grip. "I'm not either, Brace," she said in a low whisper.

"No?" He lifted her hand and bent forward, his mouth touching the soft skin on the backs of her fingers. "I'm beginning to think differently."

"I have too many problems," Sarah told him. "Along with Stephen, I have a brother-in-law who's out for my skin. And he won't care who he has to get rid of in order to make me pay for taking his son."

"He'll never touch you," Brace vowed. "That's why you're here, Sarah. I want you safe. Don't you believe I'll take care of you and Stephen?"

She nodded. "I believe that's your plan. But things don't always work out the way we want them to."

"Well, I've got a couple of ideas up my sleeve," Brace said. "I'm about ready to make you an offer, Sarah. I hope you'll think it over before you give me an answer."

"An offer?" She paled at his words and snatched her hand from his grasp. "Don't ask me to marry you, Brace. I won't let you take on my mess."

"Ah, but the deal is, I'll get you as my wife. Right now I can't think of anything I'd like better. And believe me, I've thought of little else since you moved in here."

"I've been thinking about taking Stephen somewhere else," she admitted. "I don't want the people here to start talking about you. If I'm the cause of you losing your job, I'd never forgive myself."

"Well, then. There's a simple solution, sweetheart. Just say the word, and I'll have the minister stop by and bring his book of prayers with him."

"You make it sound so easy," she said with a grimace. "There's more to it than that, Brace. You need to think of the days and years ahead, when you're stuck with a wife you hadn't planned on. What if you change your mind?"

"I'm not impulsive, usually," he said. "But I knew when I saw you that first night that you were the most appealing woman I'd laid eyes on in a month of Sundays. And your being here has reinforced my opinion. I want you, Sarah. Not just in my bed, although that's a part of it. I want you to live in my house and take care of me and make me feel like a man with roots—a family, and a woman who cares about him."

"I'm here now," she told him. "I'm taking care of you and I care about you. You don't have to offer marriage."

He shot her a glance that made her cheeks burn. His gaze fell to rest on the soft curves of her breasts and dwelt there for a long minute. "In order to have you where I want you, I have to offer marriage, Sarah. I won't have you in my bed any other way."

"In your bed." She pressed her lips together firmly, then looked down at the tabletop. "I don't think I'll ever be very good at that part of marriage,'' she said. ''From what Sierra told me, it sounds like a nasty business, and a woman is at a disadvantage.''

Brace laughed, a soft chuckle that made her look up at him. ''I don't know what sort of marriage your sister had,'' he said, ''but any man who puts his wife at a disadvantage is not much of a man at all. As to the 'nasty business' part, I'll be happy to show you otherwise, once we get a ring on your finger.''

He reached for her again, rising and lifting her from her chair. His arms encircled her and he held her firmly against his body, aware that his arousal had to be evident to her. She might as well get used to it, he figured. It wasn't going to ease up until he had his way, and she was persuaded to do as he asked.

Sarah leaned into him, as if she sought his warmth and strength, and he tucked her neatly to his length, then lifted her chin, the better to see her face. ''I'm not going to tell you I love you yet,'' he said with obvious honesty. ''But I sure do like you, and I've got a hankering for you that won't leave me alone. I think I could spend my whole life with you and never regret my choice.''

He bent his head and his lips were gentle against hers. And then, as if a fire had come to life between them, he held her closer and his mouth opened a bit, his tongue begging entry. She allowed his foray, silent and almost unmoving as he set about a tentative survey of her mouth. She was unused to such love play. He was certain of it, recognizing that her trust in him was her sole reason for allowing his exploration.

His kiss softened and he transferred his attention to her cheek, then her temple and forehead, leaving a trail of kisses that she appeared to welcome. Eyes closed, she stood in his arms, and her breath was rapid against his face. Her breasts rose and fell quickly and he relished the feel of her shapely form against his chest. One hand found its way into her hair, and somehow he managed to undo the twisted coil she had formed on the back of her head sometime today. He pulled several pins free, and the long length of waves fell down her back.

"My hair." Her voice was a mere whisper as she jerked in his arms. "You've taken down my hair."

"Yeah, I surely did," he told her, holding her a few inches from him, the better to see her. His fingers made inroads into the thick, dark mass, and against his skin it felt like the finest silk. "I've been wanting to see it like this ever since I met you. It was loose that night, too."

"I couldn't find my pins," she said. "Once I got here, I located them in my saddlebags."

"And you've kept it in a damn knot ever since," he told her. "Hair like this should be seen."

"It's not seemly," she told him. "A lady wears her hair up in public."

"Well, this lady is going to wear it down when she's with her husband," he stated firmly. "You're too pretty to look like an old maid."

"I am an old maid."

"Not quite," Brace said. "You aren't old enough, to begin with, and I'll warrant there's been more than one man chasin' after you."

She blushed again and dropped her gaze. He tugged her closer and held her captive before him. His hands slid the length of her back, then returned to where her curls and waves fell to her waist. He gripped her hair in both hands and used it as a lever, pulling her head back enough for him to seek out her mouth again.

With a muffled sigh she lifted her arms and encircled his neck, leaning into his strength and relaxing her body, allowing her softness to blend with his muscled form. She fitted herself against him then, and he felt a rush of desire that caught him broadside.

Sarah might be inexperienced and was no doubt a virgin, but she had a natural sensuality that caused his blood to rush to the appropriate places in his body, and he found himself more than ready to carry her up the stairs to his bed.

As if she knew his mind, she stepped back, folding her arms around her waist. "I don't think this is a good idea, Sheriff," she said firmly. "I'm going to bed. Alone. And I'm going to try real hard to forget all this ever happened."

Yet half an hour later as she lay in her bed, Sarah was conscious of a strange heat that possessed her as she recalled his smile and the tilt of his head as he'd released her from his hold.

"I don't think you'll be able to forget it so easily, Miss Sarah," he'd said.

And he was right. For the first time in her life she began to understand why a woman might find marriage attractive. Why a man might appeal to the baser instincts that a woman usually kept under lock and key. Heaven knew, she hadn't protested when he'd kissed her. Or hugged her and pressed her against his body. Quite the opposite, in fact.

She felt a shiver of delight as she thought of his big hands on her, and wondered for a forbidden minute how those same hands would feel against her skin. Not her hands or face, but the skin hidden by her clothing. An image of his long fingers against her breast made her sit upright in bed, and she groaned. She was becoming a wanton, and it was all his fault.

Tomorrow—tomorrow she'd turn over a new leaf. She'd be aloof and keep their relationship purely friendly. She'd give him no encouragement in his pursuit of her. Lying back down, her head on her pillow, she sighed. It sounded like a difficult assignment. For right now she could think of nothing she'd like better than to feel Brace Caulfield's arms around her again.

Chapter Five

The general store held a mixed assortment of shoppers, and Sarah felt comfortable in their midst. Several ladies smiled and nodded at her, and two gentlemen tipped their hats in her direction. Living in Benning, Texas, seemed an answer to her dreams. The thought of having a home and family in such a place had long played a big part in her fantasies, and the reality presented itself now as if a gift-wrapped package had been delivered into her hands on Christmas morning.

All she had to do was answer in the affirmative the next time Brace brought up the subject of marriage, and she could be a part of this community. In fact, she already felt that a comfortable niche had opened for her. And the man who had provided her with a home and the shelter of his position was also the means of her achieving her dream.

Mrs. Brace Caulfield. The name sounded solid. The man was to be trusted. His home was all any woman could want, and it seemed Brace's feelings extended to include Stephen in the magic circle of his thoughtfulness.

Sarah smiled at the storekeeper, Mr. Metcalfe, and

handed him her list of necessities, one she had pondered over for long minutes. Unwilling to spend Brace's money foolishly, she'd crossed off several items she considered to be pure luxury. Now she waited while the man behind the counter brought boxes and bags of supplies to rest before her.

"Find everything you need?" The low voice in her ear startled her but served to bring a smile of welcome to the storekeeper's face.

"Hey, there, Sheriff. Didn't expect to see you in here this morning." His gaze fluttered back and forth between Brace and Sarah, and his smile was jovial as the man drew his own conclusions about the couple.

"I thought I'd see if Miss Murphy found everything she needs. I knew she'd made out a list and I wanted to be certain there was no problem." Brace thrust his hands into his back pockets and took a stance beside Sarah, his dark gaze touching her as he spoke.

She felt a flush cover her cheeks and was tongue-tied for a moment. "I think everything's in order," she said finally, her voice sounding choked.

"Let's see the list," Brace told the storekeeper.

"No problem," the man replied, handing Brace the smudged and altered bit of paper upon which Sarah had made adjustments as she took inventory of Brace's kitchen.

"How come you crossed stuff off?" Brace asked the woman next to him, his frown pulling his brows down.

"There were a few things I thought I could do without," Sarah said, her voice low, her demeanor stilted. "I don't want to take advantage of you."

His brows rose as if pulled from above by two wires. "That's not likely, Miss Sarah. You can buy out the whole store if you like. So long as you keep on cooking the way you have, I'll be glad to fund the venture.''

As though he'd been granted permission to decipher the crossed-off items, Mr. Metcalfe scanned the list and hastily added the missing ingredients to the pile on the counter. His fingers were busy as he added up the total and inserted the amount in his black book. Boxes were found and bundles were wrapped as Sarah waited, her hands clutched tightly before her.

Several ladies nearby looked askance at Sarah as Brace spoke of her cooking and his willingness to buy her anything she desired. She lowered her eyes to the floor, unwilling to be privy to their disapproval.

''Ladies?'' Brace called their attention to himself and Sarah and they all stepped closer, the better to hear him.

''Have you heard the news? Miss Murphy has almost agreed to marry me.''

''Almost?'' one of the women said, her voice rising. ''What's keeping her from snatching you up, Sheriff? You're a fine specimen of a man, so far as I can tell. If I didn't already have Howard parked in my kitchen and takin' up room in my bed, I'd grab you in a minute.''

Brace laughed aloud. ''Well, I've been taken, Mrs. Johnson. Sorry to disappoint you. Hopefully, Miss Sarah will set a date right quick.''

''I think I need to take the supplies back to the house,'' Sarah choked out, thoroughly embarrassed by the attention they had drawn.

''Have you thought about a date?'' Mrs. Johnson asked, pursuing the idea like a dog with a bone.

Sarah inhaled deeply. ''A week Saturday.'' She quietly spoke the words that would seal her fate. She glanced up at Brace, his mouth agape.

''A week Saturday?'' he repeated, then quickly gathered his senses. "Sounds like a good idea to me. I'll talk to the minister today and see if he can manage it."

"I'll guarantee it," another voice chimed in. From several feet away the minister's wife put in her two cents worth, and as far as the townsfolk were concerned, that cinched the matter.

Sarah bit her tongue. She'd really done it this time. Her penchant for speaking before she thought had launched her into wedding plans almost before she had thoroughly digested the idea. This wasn't at all the way she'd thought it would be arranged.

Mr. Metcalfe leaned across the counter. "I've got some lovely dresses, ma'am. You come back without the groom and I'll show them to you. We need to get you all gussied up for the wedding."

Blushing furiously, Sarah gathered what supplies she could in her arms and looked beseechingly at Brace. "I could use a hand," she said.

"You got the wagon here?" he asked, and at her nod he hoisted a box to one shoulder and then picked up the remaining box with his other arm. Someone opened the door for them as they left, and Sarah made her departure with haste.

Brace loaded the supplies in the back of the wagon and hoisted Sarah up onto the seat. "I'll follow you on my horse and carry things in for you," he offered, and turned away before she could thwart his plan.

The drive back to the house was short, and Sarah barely had time to sort out her thoughts before Brace's horse was beside her near the back door. He dismounted and approached her with outstretched arms. "Let me help you," he said, his eyes aglow with a light she recognized.

Her hands clutched at his shoulders as he lifted her

down, and he held her for a moment in midair, looking into her eyes with a strange expression.

"What?" she asked quickly. "What's wrong?"

"Absolutely nothing," he answered. "I just wish you'd chosen to accept me last night. Then I'd have been able to properly appreciate the occasion."

"Properly? How's that?" she asked, her toes reaching for the ground.

"Like this," he said softly, lowering her to stand before him and sliding his arms to encircle her waist. He bent his head as she lifted hers and their lips met in a kiss that seemed oddly familiar and yet startlingly new. It was a possession she could not fault, for the man was to be her husband, and his embrace offered her a peek into the unknown world of marriage. Yet she was a novice at this game, and he seemed to expect much of her. She was floundering, with no notion of how to respond.

His hands were touching her everywhere they could reach—from the nape of her neck to the fullness of her hips, from the width of her shoulders to her waist, then slipping around to the front of her dress, gliding carefully over the lush curves of her breasts as if he had already laid claim to the soft flesh beneath her clothing.

"Brace?" Her voice was hushed, the tone filled with apprehension as she spoke his name.

"Don't worry, sweetheart," he murmured. "I don't expect anything from you now. Not until that ring is on your finger. Just a kiss or two will satisfy me today. But a week Saturday you can expect a revelation to take place in your life. You'll be Mrs. Brace Caulfield, and I'll make you mine."

"Don't say that," she protested. "That's what Lester

told Sierra. That he owned her, body and soul, and she must always bow to that fact.''

"That's not what I mean," Brace told her. "I'm saying we'll belong to each other as husband and wife, that my first thoughts will be for your happiness and well-being for the rest of my life. That you'll belong to me in a way that defies description. We'll be as one person, one soul, with all the same wants and needs and expectations.''

"I didn't know you were so eloquent," Sarah said, leaning against him fully. He was tall and strong and held her with arms that promised fulfillment of the words he spoke.

Perhaps Sierra's experience of marriage had been because of Lester's foul behavior. Maybe this wouldn't be the disaster Sarah had feared. Brace and Lester were nothing alike. It was not fair to tar Brace with the same brush, just because he was a man and was, no doubt, given to the same desires as other men.

"I'll make you happy, Sarah," he promised, his mouth against her forehead. "I'll do whatever it takes to keep you content. We'll raise Stephen as our own. Whatever is involved in getting custody of the boy will be our first priority.''

That cinched it. Sarah wrapped her arms around his neck and lifted her face fully to his. "You couldn't have said anything to make me happier," she told him. "Stephen is important to me.''

"I know that." Brace bent to kiss her again, and his lips claimed hers with a warmth and possessive need she responded to without hesitation. Even if the bedding that was to come was as Sierra had described, it would be worth it, she decided. Selfish as it sounded, even to her own hearing, anything that would gain her legal control over Stephen made this choice worthwhile.

Brace hadn't said he loved her. In fact, just the opposite. But there was, in the hidden depths of Sarah, a spark that threatened to burst into a flame. She was filled with the knowledge that this man was the right choice for her, that she loved him freely and without restraint. He was all that was good and honest and forthright. If he failed to love her, she could live with that lack. He liked her, he cared about her well-being and, best of all, he would be a good father to Stephen.

After ten days, ten very busy, exciting days, the house began to fill early on that designated morning. Ladies from town, led by the minister's wife, invaded Sarah's kitchen, carrying bowls and platters laden with food.

"I understand the wedding's at noon," Mrs. Johnson said importantly, as if she'd been gifted with that knowledge by the groom himself. And so she had, Sarah thought. For Brace had told her last night that to tell Mrs. Johnson something was to alert the whole town—at least the female half. Yet she was a most likable woman, and her joy at the forthcoming ceremony was genuine.

Now the ladies bustled around her kitchen and dining room, laying out the pristine tablecloth Sarah had washed and ironed in preparation for this day. They unloaded silver and plates from the dresser and set the table, adding dishes from their own homes to complete the display. The stacks of plates were enormous, Sarah thought, and said as much.

"Everyone in town will be here," Mrs. Johnson answered, her words placid, as if it were a known fact that no one in Benning wanted to miss seeing their Brace wed.

"Folks were talking about you living here," she confided to Sarah, "but I let them know that there wasn't any hanky-panky going on. I said you were a good girl, and Brace was simply biding his time till you gave in and married him."

"Thank you," Sarah told her, and meant the words. That the people in Benning should think badly of Brace would wound her dreadfully, and she was thankful for the staunch support of some of the womenfolk.

"Still, I'm glad you decided so quickly to make this thing legal," Mrs. Johnson said.

"He swept me off my feet," Sarah told her, the words having meaning for the first time in her life. For indeed, the tall, dark man had literally taken her by storm, and she felt a sense of fate intervening in her life, so certain was she of his promises and the security she and Stephen would find here in this house with Brace Caulfield.

"What every woman wants," another lady said with a laugh. "A man who knows what he wants and knows how to get it."

"He'll be getting it sooner than you can snap your fingers," a third woman said with a knowing grin. "And I'll warrant our Sarah will be well loved. Brace is a good man, and he'll take care of her."

Sarah felt hot through and through. These women spoke so boldly, so knowingly, about intimate matters, and she was so much in the dark about such things that their words sounded almost like a foreign language. She simply knew that their predictions made her warm and flushed, and her hands rose in an attempt to conceal the blush that covered her cheeks.

She'd chosen a white dress from the general store, with the help of several of the ladies who'd been out shopping that day. It was soft and frothy, with a full skirt swishing around her legs, and a bodice that sported a sweetheart neckline and embroidery on the sleeves. It fit her like a glove and made her feel like a bride, a fact that had finally come home to her as she dressed in her bedroom early in the day.

Now, surrounded by the phalanx of supporters who by the merit of being womenfolk were thus firmly grouped together in this venture, she entered the parlor, where Brace and Stephen waited. The tall, youthful minister stood beside them, and with one long finger he beckoned Sarah forward to stand next to the two males who would make up her family, Stephen in place between Sarah and Brace.

Mrs. Johnson, chosen as a witness, stood beside her, and Jamie took up his place next to Brace. The deputy was excited about his role in this endeavor, and his eyes shone with excitement.

"You've got the ring, right?" Brace whispered loudly, and was obviously reassured by Jamie's fervent reply.

"It's the only thing I've heard from you for three days. Nag, nag. Don't lose the ring. Make sure you keep it on you all the time. Don't let anything happen to it."

Around them, the menfolk laughed at the exchange, and Jamie turned to direct a glare at them. "You don't know what a pain he's been for the last week or so. Can't get his head out of the clouds."

At that, someone began to clap, and soon the room resounded with the sound of hands offering their blessings on this union.

The minister gathered his small cluster of participants

together and opened his book of prayers. The ceremony was short but meaningful, and Sarah listened to the words as if they were pearls of wisdom coming from the young preacher's mouth. She responded at the appropriate times and heard Brace's deep voice tremble as he promised to love, honor and cherish her.

He would keep his vow. She knew it from somewhere deep inside her, where all such important knowledge resides, where her own decision to marry the man had been made. And when the minister pronounced them man and wife and instructed Brace to kiss his bride, she was swept into his arms, almost crushing Stephen in the process, and offered a kiss that blended affection and respect and a touch of impatience, all in one. The crowd responded with shouts and clapping, then gathered around to offer their individual congratulations.

"Are we really married now?" Stephen asked in an undertone.

"We certainly are," she replied, bending a bit to answer him.

"I like being married, Aunt Sarah," he confided. "I'm glad we chose Sheriff Caulfield."

Sarah was silent, her heart too full for words, aware that, were it not for Brace, she and Stephen would not have remained together to share this day.

She couldn't have asked for more, couldn't have wished for a happier wedding, Sarah decided. And definitely could not have wanted a more handsome groom, or been more pleased with Stephen's acceptance of the whole ceremony. He'd expressed his joy to her the night before, assuring her that Brace would be a fine choice, and hugging her with the full strength of his boyish arms. Barely showing signs of muscle, long and gangly, they had wrapped around her waist and he'd squeezed her tightly.

"I sure love you, Aunt Sarah," he'd said soberly. "Thank you for finding me a brand-new daddy, somebody who's gonna love me."

She almost wept now as she watched the boy clinging to Brace's hand, his eyes looking upward to the warmth showered on him by the man who'd become his hero. This alone made the whole thing worthwhile, Sarah decided. Having Stephen with her was somehow fulfilling her debt to Sierra—not that she really owed her twin anything tangible, except for the acceptance of the tie that bound them together, even after death.

Plates were filled and chairs occupied as the townspeople took their places all over the house. Sarah found herself on the stairs, Brace by her side, greeting a whole line of those who offered their best wishes and bestowed their blessings. Later she ate little, but was instead sustained by the joy of the moment.

The ladies cleaned up the remains of the food, doling it out and leaving a generous supply for Sarah's use, then joined their families for the walk home. Those who lived farther away had brought wagons, and laughing children piled into the backs as the community of friends took their leave, Sarah and Brace in the doorway to bid them farewell. She waved and smiled for long moments, then slumped against the man whose arm encircled her waist.

"Tired, sweetheart?" he asked bending to her. His mouth brushed her cheek and she smiled.

"A little. Just happy, mostly."

"Are you? Really?" he asked. "You don't feel like you got talked into anything? I didn't rush you too much?"

She shook her head. "No. This is what I chose to do." She looked up at him, her tone earnest as she confided her thoughts quietly. "You know, last night, when I helped Stephen get ready for bed, he thanked me for marrying you and giving him a new daddy."

Moisture glittered suspiciously in Brace's eyes as he absorbed that statement. And then he swallowed and looked away. "I can't tell you how much that means to me," he said. "And how about you? Are you happy to be Mrs. Caulfield?"

"More than you know," Sarah told him.

"I hope you'll still be happy tomorrow," he said, kissing her again, a chaste touch of his lips on her temple.

"I will," she said firmly.

"I'll do my best to—"

"Stop," she said. "You don't need to explain yourself to me, Brace. I know you won't hurt me, and I know you'll be all I ever wanted. That's all I can ask."

His eyes darkened with a touch of anger. "Of course I won't hurt you, sweetheart. I'd never do such a thing. It's a possibility, if a man is careless or hasty. I don't plan to be either, not with you."

She turned into his arms and rested there, feeling a tranquil peace creep into her very soul. "I trust you," she said, the statement a positive pronouncement of her feelings for him. "I've given myself to you for all the years to come. For life, Brace."

"Well, you haven't yet. Not quite," he said. "But soon." And his eyes lit, dissolving the anger he'd shown just moments before. "Soon, Sarah."

Sarah listened to Stephen's prayers, as she had since Sierra's death when he'd come to her, noting with joy his inclusion of his *new father* instead of the usual blessing on Brace. From the doorway Brace watched, and Sarah caught a glimpse of joy written plainly on his face. Then he entered the box room and approached Stephen.

"Are you too old for good-night kisses?" he asked. And as if he offered the boy no choice, he bent low over the bed. Slim arms reached up to hold him fast as Stephen planted a noisy buss on Brace's cheek.

"Kids never get too old to kiss their mom and dad," he said soberly. "I've decided that Aunt Sarah is still my aunt, but she's really gonna be my mom from now on, and I'd already decided you were gonna be my new daddy. Is that all right with you?"

"Certainly," Brace told him. "I feel honored."

"You gonna sleep with my new mom?" Stephen asked in the midst of a yawn.

Brace looked taken aback. "Yeah, as a matter of fact, I am."

"I just wondered. My mom and dad used to sleep together, and you and Aunt Sarah each have your own bedrooms. I just wondered."

"Wonder no more, son," Brace said, laughter tingeing his words with melody. "Your aunt Sarah is moving into my room, as of tonight. We're married now."

"I'm glad," the boy mumbled, his eyes closing as he drifted off to sleep, his world secure, his mind at rest.

"Your room?" Sarah asked softly as they moved into the hallway.

"My room," Brace said firmly. "It's larger, room for all your stuff and mine, too. I've even got a decent-sized closet, and my bed's bigger."

Sarah nodded. ''Sounds to me like you've got your arguments all lined up.''

''No argument, just the facts,'' he told her. Reaching the door to her room, he shooed her inside. ''Get what you need for tonight,'' he said, ''and then come across the hall to me.''

''I'll put on my gown. I won't be a minute,'' she told him, thankful that he'd given her these few moments of privacy.

''Five minutes, Sarah. That's all I'm willing to wait, and then I'll come back and get you.''

She made haste, undoing her dress, stripping off her stockings and underwear and pulling the full white nightgown over her head. Her chores behind the screen in the corner took but minutes, and when Brace opened the door, it was to find her in the middle of the room, her hands in her hair, busily taking out the pins.

The sight of dark waves and curls cascading down her back was almost his undoing, and in two long strides he was in front of her. ''I'll do that,'' he said gruffly. ''I've been looking forward all day to taking your hair down.''

He took the pins from her and walked to put them on her dresser, then returned to her, brush in hand. ''Turn around,'' he said, his voice almost harsh, and he tried to soften his tone. ''I'm impatient, Sarah. I promised myself I wouldn't be, but it seems I don't have a lot of self-control where you're concerned. In fact, the past week has been a lesson in behaving myself.''

''You've had your hands all over me,'' she said sharply. ''You call that behaving yourself?''

''Little do you know, sweetheart,'' he murmured, using the brush with long, slow strokes to tame her curls.

The tendrils licked out like flames of dark fire, touching his callused hands and clinging to his hard skin.

His hands were dark against her white gown, and he felt a moment's regret that his skin was rough, his body showing the results of a hard life. Sarah deserved so much, and he was so in need of pleasing her. He willed his hands to relax, praying for patience enough to pet her and caress her as she deserved. The arousal in his trousers was becoming more rigid, and he sensed his control was near to breaking.

"Come to my room," he whispered, pulling her against him. She leaned in, gladly, he thought, as though she relished the feel of his long body against hers.

"All right," she told him. "Just let me get my robe. I'll need it in the morning."

He laughed softly, his thoughts speeding ahead to daybreak. By the time he let her get dressed in the morning, it would be later than her normal rising time to face the day. She was most assuredly not rising at the crack of dawn as was her usual practice. He had other plans.

Quietly, watching for the squeaky board in the hallway, they crossed to his room, and he closed and latched the door firmly behind them. A lamp glowed softly on the table beside the bed and he led her there.

"I'll pull back the covers," she said, as if she must make conversation in order to keep her thoughts from the coming night. "Everyone had a good time, didn't they?" She looked up, awaiting his reply.

"Yeah, I'd say so. Old Mr. Johnson had a gallon of corn likker in his wagon, and if he'd had his way, they'd have had a regular party out there."

"I didn't know that," she said, wide-eyed as she turned to him.

"Mrs. Johnson did," Brace told her. "I'll bet he got what-for all the way home."

"They brought us some lovely gifts," Sarah murmured. "The quilt from Mrs. Metcalfe is beautiful, isn't it?"

But his eyes were fixed on the vision of loveliness before him as Brace nodded agreeably. "Lovely. But not nearly as beautiful as you," he said impulsively, watching as a flustered look filled her features with confusion.

"I'm not beautiful," she said quickly. "No one's ever thought so."

"I do," he said quietly. His hands trembled as they touched her face, his fingertips sliding over her nose and cheeks, cupping her chin as he murmured his opinion of that piquant feature.

"You have such a stubborn little chin," he said. "And your blue eyes are dark tonight."

She blinked at him and he almost laughed aloud. His hands twitched as he dropped them to her shoulders, and then he slid his palms down the slope of her breasts, soft, yet firm and full beneath her nightgown. He cupped them carefully, not willing to rush her or put any trace of fear into those liquid eyes.

"I've never known such a woman," he said quietly. "I've never wanted another woman as much as you. You're exactly what I've needed for a lot of years."

"I'll talk to you about that in a year or so," she said with a shaky laugh. "I may not wear well."

"Oh, I think you will," he answered, his hands moving to the line of buttons that held her gown together. He was deft as he undid them, and then noted the anxious look she wore.

"Please turn out the light," she said. "I feel..."

"Whatever you say, sweetheart," he said reassuringly, although his eagerness to see her in the light almost prevailed. Had he begged for the lamp to remain aglow, she might have acquiesced, but for tonight he would do as she willed. If Sarah was more comfortable in the dark, then they would discover each other with the faint glow of moonlight guiding their lips, hands and fingertips. Another night would see their lamp lit well into the hours after midnight.

Sitting on the edge of a chair, he took off his boots, then slid off his stockings. "I'll just be a minute," he told her, watching as she folded back the sheet and quilt, fluffing the pillows as she prepared his bed. He stood, peeled his jacket off, then unbuttoned his shirt and tossed it across the chair.

Sarah picked it up, folded it neatly and replaced it there. She looked up at him then. "The light?"

"Right now," he said, and walked to the side of the bed to blow out the bright glow. The room was cast into darkness and Sarah was but a blur against the blackness behind her. Her white gown seemed suddenly to take on a life of its own, and Brace stepped closer to her as he slid his trousers from his waist, taking his drawers with them. He stepped on them carelessly, freeing his feet from them as he reached for her.

"Your trousers," she said against his chest. "Let me fold them up for you."

"Leave them where they are. I'll take care of them in the morning."

"I'm your wife now, Brace. I need to do this sort of thing for you."

He laughed softly. "If you think that's all a wife's

responsibilities cover, I've got news for you, Mrs. Caulfield.''

"I know that. I just don't like to think of your good trousers on the floor all night." She bent, her hair brushing against his naked chest and belly, and he felt a thundering within him that signaled his readiness. It was all he could do to stand still as she folded the rest of his clothing and placed it on the chair atop his shirt.

"All done?" he asked, and rued the impatience in his tone.

She turned back to him and he peered down at her, wanting to see her expression. "I'm done for now," she said. "I don't mean to be such a fussbudget. But I think you'll have to get used to me."

"I'm looking forward to it." His voice held an undertone of determination and his arms were firm and steady as he picked her up and placed her on the bed, tucking her feet beneath the covers. Circling the footboard, he found his place beside her and slid beneath the sheet.

Her leg brushed against his, the fine fabric of her gown between them. Then her hand reached to touch him and brushed against the mat of hair on his chest. "That's what I thought," she said, aware of his lack of covering. "You're not wearing anything."

"I never wear anything to bed." It was a fact. "I guess you'll just have to get used to me, too, Sarah."

"I'll try."

He turned his head on the pillow and caught a glimpse of her pale features in the moonlight. The stars were bright, the moon full, and he blessed the faint gleam that allowed him to watch her, even though he'd have preferred the lamplight. His arms encircled her and he drew her into his embrace.

"I've never slept with a man," she said, as if she must explain her lack of experience. "No one else has ever touched me the way you do."

"I know," he answered. "I'm glad. That gives me the chance to be the first. And the last, Sarah. This marriage is forever. I hope you realize that. I don't begin anything I don't intend to finish."

"I figured that out already," she told him, allowing herself to conform to his longer length, his firm muscular chest and the flat planes of his belly. He felt her feet touching his shins and the enveloping folds of her gown keeping her warmth from him.

"I'm going to take off your gown," he told her gruffly. "I hope you don't mind."

"Would it matter if I did?" she asked, humor lacing the words.

"Probably not," he admitted. "I can't touch you through all the material. And I want to have my hands on you."

She inhaled sharply and then he watched as she nodded—almost reluctantly, he thought.

"All right," she whispered, and sat up beside him. Her hands were busy pulling the gown from beneath her and then she stripped her arms from the sleeves and he sat up and took over, lifted the garment over her head and placed it at the foot of the bed.

In the moonlight her breasts were exposed to him, limned in the glow of stars, lifting from her chest, seeming to him to be twin offerings presented for his pleasure, making his hands twitch as he considered how he would test and discover the essence of her skin. It was something he determined to do without waiting. Her breasts would be his, his to hold and touch and kiss. He trembled again as he considered the idea, inhaling her fragrance as it rose from her body.

But first, he decided, he would woo her, teasing and petting her until she was eager for him, ready for his possession.

Chapter Six

Sarah turned her head in Brace's direction. His eyes gleamed in the light of the moon and stars, his gaze was focused on her breasts, and Sarah felt more naked than she'd ever thought possible. Her gown was too far away to reach and she wasn't quite certain she wanted it back on, anyway. The freedom of being unclothed was exciting, and the knowledge that her body had the ability to entice Brace and make him eager for her was beyond description.

He'd let her know in small, subtle ways that he liked her form, that she was attractive to him, but this was different. Now he looked with the eyes of a conqueror upon her unclothed body, his hand rising, even as she watched, to touch the underside of her breast. Her breath caught as he formed his palm there, and then she felt it slide upward to enclose the whole of that soft mound in his hand.

A sound slipped from his lips, a soft acknowledgment of his approval, she decided, although what was so exciting about a woman's breasts was more than she could understand. They were just *there*, part of her anatomy. Yet Brace sat beside her and viewed her in the starlight with a look of rapt absorption that made her feel as if she were a treasure he had just uncovered and was planning to claim as his own.

He pressed on her breast, his other arm behind her shoulders, and lowered her to lie beside him on the bed, his shoulder becoming a resting place for her head. She was silent, unwilling to admit her total ignorance of the mating that was to come. Sierra had told her in no uncertain terms that it was filled with pain and an uncomfortable messiness. That knowledge had totally put her off any pleasant anticipation of the venture.

Lester, apparently, was not of the same nature as Brace. *Impatient* and *selfish* were the words Sierra had used, and even with so little to go on, Sarah knew instinctively that Brace did not deserve either of those two designations. Even now, as his body readily gave evidence of his desire, his arousal pressing against her leg, he was careful of her tender flesh and placed soft kisses against her cheek.

She wanted more. Just what *more* consisted of, she wasn't entirely certain, but she knew a yearning for his big body to cover hers, a need for his hands to touch the hidden places that wept for his possession. As though he'd read her thoughts, he slid his hand from one breast to caress the other. Then, lifting himself on one elbow, he bent low and kissed the puckered crest, a soft, undemanding touch of his lips, and then with an openmouthed caress he nuzzled at that small scrap of flesh that seemed to swell and grow taut as if it held a vast amount of tension within. Tension that was doubled by the touch of his tongue against her.

She wiggled against him, one hand rising to clutch at the back of his head, holding him against her breast, as if she would express the urgency of her need.

He murmured soft words and his hand held her in place, fingers spread wide across her stomach as he suckled the flesh he'd exposed. Sarah moved restlessly beneath his hand and he laughed softly, a sound that pleased her.

"You like that?" he drawled in a lazy fashion, as if he could remain where he was for the whole night to come.

Her reply was but a muffled assent, but he seemed to understand the message and his palm moved lower, touching her hipbones, caressing the small rounding of her belly and moving lower still—until he reached the triangle of curls that guarded her female parts. Parts so very different from the hard pressure of his masculine need against her thigh.

She shivered as he carefully touched her damp flesh, shuddered as his fingers slid ever closer to the channel where he would place himself, and caught her breath as one long finger slid into her body.

"Brace?" A question shivered in her voice as she called his name, and she tensed against his hand. He soothed her, whispering assurance in her ear, leaning over her to kiss her skin in a myriad of places, from her forehead to her lips, then back down to the breasts that seemed to be especially appealing to him.

Words of praise rolled from his lips and she listened with awe as he described her in an undertone. "Pretty… soft…sweet smelling…" And the list went on, as though every word that described beauty was suitable to be used in his evaluation of her. She felt a thrill of excitement pass through her body, centering where his hand was discovering the womanly parts of her.

His fingers slid readily where they would, for her flesh was damp and slippery, a fact he seemed to be pleased with, for he mentioned it just at the moment she'd decided to be embarrassed because of it.

"It means you're ready for me," he whispered, his hand moving ever closer to a small nubbin that yearned for his touch. It felt swollen and in need of something, and she moved again beneath him. "Let's see how this works," he said softly, lifting himself to part her legs and insinuate his body there.

He was big, his shoulders wide above her, and his weight was almost frightening, although he held himself from her, leaning on his forearms on either side of her head. "Am I too heavy for you?" he asked. "I can do this another way if you want me to."

She felt overwhelmed by the moment of decision and simply gave her consent to his preferences with a simple nod of her head. He seemed to understand her dilemma, and chuckled softly. "I know I'm heavy, sweetheart. Let's do it this way."

In a lithe movement he knelt between her legs and lifted them to lie across his thighs. She felt exposed, more naked than she'd thought possible, but he bent and kissed her gently, murmuring words of assurance.

"I'll try not to hurt you, baby," he whispered. "The first time is painful, I've heard, but, God willing, I'll be careful and take my time."

She shivered as her body chilled without the warmth of him against her skin. And then he lifted her bottom and adjusted her against his hard arousal. One hand opened her, the other eased his member into the tight opening, and he slid his way within.

Sarah caught her breath, feeling a fullness she had not expected. In fact, she hadn't known what to expect, except for Sierra's warnings, but none of her sister's words had prepared her for this thrill of being possessed by the man she loved. Nothing had readied her for the pleasure of his body there, in the depths of hers, and the knowledge that he was truly becoming her husband, even as he pressed farther into the place that had been designed for him to claim.

"Are you all right?" he asked, his voice strained, his arms trembling as he leaned over her once more. It seemed that he was well in possession of her, for she felt the fullness almost beyond bearing. Then there was an edge of pain that drew her deeper into the chasm into which he'd thrust her, and finally, a sharp knifelike shock that drew a gasp from her lips and a cry of distress from her depths.

"I'm sorry, Sarah," he whispered against her ear. "It'll never hurt again. Just this once." And so saying, he thrust farther, beyond the barrier of her virginity, into the farthest reaches of her womanhood. His groan was one of completion, his movements strong and fervent, and she clutched at his back, aware of a new yearning, one that seemed to be centered there, where he'd secured himself in her, where his flesh was so securely meshed with her own.

She wiggled against him and he moved again, thrusting against her, where her body cradled his weight. He lay above her, sheltering her beneath the cover of muscles that flexed and provided a haven in which she was secure. Broad hands lifted her against him as he knelt once more and his palms spread wide over her slender form, his fingers exploring every inch of her body, even as his arousal seemed to come to life once more deep inside her. She felt new waves of pleasure begin as he found those secret places that responded to his touch, and then stilled herself as the response of her body swept her upward. She cried aloud as spasms of pure joy took possession of her, filling her with an ecstasy she could not have imagined.

"Sarah…" His voice broke, as if he were touched to his depths by her pleasure, and Sarah reached for him again, tugging him to lie upon her, holding him fast against her body.

"I love you, Brace," she whispered. "You don't have to love me in return. Just know that I'm happy right now, that you've been all I ever wanted, all I ever thought to have as a husband."

He held her, rolling to his side and carrying her with him. "Ah, Sarah. I knew there was a storehouse of passion in your warm little body. I had no idea it was so easily aroused and so readily satisfied. You're perfect." He lifted himself a bit and his mouth touched her eyebrows, then her temple and cheek, finally possessing her mouth with an avid kiss that told her, more readily than words ever could, that he was pleased with her.

The knock on their bedroom door came early. "Aunt Sarah. Aren't you going to cook breakfast this morning?" Stephen's treble voice sounded loudly through the wooden panel and Sarah sat bolt upright.

"I'll be down in a minute, Stephen," she said. "Go on downstairs and wait for me."

"All right. I'll put two pieces of wood in the stove, just the way you do," he said cheerfully.

"This wasn't what I'd planned," Brace grumbled, tumbling her back into his embrace. "I'd planned a long session of loving you before I let you out of the bed."

"Weren't three times last night enough to last you for a while?" she asked, feeling the heat of embarrassment flood her cheeks and then move down to her breasts.

"No, not hardly," he told her. "I'll never get enough of you, Sarah. I waited a long time to have you in my bed."

"Not long," she countered. "I've only been here a short while."

"I know that," he said, "but some things can't be measured by weeks or months. I always knew there was a woman out there somewhere made just for me, and it took a long time to find you."

"You truly believe that?" she asked, cuddling closer, unwilling to leave the warm nest of their bed.

"Yeah, I guess I do," he said. "My mother told me when I was just a boy that somewhere, sometime, a woman would love me just the way I am."

"Well, I do," she said firmly. "I wouldn't change a hair on your head."

"You make me feel like a king, as if my life has taken a total about-face, and I've been given a kingdom right here in my own home, with you and Stephen."

"Stephen." Sarah jerked upright again. "I've got to get up. I told him I'd be right down."

"I'll go with you," Brace said. With easy movements he slid from the bed and found his clothing. The fact that he was buck naked seemed to be no deterrent, Sarah noticed, and he donned his clothing without haste. She, on the other hand, held the sheet close as she groped for her gown at the foot of the bed and pulled it over her head. Her robe was nearby, and she wrapped it around herself, tying it firmly in place.

She was out of the room first and halfway down the stairs before Brace caught up with her. He waited until they reached the hallway below before he seized her and turned her to face him.

"You haven't kissed me yet this morning," he told

her, pulling her to rest against him and remedying the situation with haste. His mouth claimed hers, and his body hardened against her.

"How can you do that already?" she asked, and he did not pretend to misunderstand her meaning.

"It's all your fault," he told her soberly. "You have this effect on me."

"I suppose I'll have to stay clear of you, then. I wouldn't want you embarrassed out in company."

"You're not going to be farther from me than the end of my arm from now on," he told her, his eyes dark with emotion, telegraphing the message. "I don't want anything to happen to you, sweetheart. I'll keep you safe, even if it means taking you with me everywhere I go," he said bluntly.

"I'm safe enough here," she said. "The doors have locks and there are three guns that I know of—one in the pantry and two in the parlor closet."

"True," he admitted. "But a man could get in if he really had a mind to."

"I think Lester has given up the fight," she told him. "Stephen and I are safe."

The stove was warming up nicely when they arrived in the kitchen, and Stephen had begun to set the table, finding plates and silverware in the buffet. He carried the butter plate and sugar bowl, placing them squarely in the center of the round table, then sat quietly atop a high stool that Sarah had moved against the far wall. His gaze never straying from her, he watched as Sarah moved back and forth, sorting out bacon and eggs and mixing batter in a large bowl.

The pancakes were light and fluffy, and Stephen made much of them and then grinned at Brace. "My mama used to say that Sarah's cookies were the best in the world. And these pancakes are almost as good as cookies. Grandma sure taught her to cook real good.''

''I'm with you on that one, son,'' Brace told him. ''I've found out already that your aunt catches on real quick to everything, and she's the best at whatever she sets her hand to.''

Sarah cast him a glance that promised retribution, but he smiled with pretended innocence and made his way to where she stood before the stove. His hand on her shoulder was firm, his body behind her warm and strong, and she was reminded of the hours of the night when he'd claimed her over and over again. He bent to whisper in her ear and she flushed, dipping her head at his words.

''Are you all right?'' he asked in a whisper. ''I'm afraid I took advantage of you last night.''

She merely shook her head, glancing up to see Stephen watching them with a wide grin.

''How come you don't kiss Aunt Sarah?'' he asked innocently. ''I thought married people were supposed to kiss and hug a lot, just like my grandpa and grandma do.''

''I like that idea,'' Brace said quickly, and slid his arm around Sarah's waist. ''I just thought your aunt was too busy with breakfast to spend her time kissing me.''

Stephen laughed aloud. ''I'll bet she'd like it if you kissed her. She always likes it when I do. Just don't get in her way while she's cookin' the eggs.''

Brace reached for Sarah's chin and tilted it upward, bending to touch her with tenderness, his mouth blessing her with but a trace of the passion of his caresses during the night just past. ''How's that?'' he asked Stephen.

''Not bad,'' the boy replied, swinging his legs from

the stool he'd perched on earlier. They were eating in shifts this morning, the pancakes being the first course, the bacon and eggs to follow.

"I'm not very organized today," Sarah said, carrying the eggs to the table on a platter. The bacon was crisp, lying on brown paper to drain, and she brought it from the warming oven to where they sat, Stephen moving from his stool to take a chair across from Brace.

"What are we doing today?" he asked, looking at Sarah for direction.

"I'd thought we might go to church," she suggested. "All three of us."

"Sounds good to me," Brace said amiably. When Stephen frowned, Brace shot him a warning look.

"Don't you think it would be a good idea to please your aunt?" he asked the boy.

"Yeah, I guess so," Stephen answered.

"If we hurry and eat, we'll have time to check out our Sunday clothes and I'll be able to iron whatever needs pressing," Sarah told them both.

As it turned out, they were very well dressed without benefit of the irons and she breathed a sigh of relief that her Sunday morning didn't have to be spent wielding hot sadirons over the ironing board. They loaded up in the wagon and Brace held the horses to a steady pace as they made their way to the small church on the other side of town. Townspeople waved and called out to them as they rolled down the street, and Sarah was hard put to look them all in the eye.

"I bet they're thinking…" Her voice trailed off as Brace reached for her hand and squeezed gently.

"I think all the men are jealous of me," he offered quietly. "I've got the prettiest woman in town, and they all know it."

"Thank you," she said. "I'm glad you think so, Brace. Even if I don't agree with you."

A tall, dark-haired man doffed his hat as they pulled up before the church and Brace climbed down from the wagon to tie his team to the hitching rail. "I hear congratulations are in order, Sheriff," the stranger said with a wide smile. "We just heard this morning that there was a wedding yesterday."

"We tried to get word to you, but your housekeeper said you'd gone back south for a few days," Brace explained. "I'd have liked to have had you and Lin there, and the children, too."

"I'm sorry to have missed it, but we're tickled to death that you've found a woman worthy of you. When Lin writes to Faith, she'll be sure to tell her. I know the news will be well received." He looked up at Sarah. "Now, introduce me to your wife."

"Sweetheart," Brace began, "this is Nicholas Garvey. He and his wife have two of the prettiest children you've ever laid eyes on. The youngest is a boy, Jonathan, a real pistol. Amanda is their daughter. And still in the wagon is his wife, Lin, who's way too good for him, but—" he leaned closer to speak into Sarah's ear "—for some strange reason, she loves him."

The dark-haired woman laughed at Brace's foolishness and waved a greeting. "I'll be by one day to visit," she said. "If you don't mind."

"I'd love to have you. Any time you can make it," Sarah said. Lin was a beauty, slender, with blue eyes that sparkled and a smile that lit up her face. Nicholas was beyond description, a handsome man with dark hair and eyes, a man whose gaze was pinned on his wife as she slid across the wagon seat.

"Hold on," he said quickly, stepping to where she

sat. "I'll help you down." And he did, his big hands almost encircling her waist, lifting her to the ground with ease. He held her before him and Sarah noted with interest the same look of intensity that so often graced Brace's features. The man was besotted with Lin. There was no other way to say it. And with little wonder. The woman was enchanting.

Together they walked into the church, a small girl holding Nicholas's hand, Lin carrying a little boy. "You should have let me carry him," Nicholas said quietly. "He's almost too heavy for you, sweet."

"I'll trade," Lin said quickly and paused, handed the boy to her husband and took the girl's hand in hers.

"I love you, Mama," the child said quietly, and lifted their clasped hands to kiss the backs of Lin's fingers. She looked up at Sarah. "Isn't my mama the prettiest lady you ever saw?"

"Indeed she is," Sarah told her. "In fact, I was just thinking that very same thing. I think she's the prettiest lady in Benning. Don't you, Brace?"

His eyes burned darkly as he looked down at her. "We've already had this discussion, my dear wife. Lin is a beauty. Of that there's no doubt, but you take the prize as the loveliest woman I've ever known."

"Hear, hear," Nicholas said heartily. "That's a man in love, if I ever heard one."

Sarah shook her head and moved quickly to the church doors. "You're a pair, you are. You should be thinking about the pastor's sermon and the hymns and the prayers, and instead you're comparing the assets of your wives."

"I think we're both well satisfied with what we have," Nicholas said smoothly. "In fact, I'll have to say that our friend here looks to be pretty content this morning. I'd say he's more than satisfied with his wife, in particular, and marriage in general.''

Brace stuck out his hand and Nicholas took it, shaking it with a ceremony that appeared to be a bonding between the two men. ''I knew you'd recognize that,'' Brace said. His gaze touched Sarah and his smile was for her alone. ''I couldn't be happier, Nick.''

Sarah appeared to relish the warmth and companionship of the church service. She'd told Brace it had been weeks since her last chance to enter into worship, and the young minister seemed to find just the right words to bring a new recognition of her faith into being. She seemed to listen to the prayers and the reading of scripture with rapt attention, and Brace vowed to himself that they would be regular attendants at the services from now on.

The townsfolk gathered around them after church, and the ladies all clucked and stewed over Sarah. ''Do you need help getting your new things settled?'' Mrs. Johnson asked. ''I'll be glad to lend a hand.''

''I'm going one day this week to spend the day with her,'' Lin said, filling the silence. ''We'll have a good time getting things sorted out, won't we, Sarah?''

It was a welcome rescue, and Sarah nodded and agreed.

Dinner was in the oven when they arrived home, a pot roast that needed to have potatoes and carrots added for the final half hour's cooking. Preparing a meal with two menfolk underfoot was a challenge, Sarah decided, but one she could cope with. Between the two of them, Stephen was by far the most eloquent, anticipating the meal to come, but Brace made his own feelings known with sidelong glances and smiles that told of his happiness.

It was too good to last, Sarah thought wistfully. And yet she determined to gather every bit of pleasure she could from the time they spent together. Stephen told a spectacularly pitiful joke he'd heard from one of the boys after church and Brace shook his head at the punch line.

"Here's a good one you can tell at school tomorrow," he offered, and then proceeded to enthrall Stephen with a long tale about a boy who caught a monstrous fish, measuring the fish between two outstretched arms and causing Stephen to laugh aloud at his antics.

The boy left the table, excusing himself to feed the cats, and Sarah watched him as he carried two dishes of food and milk out the back door.

"You really like him, don't you?" she asked softly, her gaze resting on Brace's smiling face.

"Of course, I do," he answered. "Who wouldn't take to him? He's a fine young man, and more fun than a picnic."

"You'd make a good father," she said wistfully. "I hope you can make Stephen your first son one day."

"I fully plan on it," he told her. "In fact, as soon as the judge sets up a hearing, we should learn how the land lies."

That day came sooner than she'd expected, beginning with the surprise appearance of Brace midmorning, walking into the kitchen, his sharp gaze scouring the room as he spoke her name.

"Sarah?"

She stepped from the pantry and approached him.

"What are you doing here?" she asked. "Is everything all right?"

"Right as rain," he said agreeably, but something about the sharp look in his eye warned her that all was not going to be smooth sailing.

"What have you heard?" she asked.

He frowned then, bending lower to look directly into her eyes. "You don't miss much, do you?"

"You're keeping secrets," she said bluntly. "And I need to know what's going on."

"The judge is in town. He's ready for a hearing tomorrow."

"Where's Lester?" she asked quietly. "Does he know yet?"

"The stationmaster said he was there late yesterday. Got a wire and seemed pretty happy with it."

"What did it say?" she asked.

"Now, you know I can't find that out, Sarah," he told her. "That would be a violation of privacy if the stationmaster told me the contents of the message."

"Would he tell you if it held a threat of danger to Stephen?"

"That's the very thing I asked him," Brace admitted. "And he said I'd better be on the lookout for trouble. He said that Lester had sent a wire out early yesterday morning, and the reply seemed to please him."

"His family," Sarah said with a sense of certainty. "He's let his brothers know he needs their help. I'll guarantee it."

"Are they cut from the same cloth as Lester?" Brace asked, but his frown seemed to assume that to be a ready-made conclusion.

"I've never met them, but I suspect he'll get as much

help from them as they can offer,'' she told him. ''He can't run off with Stephen, can he?''

''He won't be doing that,'' Brace told her. ''The judge won't allow it.''

''There's no guarantee of that,'' Sarah said sadly. ''He has no idea of what Lester's like, or what he's likely to do to Stephen.''

''I think the doctor's testimony will bear fruit,'' Brace said. ''Let's wait and see.''

Chapter Seven

Judge Bennett was a stern-looking man, dressed in a dark suit, his features harsh, as if hewn from stone, except for a moment when he looked down at Stephen and his face softened. The boy sent a quick glance in the magistrate's direction and then whispered to Sarah in an undertone.

"He looks nice, don't he?"

"Do you think so?" Sarah asked.

"Yeah. He kinda smiled at me."

But the visage the man presented to Brace was that of a man well equipped to settle the hash of anyone who crossed him. "What seems to be the problem, Sheriff?" he asked sharply. "I heard from—" he looked at a paper before him "—from Lester Clark this morning that you've taken custody of his son without cause."

"I suspect that depends on your viewpoint, sir," Brace said respectfully. "It was obvious that the boy had been abused, and the father showed no signs of the concern a boy that age deserves." Brace looked over at Stephen, who wiggled his way a bit closer to Sarah.

"Stephen is a child. He wants to stay with his aunt,

and has instead been taken from the grandparents' family home, where he'd lived after his mother's death, to travel under less than ideal circumstances with his father.'' Brace paused again and placed a sheaf of papers before the judge.

"I'd like to appeal to the court to allow his aunt full custody.''

"That's against the law!'' Lester rose hurriedly, knocking his chair over as he rose, his face crimson with anger, his hands clenched at his sides.

The judge peered at him calmly. "Sit down, Mr. Clark. I'll set the standards here.''

Brace stepped closer to the well-used table he'd borrowed from the saloon, which was serving as the makeshift bench. "I'd like to call Stephen Clark to testify, sir,'' he said quietly. At his words, the man nodded at Stephen and extended a hand.

"Come up here and talk to me, boy,'' he said kindly.

Stephen rose and shot a quick glance at Sarah, as if asking permission, and she nodded and brushed his cheek with her fingers. Without a look in Lester's direction the boy stood before the judge.

"Sit in this chair,'' the man directed and Stephen complied, perching on the edge of the seat. "Now, why don't you tell me about this whole thing?'' Judge Bennett asked. "Where was your father taking you when you stopped in Benning?''

"I don't know,'' Stephen answered softly. He cleared his throat and seemed to search for words. "He said we might find Aunt Sarah again but that his family would give us a place to live from now on.''

"Do you know his family?'' the judge asked, leaning back in his chair.

Stephen shook his head. "But,'' he confided, shooting a glance at Lester, "if they're anything like my pa, I don't want to live with them."

"And why is that?" White brows lowered as the magistrate gave his full attention to Stephen.

"Pa is kinda…" Stephen halted, as if fearful of saying too much.

"Is he mean to you?" his questioner asked.

Lester stood up again. "I'm his pa. I have the right to make him behave. Sometimes boys need a heavy hand."

"Sit down, Mr. Clark," the judge said sternly. "I'll listen to you in a minute."

"You can't take a child's word against his parent," Lester muttered loudly. "The boy has been spoiled by his aunt, and needs to be taken in hand."

Stephen visibly shrank in the chair, his trembling lips making it difficult for him to speak. "He hits me sometimes," he said, his words quivering as they left his mouth.

"Do you deserve it?" the judge asked, and then shot a warning glance at Sarah as she would have risen. She sank back onto the bench she occupied and attempted a smile in Stephen's direction.

"I try to be good," Stephen answered. "I just want to be with my aunt Sarah and the sheriff. They got married, and he's gonna be my new daddy."

"I see," the judge said slowly. And then looking at Brace, he allowed a smile to form. "Covering every possibility, were you?" he asked. "A ready-made family for the lad sounds like just the ticket."

"He's my son," Lester said boldly.

"I'd rather live with the sheriff and my aunt," Stephen said mournfully. "We got a nice house to live in, and Aunt Sarah cooks real good."

"Pretty handy, finding a man to marry you," Lester said snidely, glaring in Sarah's direction.

The judge cleared his throat and allowed Stephen to go back to the bench beside Sarah. Lester Clark was called forward and spoke his piece, emphasizing his concern for his son, and his plans for them to live in west Texas with his family.

The judge asked several pointed questions, and then leaned back in his chair. "I'd like to speak privately with the boy, and then the aunt. I'll make a decision shortly."

Brace rose and cleared his throat. Judge Bennett looked at him expectantly and waited. "Perhaps Your Honor would read the doctor's statement first," Brace suggested.

"I intend to, Sheriff Caulfield," the man replied, sorting through the papers before him. With but a glance at the document, he looked at Lester, his gaze sharp, his eyes cold. "I'll peruse this a bit longer in a few minutes, but it seems pretty conclusive."

With a signal from his index finger he urged Stephen from his spot on the bench and rose from his own seat at the table. "The boy and I will be back very shortly," he said, directing his words at Sarah. She nodded and cast a smile at Stephen, and he wiggled his fingers at her in a farewell, then walked beside the judge from the room.

Lester stood and inhaled deeply, obviously intent on speaking his mind. Brace shook his head at him.

"One word and you'll be in a cell," he warned him. "Just sit down and wait for the man to return."

It was a long ten minutes before Sarah's name was called and she rose to follow the clerk who'd signaled her. He led her down a corridor and into a room holding several chairs, one of which the judge occupied. With a wave of his hand, he included her in his conversation with Stephen.

"I understand your nephew is adamant about staying with you, Mrs. Caulfield. He's been very specific on that point." The man smiled, but his eyes scrutinized Sarah and she felt his judgment weigh heavily on her.

"Yes, sir," she answered. "My sister, before she died, was set on extracting a promise from me to look after Stephen, should anything happen to her."

"And you think her death was not as presented to me by Mr. Clark?"

"If I may speak to you alone, Your Honor," Sarah began haltingly, "I'd like to elaborate on that."

"Certainly." With a nod of his head, he dismissed Stephen from the room. "Wait in the hallway for us, young man," he directed the boy, and with a lingering look in Sarah's direction, Stephen left the room.

In a few short sentences Sarah gave her version of Sierra's death, telling of her suspicions where Lester was concerned, and spoke of her own part in the situation. "I knew that Stephen would be in peril if I didn't catch up to him," she said fervently. "I was fearful of what Lester had planned for him. He's always been too willing to punish the boy, whether or not Stephen was deserving of it. He wore bruises from the time he was but a baby. Sierra tried her best to defend him, but Lester had her terrified."

"And he doesn't frighten you?" the judge asked.

"Not anymore," Sarah said boldly. "Brace has promised to look after Stephen, and I think he's capable of handling Lester."

"And you married Sheriff Caulfield in order to gain custody of your nephew?"

Sarah felt a blush climb her cheeks. "No, sir, not entirely. I love Brace. With or without Stephen in the picture, I'd have married him anyway."

"I believe you, young lady," the judge said kindly. "Now, let's go back to our makeshift courtroom and see what sort of decisions we can come up with."

Lester blustered and fussed loudly, but his arguments did him no good. The judge was determined that his word should be final, and with happiness etched on her face Sarah listened to the words he spoke.

"The boy will remain with his aunt and Sheriff Caulfield, and the father shall have visiting privileges under the court's jurisdiction. He may stay here in town and see his son twice a week for the next month."

"That's not even legal," Lester said harshly, rising and turning his anger on Sarah. "She's got the sheriff bamboozled, and you, too," he said.

"You'd better watch your mouth, sir," Judge Bennett told him. "My word is law here, and you're about halfway into a jail cell right now."

Lester was silent, his hands twitching at his sides, watching his son and Sarah with venomous intent. Stalking past them, he left a final threat behind. "You haven't heard the last of this," he muttered blackly. "I always win."

Stephen shuddered and clasped Sarah's hand as if it were a lifeline. "What can he do?" he asked.

"Brace will take care of us," Sarah assured him staunchly. Yet her heart beat rapidly as she considered the man who represented all that was cruel and vile. He barely gave the judge a glance as he went from the room, jamming his hat on carelessly.

"I'll set up visitation for the father," Brace told

Judge Bennett. "I'm assuming he'll still be staying at the hotel."

"Watch your back," Judge Bennett told him. "I'll return next month to make a final decision on this."

"Yes, sir," Brace said. "We'll be looking forward to it."

"Now what?" Sarah asked softly, grasping Stephen's hand in hers. The boy clung to her silently, his eyes large as he watched the judge leave just a few steps behind Lester.

"Now we go home and try to live a normal life," Brace said. "We allow Lester to see Stephen in my office twice a week for the next month, and the rest of the time we work on being a family."

"You make it sound so simple," Sarah told him, doubt tingeing her words.

"Nothing that really matters is ever simple," Brace said. "And this really matters. To all of us. We'll just take it one day at a time and make a home together."

A chill of foreboding ran the length of Sarah's spine as they left the building and paused in the sunshine, just outside. A malevolent gaze was upon her. She knew it from her depths, even though Lester was nowhere to be seen. The man was evil. Her skin almost crawled from the intensity of his presence. A deep-seated fear settled in the pit of her stomach, and she cursed silently as she considered what he was capable of.

"What is it, Sarah?" Brace spoke quietly in her ear, one arm wrapped firmly about her waist, holding her fast against his side.

"Lester is watching me," she said, and was thankful that Brace did not argue the fact with her.

"I don't see him," Brace said after a moment, "but

that doesn't mean anything. He's too smart to be out in the open.''

She looked up at him and then away. ''I was afraid you might think I was imagining it,'' she said. ''But I know he's watching.'' She stepped faster down the sidewalk. ''Let's go home.''

''That's the best idea I've heard all day,'' Brace said, a subtle tone in his voice that bid her meet his gaze, and she was held captive by the desire burning from his dark eyes. ''I'm in a hurry to have you to myself,'' he murmured quietly in a voice that traveled no farther than her ear. ''Tonight I'm leaving the lamp lit.''

As though he had nothing more important to do than spend the afternoon at her beck and call, Brace stayed in the house with her, sitting at the table with a book while she cooked, drinking a cup of coffee and testing the first sample of her batch of bread. ''I didn't realize how talented you were,'' he said, slathering butter across the thick slice he held. A jar of jam was presented to him and he used it generously, then took a bite.

''Good?'' Sarah asked, watching with satisfaction. ''My mother thought every woman should know the basics of homemaking, and the most basic is finding your way around a kitchen.''

''You were no doubt her star pupil,'' Brace commented. ''I've never been so pampered in my life. Not only do I find clean clothes to wear every morning, but I'm privileged to sit down at a meal fit for a king every evening. And in between, I've managed to snag myself the prettiest girl in town.'' He leaned back in his chair and ran an approving look down her length, from the top of her head to where her toes peeked from beneath her skirt.

"Where are your shoes?" he asked, frowning as he realized she was barefoot.

"I took them off," she said, glancing down and extending one slender foot. "My boots are too heavy for the house and my shoes are too tight."

"Then buy some new ones," Brace told her bluntly. "I can afford anything you want from the Mercantile." He looked sternly at the evidence of her frugality, and she felt her toes curl instinctively.

"I like to go barefoot," she told him.

"But when we leave the house, you wear shoes that are too small," he said, reminding her of her own words.

She grimaced, acknowledging his words as truth. And then, relenting, she turned back to him. "I'll pick out new shoes if you'll let me buy you some lighter-colored shirts. Do we have a deal?"

His frown would have appeared oddly somber if he hadn't looked so perplexed at that idea. "I like black shirts," he said simply.

"I know," she told him agreeably, "but I'm tired of seeing you in black. I'd like something lighter, maybe blue or tan."

He thought for a moment and then nodded. "All right. It's a deal. Tomorrow we'll go to the Mercantile and do some shopping."

"Will you always be so agreeable?" she asked him.

"Will you?" he countered, and then smiled at her raised eyebrows. "I know. You asked me first."

"I like agreeable men," she told him. "Especially the one I'm married to."

"Anything else I can do to please you?" he asked,

his look warming her, promising her without words that he would give her his undivided attention once the sun had set and Stephen had gone to bed.

"Just be mine," she whispered, the words seeming to come from some deep well of need, some aching demand for the security of his absolute affection. And if she only knew, he thought, he was more than willing to fulfill that yearning he sensed in her sometimes. He wanted to love her wholly, unashamedly, in a way that would assure her of his devotion, make her aware of the tremendous need existing within his soul.

She had become his very life, the air he breathed, the first thing he saw when he awoke in the morning, and her presence was the object of his searching when he entered his house every afternoon.

Yet she would think him daft should he use such flowery language in her hearing. And where the words came from he did not know, but the truth was simply that Sarah was the beginning and end of his existence.

"I *am* yours," he said, his voice breaking as he reached for her. It was not enough to look at her, to admire the sunshine of her smile, the hidden laughter in her eyes. He must have his hands on her, must feel the warmth of her flesh through the clothing she wore. She fitted against him neatly, her breasts warming him, her hips firm and womanly in his hands. His mouth sought hers and he was lost in the magic that was so much a part of her.

Sarah. His wife. His reason for living, breathing the air she breathed, sharing the space she occupied with her feminine presence.

"I'm yours, Sarah," he said, repeating the vow in a way she could not mistake. "Don't ever think otherwise. I'll take care of you and provide for you for the rest of our lives.''

"I know that," she murmured. "It gives me such a feeling of security, of peace, to know that I'm safe with you." Her lips formed to his, her arms linked around his neck and she offered herself completely to his will, her every movement enticing him to gather her closer, to carry her to their bed.

"How long before school is out?" he asked roughly, and then glanced out the kitchen window. It was still early afternoon, he decided, and the bed that awaited them at the top of the stairs was issuing an invitation he could not resist.

"You probably have an hour or so before you pick up Stephen," she said, her index finger tracing the line of his jaw. "What did you have in mind?"

"You don't know?" he asked. "Shall I tell you exactly what I'm going to do, or should I make you guess?"

"I think I have a good idea," she told him, her smile beckoning him further down the path of seduction he was traveling at breakneck speed. In moments her apron was tossed over the back of a chair, the bread was wrapped in a dish towel and she stood before him once more, this time occupying herself with the line of buttons that held the front of his shirt together. Her fingers were nimble, and in mere moments she'd undone all of them, exposing his chest to her eager hands.

Her palms spread wide across the width of muscled flesh, her fingertips almost hidden in the thick mat of hair that curled there. And then she moved them, up to his shoulders then back to where tiny buttons stood erect, testifying to his arousal. She touched them gently, then bent forward and licked at each small nubbin of flesh with the very tip of her tongue.

He could barely resist scooping her off her feet, so great was his need for her. But she intrigued him in this moment, looking like a blend of innocence and some other quality he could only describe as bewitching, tempting him with the brush of her body against his, the soft smiles of feminine temptation she offered, the kisses she bestowed.

Her mouth was full, swollen from his kiss, and her eyes flashed with an excitement that drew him ever closer. And in the midst of it all, she leaned into him, her lips seeking the flesh of his throat, her invitation unmistakable as she suckled for a moment on the skin just beneath the edge of his collar.

It would not show to an observer, but he would know it was there. When he shaved on the morrow, when he washed for bed tonight, he would see the small reddened mark she'd left behind, and remember this moment.

With a show of strength he seldom displayed, he lifted her, holding her close against himself, then sought the stairway that led to the second floor. Their bedroom door stood open, but not for long. He caught it with his foot and closed it firmly, then lowered her to the floor and set the latch securely.

She stood before him, a strange half smile curving her lips, her eyes half-closed, her breasts rising and falling as she breathed deeply, in an erratic fashion.

"You're a witch," he said, his voice rough. "A woman who should know better than to tempt a man beyond his control."

"Have I done that?" she asked sweetly, her eyes rounding as if in surprise.

"You know very well what you've done, and you're about to pay the price," he told her. His hands were quick as he stripped her clothing from her and then held her at arm's length, his gaze measuring each inch of her flesh. She was like an ivory statue, he thought—not tall, but well formed, slender, yet rounded in all the right places.

She was perfect. Absolutely perfect. His hands circled her waist and he lifted her, his face seeking the soft cushions of her breasts, his mouth open against her skin, his words muffled as he sought and found the curves that enticed him. It mattered little that she did not understand the words he spoke, for his meaning was clear, his need for her obvious. He kissed and suckled, rubbed his nose and cheek against her softly rounded breasts and then lowered her a bit until he could reach her mouth, that soft arrangement of lips and teeth and tongue, that welcoming place she opened in anticipation of his kiss, from which she uttered soft words of satisfaction, sounds of pleasure and expressions of wonder.

Her legs twined around his waist and hips, and she gripped him with the strong muscles of a woman who has ridden a horse and learned the skill well. He felt her body adapt to his, shuddered as she moved restlessly against him and then crushed her to him in a frenzy of desire that made him fear for her.

"I don't want to hurt you," he growled against her skin. "I'm afraid I'll be too rough."

"No. You won't hurt me," she assured him, sliding down his body as if she would imprint her curves and hollows on his masculine form. Her arms circled his back, her hands beneath his shirt, her fingers seeking purchase in the muscled width of his torso.

"I need to take a deep breath," he said. "Back off a little. I can't take a chance on bruising you, Sarah."

"I don't care," she whispered, bending forward and setting her teeth in a ridge just below his shoulder. She bit, not gently but with barely enough strength to cause pain, and he growled deep in his throat.

"I don't care," she repeated, her nails digging into his back.

His boots hit the floor with two solid thumps, then his trousers were quickly dealt with and his shirt was stripped off. Before she could catch her breath, she was flat in the middle of the big bed and he was looming over her. Without warning, with no pretense of gentle persuasion, he touched her, his hands exploring her body, his fingers taking measure of her breasts, her belly, and then into the feminine warmth below.

She lifted herself to his touch, cried out in abandon as he sought the treasures gifted her by her Maker, brought pleasure to each place he visited, and then followed the path his hands had taken with the heated passion of lips and tongue. She cried out again, not in fear or pain but in triumph, and he caught the sound with his mouth, tasted it and felt the joy of bringing her to a height of desire and pleasure that brought tears to her eyes and the moans of a woman who has known satisfaction to her lips.

"Sarah." He spoke her name, breathing the syllables against her ear, and then moved between her legs, seeking to find welcome there. With slow movements he claimed her; with deep thrusts he made her shiver with delight, taking her once more to the peak of passion. Then he joined her as she clung to him, whispering his name, holding him close in the clasp of arms and legs that seemed unable to release him from her hold.

If she was fearful of his passion she did not reveal it, for her face glowed with a look of satisfaction he could not fail to recognize. If she had been roughly used, she appeared not to be wary of him, for she held him ever tighter against herself. And if his movements and the caresses he'd bestowed upon her had been too abandoned, she seemed to have thrived on them. Her eyes were half-closed, her swollen lips soft and inviting, and he bent to claim them once more.

"I didn't hurt you?" he asked, and she shook her head and then laughed, a soft, enticing sound that brought him to readiness once more. But it was too soon. He would wait, wait until supper was tended to, until Stephen was in bed and until Sarah was once more ready for his loving.

It would strain his patience, but he had learned well over the past few weeks that that quality was a virtue with much value, especially as it applied to his relationship with Sarah. And so he kissed her and rolled to one side, holding her close, fearful of crushing her, yet needing to remain as one with her.

His hands were gentle, his fingertips straying tenderly across her flesh as he brushed back her hair, caressed her cheek and traced the curl of her ear. She was all that was warm and womanly, all that any man could ever hope to possess as his own.

Sarah.

Chapter Eight

It was two weeks after the hearing when Brace, who had felt able to breathe better and stop looking over his shoulder, heard of two strangers in town. Now, in the hotel lobby, they met a third, held a hurried conference in a dimly lit corner, then hastened up the wide stairway to the second floor. From the desk, Bart Simms watched with barely concealed curiosity, and when the men had disappeared into the upper hallway he sidled out from behind the wide desk and made his way out the front door and across to the jail.

"Sheriff?" He called out Brace's title with a breath-less, subdued cry that brought the lawman hastening from the back of the jailhouse. At the sight of Brace's face, Bart Simms seemed to relax and plopped down in a chair in front of the battered desk.

"Two fellas just rode into town, come a-visitin' that Lester fella in his room at the hotel. They sorta put me in mind of him—long noses and sharp, beady little eyes. I wouldn't be surprised if they're kin of one sort or another."

"Probably his brothers," Brace said quietly. "I fig-ured he wasn't just hanging around to see Stephen. I've been waiting for something like this to happen. I suspect they're a nasty bunch, the whole kit and caboodle of them.''

"Well," Bart said with a sigh of relief, "I just wanted you to know what was going on. Thought you'd be interested. I rented rooms to the both of them.''

"Damn right I'm interested," Brace said, the words vehement. "I'll have to ride home and make sure my wife is safe and sound. I think they're set on making a misery of her life.''

My wife. The words sounded sweet to his ears, and Brace recognized in the next few minutes that it was a joy to head for the big white house just past the edge of town. Spending hours with Sarah was his favorite pastime these days, and the mere suggestion of harm heading in her direction made him angrier than he'd thought possible.

"Sarah? You here, honey?" he called out, finding the back door open and entering the kitchen with haste. The room was empty, but then she would have gone on to other pursuits once the breakfast dishes were done. Now, with the added danger of Lester's brothers in town, he'd have to caution her about leaving the house open.

"What's wrong, Brace?" she asked, mere seconds after he heard her shoes clatter down the staircase. Her hair falling about her face and shoulders, she held a hairbrush in one hand and a length of ribbon in the other.

"Are you all right?" he asked, his gaze doing a complete survey of her neatly clad figure. Except for her hair being free and waving, she was the picture of ladylike elegance, even if a simple housedress was her attire. She lent it a dignity he admired, and she looked every inch a wife. A wife he'd spent long hours cherishing just the night before, holding her close to his side, luxuriating in her scent and the feel of soft curves pressed to his long, lean body.

"I'm fine," she said with a sharp look over his shoulder at the closed door. "I didn't hear you come in."

"The door was unlocked," he told her, and recognized that his worry on her behalf sharpened his tone.

"Hmm," she murmured. "I'd have sworn I locked it before I went up to get dressed."

"Well, you didn't," he said, stepping a bit closer and reaching for her. "Scared me, I don't mind saying. You need to be careful, sweetheart. We've got problems."

"Lester?" she asked. "What's he done now?"

"He has company," Brace said shortly. "Two men rode in today and took a room at the hotel. Bart Simms said they have a family resemblance. Probably some of Lester's kin."

"What can they do?" she asked, fitting neatly into his embrace. She sighed, and he felt her body relax in his arms. Leaning a bit, she nestled her head in the curve of his shoulder and tipped her head, the better to see him.

It was a temptation, and Brace could not resist. He bent to take her lips and she sighed again. "I like being Mrs. Brace Caulfield," she whispered. "You're so good to me, Brace. I could get used to being pampered real quick."

"You'd better get used to it," he growled. "'Cause I intend to have you right beside me for the rest of our lives."

"Well, not when you're at work," she said, her breath sweet against his mouth. "But I'll be happy to spend the rest of my life with you." And then she jerked away from him. "Is Stephen all right? Can they get hold of him while he's in the schoolhouse?"

Brace shook his head. "No, I've put his teacher into the picture, and that sweet little spinster carries a big gun. She's not afraid to use it, either. Taught her how to handle it myself."

"Well, aren't you a handy man to have around?" Sarah said with a chuckle.

"It seemed like a good idea when she took over at the school a couple of years back. She's got a lot of responsibility over there, keeping those young'uns safe."

"Especially our young'un," Sarah mused. "I wonder if he'd be better off staying home for the next little while. I can work with him here."

"No. Let him stay in school," Brace said with finality. "He's as safe there as anywhere. You're the one I'm concerned about right now."

"I haven't used my gun much, except for practicing, years back," she admitted. "I'm not sure I'd be very good at shooting it, even if I had to. But I'll try, if you like."

Brace considered her, noting the calm assurance she portrayed, the loveliness she wore as if it were an innate part of her. For so it was, an appeal she seemed unaware of, a beauty she apparently took for granted. And it was his, all his.

Happiness seemed to surround him in this moment and he kissed her again, offering his love with such apparent ease, it surely must be visible to her. "You're a special woman, Miss Sarah," he said quietly. "I can't believe my good fortune."

"Does a meal of chicken and biscuits for supper tonight sound like good fortune enough to suit you?'' she asked pertly.

''Yes, ma'am, it surely does,'' he answered, aware now of the scent of the meal she'd begun, apparently right after breakfast. ''What's for dinner at noon?''

''Whatever is left from yesterday,'' she said, her brow furrowing as she considered the subject. ''Probably roast beef sandwiches with gravy.''

''Is it almost noon yet?'' he asked hopefully, subtlety not his strong suit.

She eased his hat from his head and ran the fingers of her other hand through his hair. ''It will be very soon.''

''I believe I'll just stick around, then. No sense in making another trip.''

He watched her from the table, noted her skill with the sharp knife as she cut thick slices of beef from the remains of last night's roast. Bread was quickly sliced to order in preparation for the filling. She heated gravy in a saucepan on the stove, with sliced beef drowning in the savory liquid, and he'd just taken his first long whiff of the offering before him when a knock sounded at the front door.

''Wait here,'' he said, adjusting his holster as he left the kitchen. ''I'll see who it is.''

''All right,'' she answered, fixing her own plate. ''It might be Lin. She said she'd be here one day this week.''

''Well, if it is, that's fine,'' he told her. Alert to anything out of the ordinary, he felt a jolt of surprise when the stationmaster's frowning face met him at the door.

''Thought you'd want to see this,'' the man said quietly. ''Jamie said you'd come home for dinner.''

''Yeah. I'm just sitting down. Want to join us?'' He

took the wire from the man's hand and held the door wide.

"No. I can't be away from the station for too long. The noon train whistle just sounded. I'll see you later. I'm sure you'll want to send a reply."

His curiosity piqued, Brace nodded slowly and closed the door, making his way to the back of the house, the message in his hand.

"I heard you talking to someone. Was it Lin?" Sarah asked as he reappeared in the kitchen.

"No, a wire came in for me a little while ago."

"What does it say?" Sarah asked, and then back-tracked. "Have you read it yet?"

"I thought maybe you'd read it to me," he said halt-ingly. His gaze fell to the paper and he frowned. "I can make out some of the words, but it'll be easier if you just read it off."

"I can do that," Sarah said. She scanned the message quickly, then looked up at Brace. "This is from the sheriff back in Big Rapids. He got your message asking for an inquiry into Sierra's death. Apparently Lester running off with Stephen put him on alert. He says they're going to reopen the investigation, due to re-newed interest in the case. He wants you to keep a watchful eye on Lester and wait for further details."

"Makes sense to me," Brace said slowly. "And if the man stays in town, it won't be too hard to do. So long as he stays away from you, I'll just watch him and continue with his visits with Stephen."

"When is the next one scheduled?" Sarah asked.

"Tomorrow. Right after school. I'll pick the boy up and take him back to the jail and let Lester know to come over."

"I hate having that man near my nephew," Sarah

said sharply. She raised a hand as Brace would have spoken. "I know. I know. It was the judge's verdict, but I'll be glad when he comes back to town and makes a final decision."

"There are no guarantees, Sarah. Lester is his legal father." She needed to be aware of all the possibilities, Brace decided. The chances of the judge giving custody to Lester were slim, but still within the range of reality.

"I won't let him take Stephen from me," she said, anger alive on her face and in her voice.

"If the judge decides in the father's favor, there's not much we can do about it," Brace said simply. "I'm sworn to uphold the law, and that includes any decision the judge makes, sweetheart."

"I know," she said fretfully, "but I can't believe a man like Lester would be given the right to take Stephen from us."

"Don't fret over it now," Brace told her, one wide palm making its way across her back in a possessive gesture. "We'll just take one day at a time."

"You're planning on spending all your spare time right here with us, aren't you?" she asked. "Not that I'm complaining." She stepped away from him and picked up his plate. "Let me heat this up for you. It's gone almost cold while we stood there canoodling."

He grinned widely and sat down. "Is that what you call it? Never heard it described that way before."

"My mother used to scold my father when he carried on hugging and kissing in front of Sierra and me. Said he was a canoodler of the first degree."

Brace chuckled, pleased that Sarah had good memories of her parents. His own weren't as pleasant, but it hadn't been his mother's fault that school had been so difficult for him. And now he was making strides, thanks to Sarah. He'd have to write to his mother, once his penmanship had improved a little more.

"I think I'd like your family," he told her.

"They're far from perfect, but then none of us really fit that description, do we?"

"Oh, I don't know," he said slowly, looking down at his reheated meal. The gravy steamed once more and he picked up his fork to sample a bite. "This is about as good as it can get," he said, "and the woman who put it together is in the same category."

Sarah sat down with her own plate and smiled, a look of feminine satisfaction lighting her features. "I like your style, Sheriff," she said, with a glance that told him she was more than pleased with him. And that suited him just fine.

Their evenings were satisfying to both of them. Brace, because his knowledge was expanding at a rapid pace, and the studying gave him Sarah's undivided attention. And Sarah found joy in watching Brace's progress, listening to his reading skills improve day by day. They spent long hours reading, heads close together in the lamplight, aware of each other in a new and satisfying way. Stephen came and went, bringing his own schoolwork with him to study across the table from Brace.

"This is fun," he said one evening, closing his arithmetic book as he finished the last long division problem. "I never used to like homework, but now we do it together like a real family."

"We are a real family," Sarah said quietly. "We're a mother and dad and a son, and that's all it takes to be a family. In fact, just a mom and dad can be a family.

It's just more fun when there's a boy around to make it complete.''

"Like me?" Stephen asked, his blue eyes hopeful.

"Just like you," Brace told him. "You're about as fine a boy as anyone could ask for.''

"What if you and Aunt Sarah have babies of your own?" he asked.

"What if we do?" Brace returned. "They won't be any more precious to us than you are, son. And remember, you were here first. That makes you special.''

"Wow. I never thought about it that way.'' Stephen's face glowed with pleasure as he considered that theory. "I think I like being special.''

"Well, it's past time for special people to go to bed,'' Sarah told him. "You won't like it in the morning when I get you out of bed before breakfast, and you're still sleepy.''

"I'll get up as soon as you rap on my door," he told her. "If you cook pancakes, I'll even fix the fire in the stove for you.''

"That's a deal I can't refuse," she said, laughing at his offer.

They climbed the stairs together, Sarah's arm circling Stephen's shoulders, Brace a step behind. And none of them was aware of the figure on the porch—a man who peered with a malevolent glare through the long glass window beside the door.

"They're all snuggled up like three bugs in a rug.'' LeRoy's face held a sneer that mocked the words he spoke, and Lester glared at his brother as the man reported what he had seen. "The woman looks like she's got both of them eatin' out of her hand," LeRoy said, and Lester nodded, obviously agreeing with the theory.

"She's a fancy one, that Sarah," Lester said, his voice lingering on her name. "I've been wanting to get my hands on her for a long time. Just thinking about that blamed Sheriff Caulfield gettin' all the goodies she's got to offer makes me sick."

"*You* want *Sarah?*" LeRoy asked, his jaw agape as he looked at Lester. "I thought you were causin' all this fuss to get custody of your boy. And if you've got any sense at all, that's where you'll be putting your efforts, brother of mine."

"What are you talkin' about?" Lester asked. "I've been doing my best to keep Stephen with me. I was trying to bring him home to meet the family. You know how big Pa is on family. I figured he'd be pleased as punch to see a real live grandson come riding up to his door. It might even be of benefit to me. He's got all that land and cattle, making money for him hand over fist. There's no reason why he can't share a little of it with the three of us. We need to make a deal."

"Yeah, well, the first thing is to make things right with Pa," Shorty, the second brother, told him. "You left home with hard feelings and Pa hasn't got over it yet."

"What are you saying? That I should go home and leave Stephen hanging here, without me seeing him?"

"Just long enough to skedaddle home for a short visit and set things right there," Shorty said. "Let Pa know you're going to bring home a young'un, sorta wet his whistle, let him think about having a grandson. You know he's been sick, Les. This might be the last chance you've got to play cozy with him."

"I'll have to think about it," Lester said, ruminating over the idea of leaving town for the trip west. It could be done in ten days or so, he figured. And might be worth the effort. He'd have to make a decision right soon if he expected to make the best use of Stephen. If his pa died without knowing of a grandson in the picture, going to all this trouble over the brat would be in vain. For the first time he had a strong reason to go home to see the ornery old coot.

And Stephen ought to be of some use this way. Maybe he could even persuade Sarah to go along. She was mighty attached to the boy, and Les felt the urge to spend his lust on Sierra's sister. It'd be almost like having his woman back if he laid claim to her twin. Not for the first time, he regretted Sierra's death. His damn temper had gotten the best of him.

The atmosphere in Brace's office was rife with tension, most of it coming from the man who watched Stephen with barely concealed anger. "So, you're havin' a good time parking your carcass with the sheriff and your aunt Sarah, are you?" Lester asked. "And I suppose you're planning on living with her from now on."

Stephen looked up at his father with eyes that held a spark of fear. "I love Aunt Sarah. You know that, Pa. She's always been nice to me, and she's good to me, just like my mother used to be."

Lester laughed, an ugly sound. "I suppose she is. Two of a kind, they were. In fact, your ma would still be alive and kicking if she'd tried harder not to follow Sarah's lead."

"I don't know what that means," Stephen said slowly. "But it sounds like you don't like Aunt Sarah any better than you liked my mother."

"I liked your mother just fine," Lester blustered.

"Then how come you were always hitting her and being mean?"

"Just when she had it coming." Lester's self-assurance was repulsive, his words those of a bully, and Brace had all he could do not to slam the man against the wall. That any husband should be so uncaring about his wife was foreign to him. The thought of harm coming to Sarah sent chills down his spine, and the realization that this brute of a man would think nothing of striking his sister-in-law, or even worse, made him all the more determined to be vigilant.

"Who was the judge of that?" Brace asked, aware that his voice was cold and threatening.

"Who better than her husband?" Lester asked with a grin. "She was my property, after all. Law says so."

"Not my law," Brace said. "Every human being has rights, man or woman. And nothing gives a man the right to hurt another person, especially one he's promised to cherish."

"Pretty fancy words from a man who's been married for just a couple of weeks," Lester said. "Wait till you get a taste of Sarah's lying mouth and deceitful ways. You'll change your tune in a hurry."

"Some things never change, Lester. The laws of right and wrong are set in stone so far as I'm concerned."

"Listen to the dreamer," Lester scoffed. "I hope you come up with your head on straight, Stephen. You'll find out one day that women aren't to be trusted."

"I don't believe that," the boy argued, dodging the open-handed slap aimed in his direction. He looked at Brace. "Have I spent enough time with *him* yet?"

"Yeah, I'd say so," Brace said. "The judge didn't set any length of visitation. This seems like a good time to call a halt for today."

"I'm writing notes on how long you're allowing me to see my son," Lester blustered. "This isn't what he had in mind, I'll warrant."

"Well, we'll just have to ask him when he returns, won't we?" Brace asked. "And that won't be too long, Lester. I expect him back in two weeks."

"Then we'll see just who is in charge of things here," Lester said, shooting a glare of warning at Stephen. "You'll find out who's boss then, boy."

Now he turned to Brace, and his voice held a whining quality that made Brace wince. "There's a family emergency come up," Lester began. "That's why my brothers are in town right now. My pa is real sick. His heart isn't ticking away like it should, and the doctor is worried that he might not make it much longer. I need to go see him before anything happens. I suppose you're gonna give me a hassle over that, ain't you?"

"I suspect the judge will understand that," Brace told him. "How long will you be gone?"

"Probably less than two weeks," Lester said, his approach more accommodating now that Brace was willing to make the way clear for Lester's trip.

"You should be back before the judge arrives, then. But I'll warn him. I'll wire the man and tell him. Will you be leaving right away?"

"Yeah. I figured on heading out tomorrow if you let the judge know."

"I can do that," Brace said, thinking that Sarah would be happier with Stephen's father out of the picture for a while.

"Just don't think this makes a difference in my seeing my boy, Sheriff. I'll be back, and I'm planning on getting my son back. Family's important to my kin. And a father has the right to raise his son the way he pleases.''

Stephen watched from fearful eyes as his father left the office, slamming his way out the door and into the street. Lester made his way to the hotel, disappearing between the wide doors, and Stephen breathed deeply.

''I'm sure glad he's gone,'' he said. ''I wish I didn't have to ever see him again.''

''I feel the same way,'' Brace assured him. ''But we have to do as the judge ordered, son. Just one more visit should do it. And that visit won't be for another two weeks. We'll wire him and let him know about your dad's heading home for a short while. Then if the judge comes in on Monday or Tuesday two weeks from now, you'll have the last session then, and hopefully that will be the end of it.''

''My pa's real mean,'' Stephen said quietly. ''I sure hope he never gets a chance to hurt Aunt Sarah. I dream sometimes that he's hurting her, the way he used to hurt my mama.''

''Hitting her?'' Brace asked, his every sense standing at attention at the boy's words.

''Not just that,'' Stephen said, almost in a whisper. ''Sometimes at night I heard her crying, and I knew he was being mean to her.''

And just what that particular bit of behavior consisted of wasn't too hard to figure out, Brace decided. The woman had not had an easy life, on any level.

The trip home from his office was short—Brace on horseback, Stephen astride in front of him. The boy was thrilled with his twice-weekly ride on Brace's black gelding, and had all but coaxed the promise of a horse of his own.

''We'll see what they have to offer at the livery stable,'' Brace told him. "And maybe Nicholas has a three-year-old ready for a saddle. I'll ask him when he comes to town."

"He's got a pretty horse at his place," Stephen said, obviously recalling his last visit to Nick Garvey's farm.

"Several of them," Brace agreed. "But that little palomino takes the cake. I doubt we can afford to get that one for you, but Nick can probably find us something. He knows a lot of horsemen."

"Can we go there?" Stephen asked, looking over his shoulder at the man who held him securely.

"Not today," Brace replied, "but maybe tomorrow. I'll see if Jamie can keep an eye on things for me, and we'll all go out to see Lin and Nicholas and the children."

It was not surprising to see Stephen run pell-mell to the back door when Brace lifted him from the saddle, his feet kicking up dust as he burst through the entry.

"Brace says we might go to visit the Garveys' place. Maybe tomorrow," he said, the importance of his news giving him unlimited energy. He danced around the kitchen, waving his hat in one hand, as if he carried a flag of victory.

Sarah laughed aloud. "You are one excited little boy," she said, reaching to corral him as he paused in one corner of the kitchen. Her arms encircled him and she bent to kiss his cheek. "That will be worth getting up for in the morning, won't it?"

"Yes, ma'am," Stephen said readily.

"Where's Brace?" Sarah asked, looking toward the door.

"He went to put his horse out back," Stephen said.

"He didn't take him to the livery stable?" she asked.

"No. Said he wanted him close, in case he had to go

somewhere in a hurry.'' Stephen turned as the door opened and Brace appeared, his gaze touching Sarah as she placed a platter in the warming oven.

Stephen grinned at him and made a statement of intent. ''I think it's right nice that we have a corral here and a barn for horses. It'll make it handy when I get a horse of my own. I'll be able to walk right out the door and pet him and brush him and everything.''

''Don't forget the part about cleaning his stall,'' Brace said with a laugh. ''There's more to it than just riding the animal.''

''I know,'' Stephen said with an air of superiority. ''I have to learn how to put on his saddle and bridle, and we'll have to find a box tall enough for me to climb up on, so I can get up on his back.''

''Well, you've got that right,'' Brace told him. ''But first we have to build another stall in the shed, maybe even think about a barn. As it is, there's just about enough room for one more, along with the extra space it'll take for feed. Hay takes up a lot of room.''

''I'd say you've got a real education coming,'' Sarah told the boy. And then she looked up at Brace. ''Why don't we make a lean-to on the side of the shed for your buggy? Seems like it would make sense to have it here.''

''I don't use my gelding to pull the buggy,'' he said. ''I usually rent a horse from the livery stable when I drive it. And I don't use it enough to warrant keeping it here. I wouldn't bother having my horse out back, but I'd like to know he's handy if I need him in a hurry. A barn would probably be a good idea, now that I think about it.''

''When is this big building project going to take place?'' Sarah asked.

"Well, not tomorrow, for sure," Brace told her, shooting a look in Stephen's direction that branded the two of them as coconspirators. "We've got some negotiating to do out at the Garvey place. It may not bear results for a while, but Stephen is about due for a horse of his own, and Nick will know the best place to find one."

"A horse of his own?" Sarah's tone suggested horror. "Is he old enough? Big enough to ride?"

"If I didn't think so, I wouldn't have mentioned it," Brace said calmly. "He's a sensible boy, and it's time to learn responsibility. He can't do better than learning to care for a horse."

"Maybe a dog?" Sarah asked, her voice breaking. "I'd think feeding and training a dog would be a good introduction to responsibility."

"We may just add a dog to the mix," Brace said easily. "I've been thinking it might be a good idea, anyway."

"A dog? A dog for me?" Stephen's joy knew no bounds as he burst from Sarah's embrace and headed for Brace. "You really mean it, Pa?"

Brace smiled and seemed almost to grow visibly, his shoulders seeming wider, his height increasing as he looked at the boy. "You make me feel like a million dollars, boy. I know we talked about being a family, but you've never called me *that* before."

"You mean, when I called you Pa?" Stephen asked, a grin splitting his features.

"Yeah, that's what I mean," Brace said, his hand reaching out to smooth back the boy's dark hair. And then, as if he had second thoughts, he reached with both arms for the child and pulled him into a warm embrace. His lips rested on the boy's head and he glanced up when Sarah coughed and then drew her hankie from her pocket to wipe her eyes.

"I like being a family," Brace said with emphasis. "I've gotten used to it real quick, and having Stephen around is a big part of it."

"Thank you," Sarah breathed. "You've ended this day with a good dose of happiness for all of us, I think."

"Nothing could make me more contented than eating our usual supper with my family," Brace said, "unless it's eating the fried chicken you fixed for tonight. Sitting down at the table with the pair of you suits me just fine."

"You cheated," Stephen said, looking toward the stove where pale gravy bubbled in the iron skillet. "You saw Aunt Sarah put the platter in the warming oven when you came in the door."

"So I did," Brace agreed. "And I noticed that it held a lot of fried chicken." He turned toward the stove. "Unless I miss my guess, this pan has potatoes in it, all mashed up with butter and milk, and this—" he lifted another lid "—this one holds a nice batch of green beans, cooked up with bacon and onions. I smelled it when I came in the door."

"You could tell by smelling it?" Stephen asked, sniffing the air as if he would sort out the delicious aromas of the supper Sarah had cooked.

"Sure could," Brace said with confidence. "I know good food when I get close enough to sample it."

"Sample?" Sarah asked, lifting a brow as she picked up three plates and placed them on the table.

"Well, maybe a bit more than sample," Brace admitted. "I intend to eat my share of it. That's the benefit of having a wife who knows how to cook."

"I'm glad I measure up to your standards, sir," Sarah said pertly.

"More than you know," her husband said, sliding his arm around her waist.

"Yeah, she's sure a good cook," Stephen said agreeably, washing his hands at the sink.

"Among other things," Brace commented, dropping a quick kiss on Sarah's cheek. "I'd say she's just all around perfect."

"We had this conversation already," Sarah reminded him.

"Yeah, we did," he said, smiling with satisfaction. "And I haven't changed my mind one iota since. You're as close to perfect as a woman can get."

"I've got some news for you," Brace said quietly, stripping off his clothing, watching Sarah as she turned down the sheet on the bed.

"Something I'll enjoy hearing, I hope," she said, fluffing the pillows and sitting on the edge of the mattress.

"Probably not," Brace told her. "Lester's brothers came here to get him. Seems his father is pretty sick. I'm thinking Lester has ideas about feathering his nest. If there's a chance of sweet-talking his pa a little, maybe finding out the financial ins and outs of the ownership of the ranch the family owns out there, he's gonna take advantage of it."

"I think he had ideas about taking Stephen there in order to get in good with his father, in the first place, when he took him from us in Big Rapids."

"I suspect he was more interested in having *you* in the palm of his hand," Brace said, disagreeing with her theory. "Although he might have been trying to kill two birds with one stone, so to speak. Though I have a notion getting his hands on you was his first priority.''

"Maybe so. He wanted me before he married Sierra. I told you that already. I suppose he thought I'd fall into his hands once she was gone. I think that's why he let me take Stephen after Sierra's death. I kept him during the day, at home with my folks.''

She crawled into the bed and covered herself with the sheet, and then watched Brace as he approached her. "I can't believe you've never owned a nightshirt,'' she said. "I'd be glad to make you one, you know.''

"I'd only keep it in my drawer, anyway," he said with a grin. "I like being ready for anything, sweet. And you feel better when I hold you without a bunch of material between us.''

"Sorry to disappoint you, but I've got on a gown,'' she pointed out.

His smile held a trace of triumph, she thought, and his words emphasized that as he reached for her, his voice rough with anticipation. "Not for long, baby. Not for long.''

Chapter Nine

"You weren't just making conversation when you spoke of a horse for Stephen, were you?" Sarah asked. She sat perched on the buggy seat, midway between the two men in her life, her smile dazzling, Brace thought. Of course, Sarah in any situation dazzled him. But right now she was especially pretty.

Dressed in a light cotton frock, her hair pulled up to her crown in an arrangement that cascaded dark waves and curls past her shoulders, she looked like a princess. At least queen of her domain, a position she occupied with dignity and grace. He felt a surge of pride looking at her, recalling the preferred attention he received from her hand. The woman had somehow learned the gift of keeping a husband happy. From where, he had no idea, but learn it she had. His life overflowed with loving, and a sense of laughter and excitement filled his days.

"I meant it, Sarah. Our boy has earned the privilege of something special in his life. If that something is a horse, or maybe a dog—"

"Or maybe both," Stephen said in a low tone, one filled with hope.

"Maybe both," Brace returned agreeably. "We'll talk about it. First thing is to find a dog somewhere."

"Lin said there was a stray in their corncrib. She thinks it might be one of Wolf's lady friends. We can check that out. She told me it's a likely prospect, anyway, a female about to have pups."

"Wow, old Wolf is a dandy dog, all right," Stephen said enthusiastically. "If she's gonna have his pups, they'd be beautiful."

"And what do you know about all that?" Brace asked, glancing quickly at Sarah.

"I know if you have a male and a female dog, sometimes they have a family, but in this case they call it a litter of pups." Stephen boasted his knowledge with a superior air, and Sarah was hard put not to laugh aloud.

"It seems your son is well versed in such things," she said to Brace. "And he's right about Wolf. I saw him one day when he rode into town on the wagon with Nicholas and Lin and their family. Rather a dangerous-looking animal, but Amanda was trying her very best to hold the beast on her lap, and he seemed to be enjoying it tremendously."

"He's a good dog—a great watchdog, and that may be what we need. I almost wish they had a litter of pups closer to full grown. Training a puppy will be a full-time job. And since you're the one who's at home all the time, Sarah, it'll fall to you to do the training."

"I'll help her, Pa. Right after school I'll take him for a walk and feed him and—" His mind searched for more promises to make, and Stephen wrapped his arms around Sarah's waist as he mumbled his words against her arm. "We can build him a doghouse, too," Stephen said. "Or he could stay in the barn with the horses."

"Horses?" Brace asked, lifting his brows as he repeated the word that suggested more than one animal would be living behind their home on the acreage that begged for expansion. "You know I'll have to find someone to come in and put up fencing, don't you, son? You can't have animals without providing for them."

"Can we afford that?" Stephen wanted to know.

"I'll need a corral built, anyway, so might as well just extend the fencing out back and make a decent-sized pasture there." Joy colored his words as Brace extolled the virtue of his plans. "It'll be good to improve the property. I've needed to use that land for something beneficial. There's five acres of hay out back, too. I'll have to have it cut and brought into the barn, come the end of summer."

"I'm thinking that becoming a husband and father is an expensive proposition for you," Sarah said quietly. "You were doing just fine without us to clutter up your life."

"But he's havin' more fun with us around, Aunt Sarah," Stephen said with confidence, "He likes takin' care of us."

"Stephen's about got it right," Brace told her, with an aside toward the boy who watched him with his heart in his eyes. It was daunting to be so admired, Brace decided, but good for his own confidence. He'd never expected to have a ready-made family, but the reality seemed sent from heaven just for his benefit.

"Well, now that we have the dog issue settled," Sarah said firmly, "what do we do about a horse? Do we just have Nicholas look for one, or do we wait till the stall can be built and the fencing in before we take the plunge?"

"We'll find out today," Brace said firmly. "I sent

Jamie out last night to alert Nicholas to our visit. Lin is expecting us for dinner.''

"You didn't tell me that,'' Sarah said, looking down at her simple dress. "I'd have gotten myself in order a little better if I'd known we were going to actually be *company.*''

"There's sort of a family thing with Nick and Lin,'' Brace told her. "They won't treat you like visiting royalty, sweetheart. You'll be just one of the family. And I need to talk to Nicholas about some business. I thought I'd let him know the latest news about Lester and his plans.''

"Well, that's reassuring,'' she said. "You'll have to tell me one day about the family connection.''

"One day,'' he said, shooting her a look that puzzled her a bit. "But for now, just enjoy yourself and plan on having a nice day.''

The ranch was tidy, with whitewashed foundations on house and barn and a pasture full of horses. Nicholas, indeed, had several horses ready for riding, and Stephen was in the throes of delight when Nick steered him toward three sleek specimens that came to the fence, as if the boy's presence called to them.

A blood bay, her coat rich brown and accented with sleek black legs, took his attention. Tall at three years old, the mare nuzzled at Stephen's hand, accepting the bit of carrot that Nicholas placed there for Stephen's pleasure and the horse's enjoyment.

"They like to get treats,'' Nicholas told the boy. "We try to keep them to a minimum, but it's hard to resist a pretty little thing like Sugarfoot.''

"Sugarfoot?'' Stephen asked, as if questioning the reason behind the mare's name.

"Lin named her when she was still pretty small. She pranced around here making a pet of herself, and Lin, especially, fell hard for her. Said the mare was sure to be an easy ride, her movements were so smooth. As sweet as sugar, she said. The name stuck, but you can change it if you like this one best, Stephen."

"The gray is bigger," the boy said. "But he doesn't seem as friendly."

"He's going to be tall," Nicholas said. "I think he'll need a man's hand to control him. But if you like him better, we can see how it goes."

With a nudge of her nose, Sugarfoot snuffled at Stephen's chest, seeming to fuss at being passed over for a superior choice. Her low-pitched snuffle made him laugh, and he rubbed his hands on her neck, causing her to nudge even more. He caressed her ears and petted the soft underside of her throat, bringing the mare deeper in thrall to him.

"She's just a baby," Stephen said, his cheek rubbing against that of the mare.

"She's a three-year-old, Stephen. Not a baby, but certainly an animal who will return your affection. If you treat her well, you'll have the chance for a fulfilling relationship with her. Animals seem to know when they're loved."

"The gray is pretty and looks strong, and the golden horse is like nothing I've ever seen before," Stephen said, "but I like Sugarfoot the best."

"Well, the palomino isn't for sale," Nicholas said, "so it's just as well you didn't decide on that one. This golden creature is a special horse, one I was given by a special friend, and both Lin and I are firmly attached to this beauty."

Stephen clambered up on the corral fence and sat on

the top rail, seemingly comfortable with his perch. Behind him, Nicholas smiled at Brace and the two men shared their pleasure at the boy.

"He'll do you proud," Nicholas told the lawman, nodding at Stephen. "He's got a good touch with the horse, and seems more than ready for the responsibility."

"Thanks," Brace returned. "It's not my doing that he's such a prime young man, but his aunt Sarah has had a big part in his growing up."

"She can be proud of him," Nicholas said firmly. "I'll feel at ease if you choose to take Sugarfoot back to town for him."

"We need to work on the shed first," Brace told him. "I'll get some wood delivered and begin putting together a stall this afternoon. I've thought about asking Joe Castorman to come out and put up the fencing for me."

"This is gonna run you a nice piece of change, Sheriff," Nicholas said with a laugh.

"Nothing good ever comes cheap," Brace told him. "Now, let's take a look at the dog I hear you've got living in your corncrib."

"She's not alone," Nicholas warned him. "Had herself six pups just a week ago. They're all carbon copies of our dog, Wolf, and he's claimed ownership. Keeps a close eye out for them."

"Can we see them?" Brace asked, noting the stillness that possessed Stephen as the two men discussed the dogs.

"I don't know why not. Their eyes should be open in a couple of days, and they'll be ready to leave home by the time they're six weeks old." He turned from the corral fence, and Stephen reluctantly climbed down from his perch to walk beside Brace.

"Will they be large?" Brace asked, dropping one hand to Stephen's shoulder, almost, he thought, as a sign of possession. It seemed that the boy was more and more a part of his life, and he felt stirrings of ownership as he looked down at the youth.

"Pa?" Stephen spoke his title readily, and Brace bent to hear his words. "I don't care if the pup is big or small. I just think I'd like to have a boy dog if that's all right."

"I think we can talk about that," Brace told him.

"They'll be good-sized dogs, male or female," Nicholas said. "The mother is not small, and our Wolf is just about the size you'd expect. Although he doesn't resemble a wild animal. He can be very protective, though, and we'll have to wait for him to decide to let us close to his offspring."

"Protective is good," Brace said, slowing his pace as the dog lying in front of the corncrib got to his feet. With a soft *woof*, the dog approached and sat down politely in front of Nicholas, silently announcing that the man was allowed to go no farther. And then, from the house, two women approached, and the behavior of the animal changed radically.

With a sharp bark of welcome and a burst of speed, Wolf approached the pair of women and one of them, Nicholas's wife, Lin, crouched quickly to welcome the animal. Wolf lay on the ground, rolling to his back as Lin spoke to him, her hand scratching beneath his chin, her words extolling his virtues.

Beside her, Sarah laughed aloud and the dog transferred his attention to her. She bent to him and he sniffed at her hand. Then his tail began wagging in a rapid movement and his tongue lolled from one corner of his mouth.

"Now, that dog recognizes a beautiful pair of women, I'd say," Brace told their host. "I suspect he's Lin's dog, isn't he?"

"How could you tell?" Nicholas asked, his fond gaze centering on his wife. "Wolf likes women. Always has. Amanda is his private property. She doesn't go anywhere without her shadow."

"Well, I think you've sold a dog, and we haven't even seen them," Brace said. "If the pups are anything like their daddy, I'll be proud to give one space in our house."

"I think his bloodlines will run true," Nicholas said.

The corncrib door was opened and Stephen stepped inside, Wolf close behind. The boy squatted beside the large box, wherein lay a large female dog, looking like a mixed breed, mostly shepherd. The female sniffed at Stephen's hand and allowed him to pet her, then lay back, as if allowing him access to her family.

The largest of her offspring nursed busily, but at Stephen's touch, released his hold on his mother and turned his head in the boy's direction. "I like this one," Stephen said quietly, one finger caressing the tiny bundle of fur.

"That's a male, all right," Nicholas said. "Probably the pick of the litter. You've made a good choice, son."

"When can we have him?" Stephen asked.

"Several weeks," Nicholas said. "He has to learn to eat on his own and be big enough to be independent. Not that he won't need lots of love and attention from you. In fact, he'll probably be a demanding little fella, if I know anything about it."

"I think we can give him a good home." From the

doorway Sarah spoke, and the three menfolk looked her way. "We'll make him a bed in the kitchen," she said, "and when he's older, he can sleep on a rug by Stephen's bed."

"No doghouse?" Brace asked with a grin.

"We'll see." Sarah's tone was agreeable, as if she would consider the idea, but it was obvious to her audience that she'd already made up her mind about the pup.

Dinner with the Garvey family was a treat, Sarah decided. Their housekeeper and cook, Katie, showed off her superb skills in the kitchen, and Sarah gave her lavish compliments as the women shared the task of setting the table.

"You can't have her," Lin said, one arm around Katie's middle. "She's like a mother to me, and we couldn't do without her in our family."

"If you find her twin sister somewhere, let me know," Sarah said with an admiring look at the older woman. "Although I wouldn't want to give up cooking for my family. They're so appreciative." She cast a knowing glance at Brace as she spoke, and he moved from the window to stand beside her.

"You could give Katie a run for her money," he said. "I've eaten at both tables, and if I didn't know better, I'd say you were taught by someone with Katie's talents, sweetheart."

"My mother," Sarah said in an undertone.

"Mothers are the very best teachers," Katie vowed. "That's where I learned to make bread and pies and all that goes along with them."

The meal was superb, the company enjoyable and the trip homeward was filled with chatter and the laughter of three people who'd spent a happy day. Stephen immediately went to the kitchen table to begin drawing a sketch of what the stall should look like, and an outline of the area they would fence for pasture.

Brace rode off on his gelding to see someone at the lumberyard about having wood delivered, and Sarah set about looking at their closets to be sure their Sunday clothes were ready for morning.

Brace, upon his return to the house, approved Stephen's plans, explained to the boy the logistics of stall building, and together they walked beyond the shed to look over the property in order to best situate the corral.

Supper consisted of leftovers from the day before, along with fresh cinnamon rolls Sarah had set to rise early in the morning. Redolent of sugar and raisins, the scent of cinnamon accompanied the rolls to the table, and the icing ran thick and creamy onto the plates as she served them.

"A fitting end to a wonderful day," Brace said quietly. "Have you had a good time, Stephen?"

"Oh, yes, sir," the boy answered. "It's been the most fun I've ever had in my life."

"You didn't know you could fulfill his dreams so readily, did you?" Sarah asked. "He's an easy child to please, but I'll have to admit that the prospect of both dog and horse in one fell swoop would be enough to delight any child."

"Well, we'll all enjoy having the dog, I think," Brace said. "And one day we'll get a mare for you, too, Sarah. I think you've done your share of riding, haven't you?"

"Yes," she said quietly. "In fact, the mare I rode into town has been a fine addition to the stock at the livery stable. I'd had her just a short while when I arrived here, but she's a splendid animal."

"Do you want me to bring her here?" Brace asked quickly. "That wouldn't be any trouble at all."

Sarah shook her head. "I think not. I really thought I wouldn't need her," she said. "Right after we got married I sold her to Amos." Her mind worked back through the day to the horses they'd seen at the Garvey ranch. "I just may go out to visit Nicholas myself one day and see what his corral has to offer."

"Say the word and we're halfway there," Brace told her.

"You're a good man, Sheriff," she said with a smile.

Brace rose from the table and cleared the dishes quickly. "If you wash, I'll dry," he offered, dipping into the reservoir at the side of the stove for hot water. Splashing it over the dishes, he watched as soap bubbles rose to cover the plates and silverware. Then another trip to the stove produced enough hot water to rinse the dishes in a second pan.

"I'll wash the table, Aunt Sarah," Stephen said cheerfully. "I don't mind helping." He looked at her wistfully. "Do you think we could read some more later on? I like it when you read to us."

"Sounds like you have the evening all planned out," Sarah told him, and then relented as his smile wavered. "I'd love to read to you and Brace, sweetheart. You go pick out a book and we'll be in right shortly." As an afterthought she called out after him, "See if you can find a copy of *Robinson Crusoe,* why don't you? It's one of my favorites."

"You handled that well," Brace told her as Stephen finished his chore and then ran down the hallway to the parlor.

"He's so easy to be with," she said, looking after

the boy as he disappeared into the room at the front of the house.

"So are you," Brace told her. He enveloped her in an embrace that pleased her, his hands careful as he touched her with knowing fingers, his mouth against her face and then her throat, tasting the soft skin and inhaling the aroma of willing woman.

"You smell so good." His words were low and whiskey-soft against her ear. "I'll have to investigate all your sweet spots a little later on," he said, laughing softly as she clung to him with soapy hands, dampening his shirt in the process.

"You do that quite often," she commented, her knowledge of his approval and affection firm. She snatched up the dish towel he'd laid aside and dried her hands. "A little too late, I fear," she said. "I've already gotten your shirt all wet."

"Ask me if I care," he said, laughing softly as she brushed at the water stains with the towel. "I'll let you take it off after a while, if you like."

"All right." Her lips found his, blending in a kiss that gave her the assurance she craved. "I'll do more than that, after a while," she promised. "Just be warned, mister."

"I can hardly wait."

Sunday afternoon, after church service and dinner had been tended to, found all three of them measuring the available space in the shed for another stall. Jamie joined them, hammer in hand, and Sarah was sent to the kitchen to put together a picnic.

Later she brought out a basket filled with the overflow from her kitchen. Cinnamon buns left from the night before, thick slices of ham from the noon meal and biscuits she'd slid into the oven just a half hour before, along with a bowl of potato salad, completed the meal and they sat on a blanket outside the shed to enjoy the abundant feast.

"The stall is pretty well done, Miss Sarah," Jamie said, placing a slice of ham on the bottom half of his biscuit and covering it with the top. "We'll be ready for Stephen's horse by the middle of the week."

Stephen wiggled excitedly. "I can't hardly wait!" he exclaimed, his grammar gone by the wayside. It was all Sarah could do not to hug him close, so appealing were his actions. He was growing up, she thought, and she'd do well to give him the respect due a young man, lest he think she saw him as a baby.

They cleaned up their picnic, and Stephen all but scooted Jamie out the front door, so anxious for another session of reading he barely observed the manners he'd been taught. It was all right with Jamie, for Brace said he'd been off sparking with a town girl for the past weeks and had already planned an assignation with the young lady for after Sunday-evening vesper services.

The continued reading of *Robinson Crusoe* came next, and the three of them decided they should devote their evenings to the story, enjoying two chapters a night. Stephen tried his best to argue for three, but gave in gracefully at a nod from Brace.

"I think it's time for bed, son," Brace told him. "School tomorrow, don't forget."

"It's almost summertime," Stephen said. "In fact, it was pretty hot today."

"We have another month before school will be out," Sarah told him.

"And then I can work at training my horse, can't I?"

"Yes, I think that sounds like a good idea. There's a

lot involved, you know. We'll have to talk to Nicholas to find out just what we need to do.''

Stephen nodded happily, kissed his aunt and hugged Brace with a strength that surprised the man. "I'm going to bed," he announced.

"Shall I go up with you?" Sarah asked.

"Naw. I'm old enough to take care of myself," he said. And then, as an afterthought as he climbed the stairs, he called back to her. "You can stop in later and say good night if you want to."

Sarah knew a moment of joy as she recognized his need of her. He was growing up, but a woman's touch was still important in his young life. She said as much to Brace and was pleased by the look of affection he cast her way.

"A boy never gets over needing a woman's touch," he said. "Speaking of which, I could use a little touching right now. Someone said something about taking off my wet shirt."

"That was last night," Sarah told him, eyeing the cotton garment. "This one is dry."

"It still needs to come off," he said. "I thought maybe—"

"You thought right," she said as he hesitated. "It's time for bed for all of us, I think. And time for you to…"

"Scout out all your sweet spots?"

"I shouldn't have reminded you of that, should I?" she asked.

"You'll never need to ask for that," he told her. "It's my pleasure to let you know how precious you are to me."

Once more, Sarah felt the rush of thanksgiving that so frequently invaded her very being. "Remember the night we met?'' she asked, thinking about the events of the past weeks. ''You scared me to death, pointing that gun at me.''

''I wouldn't have shot you, no matter what the circumstances,'' he told her. ''In fact, I'd never pointed a gun at a woman before, and when I realized you were a female, it just about did me in.''

''You sure didn't have any qualms about putting me in jail,'' she said. ''I thought you were pretty businesslike about the whole thing.''

''I didn't want to let you get away,'' he admitted. ''There was something special about you, Sarah. I couldn't take a chance on losing you. Even then.''

''And now?'' she asked.

''You'll notice I married you as soon as I could figure out how to get a ring on your finger,'' he told her, laughing as he recalled his haste.

''You don't stand a chance of losing me, Sheriff,'' she said. ''I'm yours for as long as you want me.''

''Let's just say *forever,* then,'' he murmured, holding her captive against him.

She nodded. *''Forever.''*

Chapter Ten

Brace came in the back door at noon, a smile that seemed to forecast good news curving his lips. His words affirmed that theory, and Sarah was breathless at the announcement he made.

"I have a surprise for you," he told her, barely taking time to greet her with a kiss before his impatience made itself known.

"A surprise?" She placed his plate on the table before him as he settled there, and bent to touch her lips to the curls that rested atop his collar at the nape of his neck.

"That tickles," he said, shrugging his shoulders and shivering.

"I thought I might coax you to tell me your news," she said, bringing her own plate to the table. Freshly picked green beans, lavish with bits and pieces of ham, were heaped generously beside slices of corn bread. A plate of newly churned butter was placed before him and he lifted his brows at the sight.

"When did you manage to get fresh butter? Did you churn it?"

Sarah nodded. "I went to the store and almost bought

some ready-made, but Mr. Metcalfe had fresh cream, just brought in from that farm on the edge of town, where the man sells milk. I like to use a churn, and I'd found one in your pantry." Her shoulders rose in a gesture that belied much effort on her part. "Try it," she said.

He did, slathering a generous amount on his corn bread and lifting it to take a bite.

"I was thinking," Sarah said. "I'd thought we might get that cow we spoke of once. Especially if you decide to enlarge the shed into a barn."

"I thought you were more interested in hearing the news I have for you than discussing a cow," Brace said with a grin.

"I am," she returned smartly. "But the idea of having our own milk and cream handy is very appealing, Sheriff."

"How appealing is a visit from your family?" he asked, unable to subdue his smile as he drew a folded piece of paper from his shirt pocket. He held it in one hand, the fingers of his other carefully unfolding it, then offered it to her.

"A wire from my father?" she asked, glancing at the bottom of the page, where the stationmaster had written the name Joshua Murphy in a firm hand.

"One and the same," Brace told her. "Read it out loud. I think I got the general idea when I looked it over, but I may have missed something."

"I doubt that," she said smugly. "You're my star pupil, sweetheart. You can read most anything in print."

"Thanks to you," he said quietly. "I owe you much, Sarah."

"No, not at all," she replied. "We're even, so far as

I'm concerned.'' Her gaze dropped to the contents of the paper she held and her voice held an abundance of happiness as she looked up after a moment. ''They're coming here. Their train will arrive tomorrow and they'll be staying for several weeks. Oh, Brace, I can hardly wait to see them. I just wish it hadn't taken them so long to make the trip.''

''Have you forgiven them for not pursuing the truth about your sister's death?'' Brace asked her tightly.

''They're my parents,'' she said softly. ''We all do things we'd like to change, and I think they probably have a lot of regrets about Sierra. But you have to remember that they were dealing with Lester's shenanigans, stealing and embezzling, and maybe holding Sierra responsible in a way. She married the man and brought him into the family, after all.''

''And how did you feel about that?''

Sarah thought for a moment. ''I think Lester had Sierra hoodwinked, and he obviously fooled my father into giving him a job and access to company funds.''

''Well, if you can put your grudge against them aside, I can do no less,'' Brace told her. ''And I think they've probably only recently realized how much they're missing, Sarah. Between you and Stephen is a bond that must be obvious to them, and I'm thinking they want to share in that. They must feel his loss terribly, on top of missing you.''

''I hope so,'' she said, carefully folding the wire and tucking it into her apron pocket. ''I've feared that my leaving had cut all ties between us. But it sounds like they've forgiven me for running off.''

''Did they realize you were hot on Lester's trail when you left?''

''They knew he was about to cart Stephen to Texas,

and had even tried to stop him. But you know what Lester is like. Nothing stands between him and what he wants to do.''

''Well, I'm sure your father talked to the local lawmen in Big Rapids before he left there. I'll warrant they've changed their minds about Lester's part in your sister's death. If anything comes of all this, they may have to go home to testify. And you may have to make the trip, too,'' he told her. ''Just know that if you go, I'll be with you, Sarah.''

''Thank you,'' she whispered, and then her frown disappeared as she rose quickly from the table. ''I'll have to think of where to put them,'' she said. ''I don't know if the bed in the back bedroom will be large enough. Maybe I can switch things around a little.''

''There's a big bed in the attic,'' Brace said. ''The folks who lived here before I did apparently had an overload of furniture, and when the lady sold out to me, she left everything behind. I think I saw a couple of dressers and chests of drawers up there, along with a rocking chair and a little cushioned chair that looks kinda fragile to me.''

''Maybe a slipper chair, made for a lady's dressing room,'' Sarah ventured. ''I'll go up and look this afternoon, and maybe we can bring things down after supper.''

''Whatever you say, sweetheart,'' Brace said agreeably. ''Just don't try to do any carrying yourself, you hear me?'' His brows drew down as he spoke, and Sarah nodded quickly.

''I'll wait for you and Stephen to help,'' she told him.

The morning train was greeted by the three of them, Stephen begging to stay home from school for the occasion. Sarah had agreed to his request, and so the three of them drove in the wagon to meet the older couple.

They were nicely dressed, Brace thought, a hat perched stylishly on Mrs. Murphy's head, her traveling gown a bit dusty, but nonetheless cut nicely to fit her stout form. Joshua Murphy was dressed as a business-man, his suit dark and well tailored.

"I'm Sarah's father," he said, holding out a hand to Brace. "This is my wife, Colleen," he continued smoothly, the two men clasping hands as he spoke. Then he turned to where Sarah stood quietly beside the lawman. "Sarah." Her father's voice broke as he spoke her name.

"Sarah?" He repeated her name and then his arms rose to enclose her. She went gladly into his embrace and her arms circled his neck, her mouth against his cheek.

"Daddy," she whispered, her eyes filling with tears as she was greeted with an abundance of emotion.

"Save a hug for me," her mother said, moving closer to be included in the embrace.

"How about me?" Stephen asked, looking expec-tantly at his grandmother. Colleen smiled at him and halted, veering from Sarah to where the boy stood. She bent to him and kissed him warmly, then brought him to her side.

"We've missed you terribly, Stephen," she said, al-lowing her tears to fall unashamedly. "Your grandfather and I were so happy to hear that you were here with your aunt Sarah," she told him.

Joshua looked up at Brace. "Thank you for letting us know what was going on here," he said with feeling. "Our sheriff in Big Rapids notified us that the case involving our daughter was being reopened, thanks to you and a friend of yours.''

"Nicholas Garvey," Brace said. "He's a good man, and has agreed to help us."

Sarah reached for Brace's hand and drew him closer. "I'm married, Daddy," she said, holding up her hand, showing the wide gold band she wore. Her fingers were almost engulfed by Brace's wide palm, but the ring glistened in the sunlight.

"The groom sent a wire, Sarah," her mother said. "I wish we'd been here for the wedding, but if you're happy, that's all that matters to us. And having Stephen here with you is exciting. We've been so worried about both of you."

"Is there anything we should know, right off?" Joshua asked Brace. "You said in your wire that the judge for this area was returning to finalize the matter. When will that be?"

"Within the next week or so," Brace told him. "Right now Lester and his two brothers have left town to visit their father. The old man is quite ill, I understand, and the three brothers have gone to the western part of the state. They should be back before the hearing. I'm hoping you can be here, too."

"I'm planning on it," Joshua said firmly. "We need to do whatever we can to secure Stephen's future."

"Thank you, Daddy," Sarah said. "And you, too, Mama. I'm so glad the both of you came to visit. Will you stay long?"

"As long as it takes to set things to rights, child," her mother said. "We didn't do everything we should have back in Big Rapids, ignoring things the way we did. The only excuse I can offer is that we were so broken up about Sierra, we neglected to investigate thoroughly. That's been taken care of now. Our lawyer is still digging up the facts, along with the town's sheriff and a marshal sent in by the government."

"Well, it sounds like things are under control," Brace said, waving a hand at the wagon he'd brought for transportation. "The wagon isn't very comfortable, but the buggy wasn't large enough for all of us to travel in," he told them. "I'm thinking of buying a surrey, one that will hold six nicely."

"You are?" Stephen looked up at Brace with wide eyes. "Boy, that would sure be great, Pa. Will we get a horse to pull it?"

"Probably two," Brace told him. "We'll have to get busy finding room for more stalls, won't we?"

"Stalls? You're building stalls?" Joshua asked.

"For my new horse," Stephen said proudly. "We're gonna get him this week, maybe. And we might make our shed into a regular barn."

"Well, I'm quite a hand with a saw and hammer myself," Joshua said. "I'd like to lend my help."

"That would be most welcome," Brace told him. He turned aside and picked up two pieces of the luggage that had been deposited on the station platform. The whistle sounded and the engine began to move. "Let's move away. The ladies won't want to get their clothes dirty when the wheels kick up cinders," Brace said.

"I'll get the rest," Joshua said, lifting his own share of baggage. Stephen scooped up one smaller bag and moved toward the wagon, placing the tapestry valise on the back.

"I'll ride back here and watch stuff," he said staunchly.

"I'll ride with you, Stephen," his grandfather said quickly. "We can start to catch up on all the news."

"Okay, Grandpa," the boy said quickly, helping the older man deposit the luggage. Brace added the two he'd carried over and then lent a hand as Colleen attempted to climb up onto the high seat.

Placing her in the middle, he deftly lifted Sarah to sit beside her mother and then circled the wagon to find his own place on the wide board seat.

The trip home was short, and in less than an hour the Murphys were settled in their room, and Sarah and her mother were busily putting away an enormous assortment of clothing in the dressers and chests Brace had moved into the room. The men headed for the back, where the wagon was placed beside the shed and the horses were staked to graze.

In less than a week the morning train from the east brought with it a man who was greeted with a hearty handshake by Brace. "Welcome, Judge," Brace said, his voice more than sincere as he thought of the issue that would be solved today.

"Is our boy in school?" the magistrate asked, walking beside Brace toward the jailhouse.

"Yessir, he is," Brace answered. "I take him every morning and pick him up when school is over in the afternoon."

"Sounds like a good plan to me," Judge Bennett said sagely. "I'd say keeping him out of danger was the first priority here."

"That's the way his aunt and I feel," Brace told him. "And keeping Sarah safe is right up there with looking after Stephen."

"Do you think she's in any danger?" The judge's eyes narrowed as he walked more slowly. "Has the father threatened her?"

"I'd say so," Brace told him. "He was blatant about it when you were here last. Made a threat when he left the courtroom."

"Well, we'll have to put in place some strict rules this time, perhaps," the judge said. "I've about decided—" His words came to an abrupt halt as he shot a look of chagrin at Brace. "I almost let the cat out of the bag, didn't I?"

"I'm sure you'll do what's best for Stephen," Brace said, pleased that Judge Bennett apparently was leaning toward leaving Stephen in Sarah's custody. Even if that meant continuing the visitations with Lester at the jailhouse.

"I'll need you to go pick up the boy from school a little early today. We should get things rolling right after noon, I'd say." Passing the hotel, Judge Bennett waved a hand at the double doors of that establishment. "Is Lester still living here?"

At Brace's nod, Judge Bennett turned abruptly about, but Brace halted him with a hand on his sleeve.

"He's not here right now," Brace said. "I gave him permission to leave town for several days. He left with his brothers. His father is ill, according to the two brothers, and I didn't feel there were sufficient grounds to force the man to stay here waiting for you. We'll probably have to put off the hearing," he added. "Didn't you get my wire?"

The judge pursed his lips. "It slipped my mind—but, yes, I did get it. I think we can make a judgment without the father here," he told Brace. "I'll come back to reinforce it, if necessary, next month. In the meantime, I don't see any reason to withhold my decision."

The two men entered the hotel, where the desk clerk recognized both of his early-morning callers and smiled expectantly. "What can I do for you, gentlemen?" he asked.

"Mr. Simms," Brace said quickly. "If you'd be so kind as to arrange for a room to be made ready for the judge for a night or two, I'd be most appreciative. I'm assuming that the three men we spoke of last week have left town for a while. Am I right?"

"Yessir, Sheriff," Bart Simms said. "They said they'd be back in a week or so, and asked me to hold their rooms for them."

"Well, it's not a likely circumstance," the judge said, "but if any of them should return today, particularly Lester Clark, please notify him that we'll be having a hearing over at the town hall shortly after noon today. I'd appreciate it."

"Sure will, sir," Mr. Simms told him. "I'll go up and leave a message."

"Thank you," the judge replied readily and did an about-face, heading for the outside door. "That should take care of that," he said, resuming his walk down the sidewalk.

"I'll go home and get Sarah, and bring her back after we eat dinner. Would you like to come along? My wife's a wonderful cook." Brace knew a moment of pride as he spoke the words. He'd done more bragging over the past couple of weeks than he had in his whole life. "In addition," Brace said, "my in-laws are here from Big Rapids. I'd like to include them in the hearing, since they have a vested interest in Stephen's future."

"I'll turn down the invite," the judge said slowly. "I can't take a chance on lending my support in your direction. Everything must be on the up-and-up, no favoritism shown to either party. But I'd like to visit in your home after this mess is all cleared up."

And it was a mess. Brace agreed entirely, not surprised when the judge turned down his offer of dinner. It was to be expected.

Sarah had a kettle of soup ready for him at noon, and he blessed the judge for denying himself the opportunity to share this meal with them. Finding his woman at the stove, apron tied around her middle and curly tresses of hair falling about her forehead and cheeks, Brace was thankful to be alone with her.

"Where are your parents?" he asked, speaking in a low voice lest he be overheard.

"Out back," she said. "I said I'd call them in when you got home. My father wanted to check out the shed and the building you've done."

Brace held her close for a few minutes, telling her of the circuit judge's arrival on the early train, explaining why the man had chosen to eat his dinner at the hotel restaurant, and finally looking at his pocket watch as he realized that the hearing was to be held in short order.

"I'll be ready," Sarah said. "I'll call in my folks now, and I don't take long to eat. You just need to wash up while I ladle up some soup for everyone." She went to the back door, and a high-pitched whistle called her parents to the house.

"Where'd you learn to do that?" Brace asked, turning from the sink in surprise.

"The boy next door taught me. Sierra was so jealous. She never could figure out how to hold her fingers in her mouth and get any sound."

From the shed, two figures hastened toward the house, and Sarah's father called out, seeing Sarah behind the screen door. "You haven't forgotten how, have you?" His smile was wide, his approval of his daughter evident.

"I've never heard her whistle like that before," Brace told him as the older man kicked the dust from his shoes on the porch. "My wife apparently has many talents I've yet to discover." He turned then to speak to Joshua directly. "The judge has come to a conclusion and is going to announce his findings at a hearing in about an hour. I'm assuming that you and Colleen will go with us. We'll pick up Stephen at school and bring him along, too."

"Definitely," Joshua said firmly. "That boy's future is uppermost in our minds. Right next to being certain of Sarah's happiness. And on that note, I think my wife and I agree wholeheartedly. Am I right, Colleen?"

With a quick look in Sarah's direction, her mother nodded, her eyes filling as if her emotions were close to the surface.

"I've never done anything so smart in my whole life as marrying Brace," Sarah said. "I practically asked him if he'd have me." Her grin was mischievous as she cast him a quick look.

"Not true," he said, denying her claim. "I'd been after her to set a date, and then she turned the tables on me, right in the middle of the general store, and announced it to the whole town. She's lucky I didn't snatch her up right then and there and go visit the preacher."

"Sounds like Sarah, all right," her father said, laughing as Brace told his story.

"I didn't want her to be alone in the world," Brace said. "I knew she had folks, but here in Texas she was without family, except for Stephen, and having him in tow made her vulnerable to Lester Clark. I knew I'd die before I let anything happen to her. So," he said with a grand gesture that turned into a bow, "and so I married her. A dandy bit of business on my part. Got me a wife, the best cook in town and the prettiest woman in Texas, all in one fell swoop.''

Joshua reached up to shake his son-in-law's hand. ''Welcome to the family, son. I couldn't be more pleased.''

They sat at the table, full bowls before them, with bread on a tray and jam Sarah had found in the pantry. ''Where did this come from?'' she asked Brace, spooning a generous portion onto her slice of bread.

''Got it from the general store,'' he said. ''One of the farm ladies makes it for sale every summer. You'd be surprised how many of those women help support their families with cooking and baking. Several of them do needlework, too, and sell the products through Mr. Metcalfe at the store.''

''I'll have to go have a look-see,'' Colleen said, obviously relishing the flavor of the jam. ''Tastes like strawberry and something else with it.''

''Rhubarb,'' Brace told her. ''It's the most popular jam they sell.''

''Never had rhubarb in jam before,'' Colleen said. ''I've only used it for pie.'' She looked sharply at Brace. ''I don't suppose you have any growing on your property, do you?''

''Out past the place where the new pasture is going to be fenced,'' Brace said, waving a hand in that direction. ''There's a big patch of it.''

''Well, make sure it isn't included in the pasture,'' Sarah said. ''I'll cut some to use, and I don't want horses getting to it first.''

''Yes, ma'am,'' Brace said nicely to his wife, and then grinned at Colleen. ''See how well she has me trained?'' he murmured.

"I'd say there's a lot of spunk left in you, young man," Sarah's mother said knowingly. "I doubt you're completely taken in by any woman, even one as…" She allowed her gaze to run over her daughter and then spoke slowly. "Even one as special as my Sarah."

"She takes after her father, you know," Joshua reminded his wife. "She and Sierra used to run us about ragged when they were small. What a pair." He ate slowly, as if the food were a feast—for indeed it was, Brace decided.

And then Joshua spoke again. "We've missed Sarah so much. When she left, it was like we had nothing left. Stephen gone, and Sarah hot on his trail, caused us no end of worry."

"We were so pleased to hear that she'd married you," Colleen said.

"I'm sorry I didn't write you," Sarah said.

"Well, I took care of that when I sent them the news," Brace told her. "I knew that a woman as extraordinary as you are must be missed terribly by those who love her."

Sarah blushed and rose quickly, her empty bowl in one hand. "That's about enough of that," she said. "I'll be getting a big head if you keep this sort of thing up. Now, let me clear up the table and then we'll go find the judge and see what's going to happen."

Brace cleaned his bowl with appreciation. "I'd kinda planned on going back for seconds," he said. "Maybe I'll have another bowl after the hearing. I'm thinking we need to be on our way." He turned to Sarah and his voice was low. "Are you worried?" he asked, and then tossed in words that might set her mind at ease. "I don't think we have anything to be concerned about. The judge sounded to me like he's about ready to give Stephen to us on a permanent basis,'' he told her. ''He almost let it slip this morning while we were walking from the train.''

Sarah's eyes lit with hope as she placed her bowl and spoon in the dishpan, then turned back to the table to finish clearing. ''Oh, I hope so, Brace,'' she said eagerly.

Brace grinned. ''Well, don't let the cat out of the bag, sweetheart. It's not something we can even talk about yet. We'll just have to wait and see.''

The hearing was delayed by Lester's arrival just as the judge was leaving the hotel. ''Thought you'd pull something on me, didn't you?'' he said caustically to the judge. ''A good thing I came back when I did. Something told me I'd better.''

The judge refused to be riled by the man, but filled him in quickly on the hearing and then turned away. ''I'd suggest you join us, Mr. Clark. I don't want to hear any more from you.''

Lester gaped as he followed the judge and Brace into the street. Then his eyes narrowed, and he approached Joshua Murphy. ''I might have known she'd go crying to her mama and daddy,'' he said harshly. ''I suppose you think bein' here is gonna help her get her hands on my boy, don't you?''

Across the street, Sarah stood at the doorway to the jailhouse, Stephen by her side. ''I thought he wasn't gonna be here,'' Stephen said, reaching for Sarah's hand.

Joshua looked her way and then at Brace. ''I'd say you don't have a snowball's chance in hell of getting the boy, Clark. You're a rascal, and it doesn't take much intelligence to figure that out. I think you'd better tag along and listen to what the judge has to say. I doubt he'll shilly-shally around much.''

His words proved to be valid, for the judge took little time in speaking his mind on the matter of Stephen's custody. "I find it in the best interests of the child that he be in the custody of his aunt Sarah and Sheriff Caulfield. This ruling will be in place until Stephen is eighteen years of age, or until a higher court rules otherwise. Just one other thing. Stephen must see his father once more in accordance with my earlier decision.'' The gavel he held hit the table before him with a satisfying thump, and those assembled before him wore various looks of approval and anger. "I will not make a recommendation for future visiting rights. I don't want the boy to have contact with his father.''

"This won't hold up," Lester said, his words spit from between his clenched teeth. "I'll see to it that I get the boy, one way or another.''

"I'd walk carefully, if I were you,'' Judge Bennett said harshly. "That could be construed as a threat, and I don't take threats lightly, sir.''

"Well, there are other courtrooms and other judges,'' Lester told him, "and a father shouldn't have to go to all this trouble to have custody of his own son.''

"If the father is not fit to raise a boy, then the court must step in and make a ruling in the child's behalf.'' Judge Bennett's words were brisk and to the point. Lester glared his hatred at Sarah, Brace and Stephen, and the older couple, then turned on the judge.

"I know men in high places. My family is well-known in west Texas, and we're a prosperous lot.''

"Money doesn't always buy what you want, sir,'' the judge said. "There are things more important than a pocket full of change. Justice is one of them. Another is human kindness between father and son. Or any parent and child, for that matter.''

"That's a bunch of fancy talk," Lester said, a sneer twisting his mouth, his eyes casting darts at those who had determined to beat him at his game. "I just now came from my pa's place clear on the other side of Texas, after seeing him on his deathbed. That's how important family ties are to me. I believe in a father's rights and having a real family, with a father and child together."

"We have a real family," Sarah said sharply. "Stephen has a mother and father who love him deeply and will take good care of him."

"Spoil him rotten, you mean," Lester said with a dark look that promised vengeance should he find an opportunity.

"Can we go now?" Stephen asked quietly, leaning close to Brace to make his wishes known.

"Right away, son," Brace told him. "School is not on your schedule for the rest of the day. That's why Sarah had you bring your books along with you. You can work at the kitchen table with your grandmother and Aunt Sarah this afternoon."

"Thank you, sir," the boy whispered. "I sure am glad that judge didn't let *him* take me with him."

"I didn't think he would," Brace said, standing and adjusting his gun belt. "Let's get on home with the whole clutch of you," he said, one long arm clasping Sarah to his side, his look including her parents. "I've got things to do this afternoon, so you'll be on your own for a while."

"We have things to do, too," Sarah told him. "We're going to start by finding a good name for Stephen's dog."

His eyes glowed as the boy heard her words. "I didn't even think about that," he said. "We'll sure enough have to really think hard, Aunt Sarah. We've got a horse to choose a name for, too. We might want to call it something different."

"So we have," she said, "and we need to begin talking about your responsibilities, Stephen, about what's involved in cleaning stalls and training your dog to go outdoors when he needs to…"

She glanced up at Brace and her father for support and together they laughed aloud. Joshua leaned down to speak directly to Stephen. "Your aunt is telling you that dogs have to be taught where it's polite to wet when they need to. Usually out in the back somewhere is a good place to send him when the time comes."

"I can do that," Stephen said. "We can have a rope for him and I'll take him out there every little bit till he catches on."

"I think we're on the right track here." A smile of approval touched Brace's lips as he agreed with the boy.

They left the town hall together, the grandparents flanking Stephen, who carried his books, while Sarah was tucked close to Brace's left side, leaving his gun free and readily available. And Brace, himself, almost wished for a chance to make use of it.

Chapter Eleven

"I feel like a heavy weight has been lifted from my back," Sarah said, sighing contentedly as she pulled the sheet over herself. The house was quiet, Stephen long since having gone to sleep, Sarah's parents nicely ensconced in their own room just down the hall from where Sarah and Brace slept. Stephen had had a few questions about the judge's decision, and Brace brought them up, unwilling to mar Sarah's good humor but aware that the subject must be opened.

"Stephen wanted to know if there was any way Lester could still get hold of him," Brace said. "We need to be vigilant, Sarah."

"Is it time for me to practice shooting a rifle or shotgun?" she asked, her voice revealing her distaste of the prospect. She rolled over in bed to face him.

"I don't think so," Brace told her, settling beside her on the feather tick. "As long as you keep the doors locked and don't go wandering off with Stephen, you'll be fine. Lester's too smart to pull anything really stupid. And having your folks here will be a deterrent, too."

"Don't count on that," Sarah said. "Look what he did back home, stealing from my father's business."

"And that's another thing," Brace told her. "I've asked Nicholas to look into the man's reputation back where you came from. Being a banker gives him access to any number of things I couldn't do on my own. Even as a lawman, I'm limited by my resources. Nicholas will make inquiries. Where money is concerned, he's tops at the game. And anyone who has left a trail can be traced rather easily. I suspect Lester didn't take pains to cover up his actions. He no doubt thought that his in-laws would overlook his shenanigans."

"Well, they didn't when they finally realized what he'd done," Sarah said. "My father turned what information he had over to the bank about the mismanagement of funds that were under Lester's control. The problem was that there was no tangible proof."

Brace yawned and rolled to face Sarah. "Nicholas will take care of it for us, sweetheart. Don't worry about anything but taking care of me right now."

"And just what do you need?" she asked, smiling at him by the light of a single candle.

"Just you, Sarah. Just you." His hands reached for her, and she was reminded once more of the passion he was able to draw forth from her body. His desire for her seemed endless and she knew a happiness she could barely contain as he held her close, pulling her atop his chest and then drawing her face close to kiss each inch of skin he could reach. "I promise to be really, really quiet," he whispered, and she stifled a laugh against his throat.

He shifted a bit, and his mouth was hot, avid against hers, his palms running the length of her body, his fingertips pausing to caress his favorite places as they searched out the secrets of her femininity. She writhed against him, his big hands urging her closer, her own need for his loving causing her to settle squarely atop his long length.

Her legs parted as she felt the pressure of his arousal against her belly, and she lifted herself to better capture that firm, seeking member. "Can I do this?" she whispered, and Brace thought her voice was the epitome of feminine innocence. His Sarah still had much to learn, it seemed.

"Of course you can," he answered, barely able to put two words together. "You can do anything you want to, baby. If you want me, you know how to fit things together."

"I didn't know it would work this way," she whispered, aware of the fullness of his arousal as it found a haven in the depths of her body.

"You'd be surprised at how many ways we can make it work," he told her, his words teasing, approving her movements.

"I don't think I know what to do next," she told him, kissing his throat and nuzzling beneath his ear.

"Just use your imagination, sweetheart," he muttered. "You'll come up with something, I'm sure."

And she did. Gracefully, and with a passion that came readily to the surface, she brought pleasure to both of them. Brace was trembling beneath her, his long frame taut, his arms holding her with an embrace that drew them together in a new way, and Sarah cried out her joy against his chest, the sounds muffled so as not to carry beyond the walls of their room. He guided her into nuances of lovemaking that had heretofore been unknown to her, and she reveled in his teaching of her untutored body, responding readily to each touch, each softly whispered instruction he gave.

"I love you," she said, and then repeated the words,

as if she could not tell him enough, as if her heart could not contain the emotion that spilled forth.

"Ah, Sarah," he whispered. "You're a wonder. A woman I never thought to find."

They nestled in the middle of the big bed, wrapped together in an embrace that involved more than just their bodies blending as one. As if the love that possessed them both, that made their lives together such a thing of beauty, would not allow them to separate one from the other.

Brace's big hands moved against Sarah, touching and caressing her hips and breasts, the curves of her legs, drawing them about himself as though he cherished the very feel of silken flesh, the warmth of her womanhood, the fire of her passion.

"Shouldn't I put my nightgown on?" she whispered. "What if Stephen or my mother come in early to wake us?"

"They won't," Brace told her firmly. "I locked the door. Besides, you always wake up before Stephen does. And if your mother gets up early, she can cook breakfast."

"I feel like I might sleep till noon," she murmured, a laugh tingeing her words. "I'm worn out, Brace. You've made a wanton woman out of me."

"So long as you only want me, that's all right," he said. "Don't ever stop loving me, Sarah."

"No chance of that," she said, her words positive, her tone firm, as though she made a vow.

"I'll take care of you," he whispered against her ear. "I won't let anything happen to you, sweetheart."

"I know that," she affirmed. "You make me feel safe and secure and well loved."

"You're all of that, and more," he told her. "Especially the well-loved part."

"When can I get my saddle and bridle and all that other stuff?" Stephen asked a few days later. His teacher had let the children out early, and Brace, called from the jailhouse, had picked him up and delivered him safely home.

Now the boy sat at the table and drew diagrams of the stall they had completed. "I think we need to have a tack room," he said. "Nicholas has a big one, with all his harnesses on the wall and saddles and stuff like that on racks. Do you think he'll have a saddle for my horse? Or will we have to go buy one ourselves?"

"I haven't thought about it much," Sarah said, aware that her answer was less than satisfactory. "I suspect we need to ask Brace what he thinks."

"I wonder if the man at the livery stable has any extra saddles for sale," the boy mused as he looked from the kitchen window. "Could we walk over there and ask him?"

"I don't think that's a good idea," Sarah said firmly. "We'll have to wait and see what Brace wants to do about it."

"I'll ask my grandpa what he thinks. Maybe Pa would like it if we surprised him and did it all by ourselves." Stephen's words were spoken in a way that sent a signal to Sarah. Stephen had been doing some thinking about this. It wasn't a spur-of-the-moment subject they explored today.

"Let's give it a rest," Sarah said. "You can talk to your grandfather, and the both of you might want to ask Brace about it tonight. Then we'll go out to see Nicholas in a day or two. I think he's about ready to let the horse go, Stephen. We'll be bringing her home before long. And just think how pleased your grandpa and grandma will be to be included in the whole thing."

"I'll bet they'd like to see the pups, too," the boy said. "I've been thinking about naming our dog Bear. What do you think?"

"Do you think he'll look like a bear when he gets bigger?" she asked.

"I thought he was pretty furry, more so than the rest of the litter. Didn't you notice?"

Sarah shook her head. "I can't say that I did. But I'll take your word for it. If you want to call him Bear, it's fine with me."

"Well, he's gonna be pretty big, I think, and it kinda goes with Wolf, doesn't it?" Stephen asked. "And I thought about a name for the horse, too. Do you think she'll like to be called something like Buster, or maybe Beauty, or maybe we should just stick with Sugarfoot? She's awful pretty, but I don't know if Beauty will work or not. Especially since she's used to Sugarfoot."

"Well, I don't know if Beauty is what we want," Sarah countered. Tilting her head to one side, she thought long and hard about the boy's choices. "Maybe we should just keep the name Nicholas gave her. I really like Sugarfoot."

"I'll probably just let her have the name she already has," he told Sarah. "That'll be easier, anyway, with just the dog to name." He sighed deeply. "I'm so glad you listen to me, Aunt Sarah, like you really care what I think about stuff."

"I do care," she answered. "I love you, Stephen, and I'll always be interested in what you think."

It seemed the problem had been solved, for Stephen turned back to his drawing pad, including a saddle in the picture he was producing. "I sure wish Pa would hurry home, and maybe we could go to Nicholas's place today," he said after a bit, during which he'd cast several longing glances her way.

"When Grandpa and Grandma come back from the general store, we can talk about it some more," Sarah told him.

Colleen sported a new shawl when she returned from Mr. Metcalfe's dominion, and it had to be admired by all, for Brace came in the door in the midst of Colleen's exhibit of her newly acquired treasure.

Joshua drew Brace toward the back door. "Are those posts going to just sit there, or are you planning on putting up a fence?" he asked dryly.

"I'm going to hire it done," Brace told him. "I just don't have enough time to get the job done before we pick up Stephen's horse. And my own animal needs to be let out during the day. I'd thought Stephen and I could help with the job, but I think I'll have to bring in someone from town."

"No such thing," Joshua told him firmly. "I'm right handy with tools, and putting up a few boards on posts already in the ground is a snap. Why, you've done the hard part already. Setting those posts was a big job."

"That's true," Brace agreed. "And if you want to help, I'll be able to put in several hours every evening."

"Stephen gets out of school right shortly, doesn't he?" Joshua asked. "He'll be a big help to me."

"Well, I won't argue with accepting a helping hand," Brace told him. "I'll have the lumberyard deliver the first load of boards tomorrow. You can just have at it."

"Pa," Stephen said impatiently, as if he'd been waiting for a break in the conversation in order to put in his two cents worth. "Can we go to the Garveys' place tonight?"

"Probably not tonight," Sarah told him quietly. "Brace will have to let Nicholas know we're coming, after all." And then she thought of her own conversation with Brace.

"Nicholas is checking into some matters for us, and Brace might want to wait and see what kind of answers we get."

Stephen rose and walked to the window, looking out upon the fence posts that stood in neat rows. "Is my real pa still in town?"

Sarah thought he sounded fearful, and she could hardly blame him. It must seem that his whole life had been spent living in fear of the man who had sired the boy. "I don't know," she answered. "He was going to see his father the last I heard."

"You don't think he'll be coming around here when he comes back, do you?" Stephen asked.

"Well, if he does, we don't have to worry," Sarah told him. "The windows are locked and the doors have bolts on them. He couldn't get in the house if he tried. Besides, with your grandpa here, he'd be a fool to make any trouble."

"It's a good thing we married the sheriff, ain't it, Aunt Sarah? And a good thing my grandpa and grandma came to visit."

"Yes, it certainly is," she said quickly, thinking that the child had no idea just what a good thing it had turned out to be, all the way around. A new relationship had sprung into being between her and her parents, and their presence was a joy she would long cherish.

The three men were crowded into Lester's hotel room, the brothers newly arrived, their cups filled with whiskey from a bottle Lester had brought with him. "What do you think, boys?" he asked. "Will Pa be ready to forgive and forget when we go back? Do you suppose he'll get out the fatted calf for me?"

"He'd be more ready to accept you back if you had the boy with you," LeRoy said. "We'll need to snatch him up before we leave town."

Lester frowned. "It might cause too big a ruckus if we take him with us. And on top of that, there's still Sarah to consider. I'd like to have a shot at her, too."

"Now, that's one fine-lookin' woman," LeRoy said agreeably. "I wouldn't mind gettin' my hands on her, myself."

"There's enough there to share, I'd think," Shorty said slyly. "She's a lot of woman for a stick-in-the-mud like our goody-two-shoes sheriff, don't you think?"

"You fellas need to find women of your own," Lester said. "We'll talk about all that later. I'm thinking it might be a good idea to get our hands on both of them, maybe see what sort of ransom Caulfield is willing to pay to get them back. He won't be too anxious to fire on us if we have his woman with us."

"And then what?" LeRoy asked. "So he pays a ransom. And we'll be without the woman and boy. That don't sound too smart to me."

"Who said we wouldn't have the both of them? We'll take Caulfield's money and skedaddle back to the ranch, with enough of a nest egg to keep us going until we make a permanent deal with Pa."

"I like the way you think," Shorty said with a loud laugh. "And the trip west, next time, should be a lot more fun than this one. I'd even share my bedroll with the woman. In fact, I'm plannin' on it."

* * *

The menfolk seemed to find a special sort of enjoyment together, using hammers and saws, cutting and nailing boards in place, as they enlarged the shed. The pasture fencing was coming along nicely, Brace said, with enough already enclosed to contain the horses.

Sugarfoot was to be turned into the pasture by the end of the week, and a larger area for horses and supplies would be finished. Even a stall for a cow had been included in the project, and Sarah was given the task of locating one.

She checked with Mr. Metcalfe and was sent to the milk farm from whence her cream had come before. Armed with enough money to purchase a cow, and accompanied by her mother, she set off in the buggy to make the purchase.

Colleen readily admitted her ignorance as the buggy passed a herd of docile-appearing cows in a field leading up to the farmhouse and barns. "I'm not much on milking, I'll tell you right now, Sarah," her mother said. "I had to do my share when I was a young girl, but it's been years since I sat on a milk stool."

"If you remember how it's done, I'll be grateful," Sarah told her, laughing at her mother's words. "Mr. Metcalfe said I should get a Jersey, a young one. He said to look for a brown cow with a pretty face, kind of on the small side."

"Sounds like a Jersey to me," Colleen said. "That's what my father had on the farm, and Holsteins, too. The Jersey we used for milking was a champ, my mother always said. Gave the richest milk in the county."

They pulled the buggy up in front of the barn, and in short order were greeted by the farmer who owned the place. "Howdy there, ladies. What can I do for you?'' He approached them with a grin. Sarah slid from the seat, and climbed down quickly.

''Mr. Metcalfe at the general store told me I might be able to buy a milk cow from you,'' she told the gentleman. ''I wondered if you have any for sale.''

''I can probably come up with a nice milker for you,'' he said pleasantly. ''What did you have in mind?''

''My mother—'' Sarah waved a hand at Colleen, who watched from the seat ''—my mother said I should think about getting a Jersey. She told me I'd get rich milk and cream.''

''They aren't known for volume,'' the farmer told her. ''But it's true that their milk is probably the best for drinking, and the cream is the best there is for churning butter.''

''I don't need enough milk for the whole neighborhood,'' Sarah told him with a laugh. ''Just enough for our family.''

In less than a half hour, as they left the farm, a dainty, light brown cow was tied to the buggy and Sarah's reticule was considerably lighter. It seemed that Mr. Metcalfe and Brace had been pretty accurate as to the value of a cow, but Sarah still had a bit of money left after the bargain was struck.

Pleased with her venture into cattle buying, she considered the calves the farmer had told her about. If raised over a period of several months, even a year, a calf would grow to a size suitable to slaughter for a family's meat supply for some months. Kept in the cold during the winter months, it seemed an economical way to be sure of beef on the table, Sarah thought.

Brace agreed with her, upon their arrival home. Approving of her purchase, he listened as she explained the value of buying a calf, and then posed a question she had not thought of.

"After you have a young calf here for a while, you'll probably want to name it, won't you?" At her slow nod, he continued. "You'll feed it and put it out to pasture every day, and pretty soon you'll become attached to it. That happens, you know," he said with a smile. "So what happens when we have your pet butchered and you're faced with cooking parts of the animal for supper all winter long? Can you do that?"

Sarah felt a sharp pang of regret. "I don't have a calf yet, and already I'm grieving for it," she said quietly. "I don't know if I can, Brace."

"I doubt you could, sweetheart," he told her. "You're a softie at heart. Buying meat from the butcher or a farmer nearby seems like a better idea to me. You won't have any fond memories of the animal to cope with."

Sarah nodded slowly. "You're probably right." And then her voice became more lively, and she smiled. "But drinking milk and making butter won't bother me at all."

"Once you learn how to milk this critter," Brace said, leading the cow into the shed, where a stall had been hastily put together for her use. A rough manger held hay and the cow seemed to feel at home there. "We'll put her in the pasture every day," Brace said. "It'll save on feed, and she's better off with fresh grass."

Sarah looked at him hopefully. "Do you know how to milk her?"

He shook his head. "It's been years since I lent my talents to that chore. But I heard from your pa that Colleen is quite a hand at it. Maybe she can give you lessons.''

"Do you have a milking stool?" Colleen said from behind them. "And a new bucket to use. You'll need a milk house or a cool place in your pantry or washroom to keep the milk while the cream rises."

Sarah felt overwhelmed for a moment. "It seems like I got us into a sticky situation, doesn't it? I'd better go see Mr. Metcalfe to find a bucket and see if he has any milking stools for sale."

"I can make you a stool," Brace told her, his smile teasing as he considered her problem. "And I've already brought home two new milk pails for you to use, sweetheart. I knew you'd need them."

"We'll have your first milking lesson after supper," Colleen told her. Her glance touched on Brace as she spoke. "And you, too, Sheriff. Let's see if you remember the skill."

"I'm game," Brace said. "Now I want you ladies to come over here and admire the lean-to we built for our new surrey. Not to mention the addition we've laid out."

"A new surrey?" Sarah asked.

"I mentioned it before," Brace told her. "The day your folks arrived. I've already ordered it from Amos, and he tells me it should be here by the end of the month."

"What about somewhere to store the wagon?" she asked.

"There'll be room inside for that," Brace told her. "We're enlarging the whole place to double its size." He bent closer and his words were hushed. "Your father has rather grand ideas, and I'm not about to stop him."

"You'd better put a bridle on him," Colleen said. "He gets carried away sometimes."

"We can use all the space he builds," Brace told her. "Sarah's mare is next on the list, and a team to pull the surrey."

Sarah's eyes widened. "You're extravagant, Mr. Caulfield."

"No," he said. "Just providing for my family."

Supper was late, what with the flurry of activity in the shed, and it was almost dark by the time the table was cleared and the dishes put in the pan.

"We'll do these later," Sarah said. "I'm anxious to see our first milk produced."

The shiny new pail they used was over half full when she carried it to the washroom an hour later. "The cream will rise nicely for butter," Colleen said. "We can churn tomorrow."

"After we take some for our oatmeal," Sarah said, thinking of Brace's affinity for the hot cereal. "And some for our coffee. I'll be so glad not to have to buy it by the pint at the general store. And Stephen can have all the milk he wants to drink." Her smile told of pride in the new venture, as Brace came in the door.

"Doesn't take much to make her happy, does it?" he asked Colleen.

"Never did," her mother answered. "She was always easy to please. Sierra was the stubborn one, headstrong and impatient if things didn't move along as quickly as she liked. Sarah seemed willing to sit back and enjoy every day as it came along." She looked at her daughter with admiration gleaming in her gaze. "I'll bet you've found that to be true, haven't you, Sheriff?"

Brace thought for a moment. "For the most part,"

he said. "But you should have been here when we first met. She was dead set on having her own way. I ended up putting her in jail, right off."

Colleen looked properly stunned. "In jail? In a cell?"

"Sure did," Brace said agreeably. "She spent a night there, while I sorted things out. She was determined to shoot Lester, and I couldn't let her follow through with that."

"No, I suppose not," Colleen said slowly, "but I wonder if it wouldn't have solved a lot of problems if someone had aimed a gun at him a long time ago."

"Now, that sort of talk will get you in trouble," Brace said with a grin. "Though I have to admit, I agree with you."

"This blood bay is a beautiful piece of horseflesh," Joshua said emphatically a week or so later as they watched the new addition racing across the pasture. "I wouldn't mind having one like it myself."

"I didn't know you rode," Brace said. "And where would you put one in the city, anyway?"

"I had a horse when I was younger," Joshua told him. "Learned to ride when I was just a tadpole. My pa put me on a pony when I was about four years old." He sighed. "I'd give a bundle to have a place out of the city, a few acres where Colleen and I could raise chickens and a garden and have some horses."

He looked abashed as Brace smiled. "I'm just a dreamer, I suspect. But it seems that life is passing us by and we're living in a big old house, rattling around in it all by ourselves. I hate to think about going home and leaving all of you behind."

"No one said you had to leave," Brace told him. "I'll bet you could find a few acres hereabouts, if that's what you'd like. Benning is a good place to put down roots, and it's never too late for that. There are a couple of small places outside of town for sale. It might be worth your while to take a look, see if either of them would be suitable for you.''

Joshua looked brighter, Brace thought, his eyes gleaming as if an idea were burning to be brought to fruition. ''Maybe I'll just do that,'' he said. ''If Colleen would be willing to leave her garden club behind and start all over.''

''She can have flowers here,'' Brace told him. ''And I'd say Benning is about ready for a garden club. I'll bet she could organize these ladies in no time flat.''

''You really wouldn't mind if we did such a thing?'' Joshua asked ''We wouldn't be in your way?''

''Not as long as you know how to use a hammer and saw, and remember how to be a grandpa to Stephen.''

''That'd be the best part of the whole thing, I suspect,'' Joshua said slowly. ''Stephen could spend time with us, and Colleen would be in hog heaven, baking cookies for him and sewing shirts and pants. She's missed him terribly for the past months, ever since Lester came one day and marched off with him.

''I thought Sarah was going to fall apart. She'd been taking care of the boy ever since Sierra died, and it was like losing her own child.''

''Well, she considers him her own now,'' Brace said. ''Mine, too. I don't think a child of my own blood could mean more to me.''

''Speaking of which, is such a thing in the offing?'' Joshua asked hopefully.

''One of these days,'' Brace said confidentially. ''I sure hope so, anyway,'' he added slowly. ''Sarah would be a wonderful mother.''

"She already is," Joshua told him. "She was born to be a mother, and being with Stephen has her well trained for raising her own."

The men worked on, sorting out the tack room, setting aside bits and pieces of leather to be mended and cleaned. A secondhand harness for the team to draw the surrey had been purchased, and Brace was eager for its use to begin.

"Shall we go in and put your idea to a vote?" he asked Joshua.

"You mean about living here permanently?" the older man asked.

"The very one," Brace said with a laugh. "I suspect it will meet with rousing approval from the rest of the family."

His opinion proved to be valid. Colleen leaned to kiss her husband fervently as he spoke of moving from Big Rapids to Benning. "I believe she likes my scheme," he said, grinning widely.

"Just stay where you are," Colleen told him with a laugh. "I'll hug you later."

"Promises, promises," her husband said ruefully. And then he cast her a look that held a vow of intent. "I'll hold you to it, sugar."

"You never called my grandma that before," Stephen said, all agog as the adults bandied words back and forth.

"You'd be surprised what your grandpa has called me over the past years," Colleen told the boy. "He's quite a romantic fellow when he gets going."

"Sugar?" Stephen said, rolling the word on his tongue. "My pa calls Aunt Sarah his sweetheart sometimes. I suppose it means about the same thing, don't it?"

"Just about," Brace agreed with a quick look at Joshua.

The adults sat at the table for an hour, discussing the possibilities of the move, until Stephen finally spoke his mind. "I think we need to just decide you'll move here, Grandpa, and then we can go in the parlor so Aunt Sarah can read to us."

"Sounds good to me," Brace said. "Let's all lend a hand clearing up and we can get our book in about ten minutes flat."

Chapter Twelve

"I've written something I'd like you to look at, Sarah." Brace held a sheaf of papers in his hand and sat down across the table from his wife. To her surprise, his hand trembled a bit as he handed her the results of his endeavors.

Sarah placed the epistle on the table before her, for indeed that was what Brace's efforts had produced. It was a letter to his family, and under the date June 15, 1901, was the salutation "Dear Mother and Dad." The handwriting was a bit sprawling, but each letter had been carefully formed, and the sentences he'd written were lined up meticulously on the unlined paper as if he'd taken special pains to be neat.

It was not standard cursive writing, but a blend of printing and the use of formed letters such as they'd practiced during long hours at the kitchen table.

Sarah read it quickly, her heart pounding in her chest, her smile giving away her absolute pride in her star pupil. As she reached the final line, she sighed and her index finger traced lightly over the words he'd put together.

"I'm so proud of you, I could burst," she said, her

voice breaking on the words as she tucked the pages into her pocket. And then she rose and walked to where he sat, bending to hold him close.

"We can do better than that," he said, laughing as though something had pleased him immensely. For indeed it had. Sarah saw the look of satisfaction on his face, noted the pride in himself he could not conceal and found herself close to tears.

Brace pushed his chair back from the table and pulled her into his lap. He held her close, her face pressed next to his, his mouth speaking against her ear, even as his lips found tender flesh there to bless with his kisses.

She curled against him, content to be close to the man she loved, uncaring if the rest of the family should find them so engrossed in each other. In fact, she had discovered over the past weeks that her own parents found great pleasure in each other's company, something she had heretofore not been aware of, at least on a conscious level. She'd always known that there existed a great deal of love in their family, but the relationship between her parents had remained a mystery to her, as though she could not allow her mind to accept their loving each other in the same way she and Brace found joy in their marriage.

Now she took her ease in his embrace, proud of the man he was and even prouder of the intelligence that had allowed him to progress so far in his education. "Can we mail it out tomorrow?" she asked, and was pleased by his quick nod of assent.

She took it from her apron pocket and unfolded it with care, then read again the words he'd taken such pains to write.

It was a summation of his life, wrapped up neatly in a logical fashion, beginning with his taking the job representing the law in Benning, and continuing on to his marriage to Sarah. He spoke with pride of Stephen, gave the details of the arrival of Sarah's parents and their plans to stay on in Benning. But the highlight of his letter was his description of Sarah herself, of her beauty, her abilities and the happiness she'd brought to his life.

Sarah read it for the second time, more slowly than her first perusal of it, and felt her eyes fill with tears as she folded it again and slipped it back into her pocket.

"I didn't mean to make you cry," Brace told her, wiping her eyes with his white handkerchief, freshly ironed that very morning.

"I'm so proud of you," she whispered. "Your mother will be pleased by this, you know."

"I hope so. I've sent mail home before, but always had to have someone else write the letters for me. In fact, a year or so ago, my family was talking about sending me a wife. I suspect they thought I wasn't bright enough to find my own bride. I think maybe that's why I wanted to let them know how happy I am with you, and what a wonderful woman you are."

"You flatter me," she said, and then grinned and kissed the tip of his nose. "But I love it." Her mouth caressed his then, and it was several seconds before the sound of her mother's voice penetrated her concentration.

"Sarah?" Standing in the kitchen doorway, Colleen looked at her daughter hesitantly. "Am I interrupting?"

"We can continue this discussion later," Brace said quickly, and Sarah was very much aware of the crimson that ridged his cheekbones and the measure of his arousal that pressed against her bottom. He held her firmly where she sat, and she did not quibble with him, satisfied to remain in place.

"What is it, Mother?" Sarah asked, aware that Colleen was excited about something, given her gleaming smile.

"Stephen's dog has arrived," Colleen said. "Nicholas just drove up in their buggy and brought him around the back."

"Where's Stephen?" Brace asked, apparently changing his mind about Sarah's spot on his lap, lifting her to stand beside him.

"Out in back. Where did you think he'd be?" Colleen asked. "Sitting on the ground with a lap full of puppy, all shiny eyed and happy as a lark."

"It's a good thing he's out of school," Sarah said with a laugh. "He's going to be one busy boy training that dog for the next little while. At least it will take a load from my shoulders, teaching him where to do his duty."

"Well, that's a polite way of putting it," Brace said with a lifted brow. "Let's go take a look, ma'am. I think he'll be wanting to show off a little."

Indeed, the boy wore a look of pride, his hands full of a wiggling, squirming pup. It had grown considerably since their first encounter—it was almost five weeks old now, Nicholas said, and very smart.

"I thought he might be too young to take from his mother, but he's caught on to eating from a pan and seems quite independent to me," he said. "I knew that Stephen was anxious to get his hands on him, so I told Lin I'd bring him into town with me." He cut a quick glance at Brace and grinned. "She had to tell him goodbye and shed a few tears over him. It's going to be hard on her when the last one goes to a new owner."

"Why don't you keep one?" Sarah asked. "A place as big as yours could use two dogs, I'd think."

"I've already *got* two dogs," Nicholas said flatly. "That female is going nowhere. Wolf is quite smitten with her, and Amanda has claimed her as her own. She calls her Sweetie-Pie, and woe be unto anyone who tries to take that female away from us."

"Well, then," Sarah said logically, "three dogs would work, I'd think."

"I may keep one and give it away down the road a ways," Nicholas said. "We got Wolf when he was full grown, and there are those folks who'd rather have a dog already trained to be a watchdog. And with Wolf as his daddy, it shouldn't take him any time at all to catch on."

"I'll bet Lin will have something to say about that," Sarah said quietly to Brace, but her words were picked up by Nicholas's sharp ears, and he shot her a quick grin.

"You may be right, but then dogs don't cost a whole lot to have around, and Lin sure has a good time with them. I like to keep the woman happy."

"Well, you've made our boy happy," Brace told him. The men watched as the pup used his tongue effectively on Stephen's face and then sniffed at his shirt before curling up to sleep in the youthful arms that held him.

"I think he's found a good home." Nicholas looked at the boy and his pup with tenderness, and Sarah saw another side of the man. Not that Nick hid his gentler streak, but this glimpse of the man Lin loved with such passion made Sarah appreciate him even more.

"How much do we owe you?" Brace asked.

"Nothing," Nick said. "This is worth a million dollars right here." He pointed at Stephen and smiled.

"I'm hoping my boy will grow up to be as terrific as yours."

"He will," Sarah said confidently. "He can't miss."

The supper table was alive with a discussion of the new pet. Joshua spent an hour making a collar from a piece of harness that was worn in spots, and Bear wore it, but not with pleasure.

"He'll get used to it," Joshua predicted as Stephen watched the puppy with a worried expression. "It takes a couple of days sometimes for a dog to settle in, Stephen. He'll do fine. Now, he might be lonesome for his littermates when it's time to go to bed, but if you sit with him till he goes to sleep and leave him something warm to cuddle up with, he'll be all right."

"How do you know so much about dogs, Grandpa?" Stephen asked. "I didn't know you had any pets."

"I did when I was a boy," Joshua told him. "And when we find a place to live hereabouts, I may be in the market for a dog, myself."

"Maybe Nicholas will still have pups then," Stephen said hopefully. "Or maybe the female will have a new litter."

"It takes a while for that to happen," Sarah said carefully. "It seems more likely that the pup Nicholas hangs on to will be ready for a home by then."

Bedtime found Stephen curled around his dog, both of them nestled on a piece of quilt behind the cooking range where the banked fire kept the space almost too warm for comfort. Although summer was well under way, the nights were cool, and Stephen had to be persuaded that the pup would be comfortable without a blanket to cover up with.

"Dogs have a coat that keeps them warm," Brace

explained carefully, ruffling Bear's fur to show Stephen the dense growth that covered the pup. Satisfied that all was well, the boy went to bed, followed closely by his grandparents.

Within an hour, Sarah and Brace were settled in their bed, and suddenly Sarah sat up, her hand covering her mouth.

"What's wrong?" Brace asked. "Are you all right?"

Sarah nodded her head, and Brace realized that she was laughing and stifling the sound behind her palm. "I just heard Stephen leave his room. I'll warrant he's gone downstairs to sleep with that doggone puppy." As if torn between hauling the boy back to bed and leaving him to his own desires, she drew up her knees and hugged them. "Do you think—"

"No, I don't think," Brace said quickly, cutting her off, aware of what she was about to propose. "You're safe leaving him with the dog. It won't hurt either of them for Stephen to sleep on the floor tonight. We can talk about putting the quilt next to his bed tomorrow. Will that suit you, sweetheart?"

Sarah looked in his direction. "You read me like a book, don't you?" she asked. "I can't even keep my thoughts to myself these days."

"I know what makes you tick," he admitted. And then he reached for her. "Forget Stephen for a while, Sarah. Just let me hold you and appreciate you, will you?"

"Appreciate me?" she asked, curling against him. "I think I like the sound of that."

The house they found was small, but as Colleen said, they didn't need stairs to climb, and two bedrooms were plenty for her to keep clean. The rooms themselves were ample, the kitchen holding a new cookstove, shiny and showing signs of loving care. She and Sarah measured the windows and set to work making curtains while Joshua and Brace got the house ready to move into.

A letter to their lawyer in Big Rapids, with instructions to sell their home there and pack up their belongings, settled that part of their moving problem, and arrangements were made for their household goods to be shipped on the train.

Colleen fretted over someone coming into her house and finding things awry, but Joshua pooh-poohed her fears. "Everything is spick-and-span," he said. "You left things just like you always do, sugar." He turned to Sarah and laughed. "She always has to clean everything within an inch of its life, just in case something happens to her and she doesn't come back. She doesn't want anyone to think she's not a good housekeeper."

Sarah laughed and then sobered suddenly. "I understand that, Mama. Scary, isn't it?"

"I knew you would. After all, we're both women," Colleen said, as if that settled that. And so it did.

By the time July was over, the new house had been thoroughly cleaned and outfitted with the houseful of furniture that arrived from Big Rapids. The leftovers were deposited in the attic, and Colleen hung curtains and laid rugs with a vengeance. A few new pieces were ordered from the catalog and delivered to the general store from Sears, Roebuck, in Chicago. Moving in was the next order of business, and the whole family pitched in with enthusiasm.

A washing machine took Colleen's fancy, and once he saw how it simplified Colleen's wash day, Brace vowed to get one for their own home, a decision Sarah did not argue with. She was thoroughly tired of the scrub board and more than ready to have the modern appliance in her washroom. Turning a crank so that the clothes were agitated inside the machine sure beat scraping her knuckles on the scrub board any day of the week, she told Brace.

It was late August when she approached him with some news he found much to his liking. In fact, so delighted was he that he picked her up and carted her without ceremony to their room. There he closed and locked the door, then proceeded to strip the clothing from her body.

"Brace! What are you doing?" she asked, breathless from his handling.

He held her before him, admiring the sleek lines of her feminine form, and frowned. "I don't see anything," he said. "How do you know there's a baby in there?"

His big hand was flat against her belly, and she laughed aloud at the perplexed look on his face as he pressed gently against the cradle nature had provided for his child to inhabit for nine months. Just seven months now, though, thought Sarah.

"I have all the signs," she told him gently. "My mother says that everything points to our having a baby in about seven months."

"Why'd you wait so long to tell me?" he asked. "How long have you known?"

"Not long," she said. "I talked to Mama about it just yesterday, and she said it seemed likely."

"I guess I hadn't thought much about it," he told her. "I should have known you haven't done that woman thing for a while."

"The absence of 'that woman thing,' as you put it,"

she said with a smile, "is one sure and certain way of knowing there's a baby on the way."

"Where will we put him?" he asked. "We'll need one of those little beds that babies use, won't we? And a high chair for him to sit up to the table, and—"

"We won't need any of that for a while," Sarah said quickly. "We can put her in a box or basket or a dresser drawer for a couple of months while we decide on furniture for her."

"Her?" He looked aghast. "What do you mean, *her?*"

"It could very likely be a girl," she said.

"And just as likely a boy," he said, speaking his mind. "Although we already have a son." He looked thoughtful for a moment. "I guess a girl would be all right."

"Well, thanks a lot," Sarah said. "I don't think it makes one bit of difference what we have, so long as it's healthy."

He reached for her at that, and held her close. "I'm sorry, sweetheart," he told her. "You know I don't care what it is. I'm just so doggone happy about the whole thing. I hadn't thought a lot about babies, but I guess I should have realized that two people who make love as often as we do ought to be prepared for this to happen."

"Brace." She spoke his name sharply and then laughed. "I guess you're right. I just hadn't thought about it that way."

"There's just one thing," he said. "There'll be no dresser drawer for our baby to sleep in. We'll buy a proper bed, or else I'll make one. I'll bet your father would help. I think, from what I've seen, that he's pretty handy with any kind of woodworking."

"He is," Sarah admitted fondly. "He made my

mama all sorts of things for the house. In fact, the next time you go out there to visit, take a good look at the library table in front of the window in the parlor, and the cabinet in the kitchen where she keeps her good dishes.''

''Well, that's settled, then,'' Brace said with satisfaction. ''We'll build a crib and buy a mattress from the catalog. And we can get some stuff for you and your mother to make baby clothes out of. That soft, kinda fluffy material. You know what I mean.''

''Flannel,'' Sarah said, providing him with the proper word. She grinned at him, her delight in the fact of her pregnancy obvious. ''I'm so glad you're happy about this,'' she said. ''We've never really talked about having babies, but I've been walking around in a cloud all day today. I feel like I've been blessed by God, Brace. Does that sound foolish to you?''

''No,'' he replied. ''Not by a long shot. I think each child that's born is a blessing. I think that's why I couldn't stand that Lester had been so mean to Stephen. I don't know how anyone could deliberately hurt their own child. Or anyone they're responsible for. It seems to me that a wife and child are a sacred responsibility, and a man should respect them and treat them as well as he's able.''

''Well, you certainly follow that principle,'' she said, touched to the core by the words that allowed her to see the noble character of the man she'd married. He was loving and good, and she told him so in plain words. And then added for good measure the feelings she'd recognized since the early days of their marriage. ''I love you, Brace. I know I've told you before, but sometimes it fills me to the brim and I can't contain it. I didn't know I could love anyone the way I do right now. You're the best man in the world, and I'm so happy you're mine.''

He looked down at her, and for the first time since she'd known him, she saw his eyes fill with tears. ''I've known that for a good while, Sarah, but it makes me feel very privileged when you say it aloud. I knew you loved me on our wedding night, when you gave yourself to me so sweetly. You couldn't have done that if you hadn't felt deeply for me.'' His body trembled as he held her, and then he spoke again.

''I've never told another woman that I loved her. Probably because…well, just listen hard, sweetheart. I love you, Sarah Murphy. I've loved you almost from the first time I saw you. I told you once I didn't love you, but it wasn't true. I just didn't recognize it at the time. I want you to know that I'll do my best to earn your love for the rest of my life.''

''You don't have to earn it,'' she said, her own tears falling like rain. ''You have it already, freely given.'' She leaned against him fully, as if she could somehow be a part of him, her mouth seeking the tender flesh of his throat.

He hugged her, his big hands measuring her as they moved against her skin. From her nape downward he traced the lush curves of her body, his hands tender as he stroked her slender frame. ''It won't be long, though, will it?'' he asked. ''I mean, before you're growing big with my baby and we won't be able to stand so close together.''

''We'll figure something out, I'm sure,'' she told him, smiling at his reasoning. ''Folks have been hugging for centuries, even when women were nine months pregnant. We won't be any different than anyone else.'' She slid her fingers into his hair. ''I'll bet you can come up with some way for us to snuggle, even with a baby to consider.''

"Yeah," he told her with a wide smile. "I'm already working on that."

The mail was delivered daily to Titus Liberty when the morning train came into Benning, and should Sarah be in town, she delighted in stopping by to talk with the man and carry home the assortment of mail Brace received on a regular basis. Some of it had to do with his job, and those letters she quickly set aside for his perusal. There was a large catalog included in the bundle this morning, she was pleased to note, anticipating an hour of wish-list time for herself once the house was in order for the day.

But by far the most important item was a letter addressed to Brace, bearing the return address of John Caulfield. Recognizing the address as the one she had sent Brace's letter to, she clutched the letter tightly, barely remembering to thank Titus for his quick delivery of her mail.

The jailhouse was her first stop, and she entered the door quietly, her gaze seeking the familiar form of her husband. He was at the far side of the room, looking out the window, his forehead pleated as if he were in the midst of some great dilemma.

"Good morning," Sarah said, greeting him in an almost formal manner, as if this were just any old day, and not an occasion that would touch Brace's heart and hopefully bring him into a closer relationship with his parents.

"What do you mean, 'good morning'?" he asked, turning to her with a smile, his pensive mood evaporating in an instant. "It was good from the very beginning, Mrs. Caulfield. If I remember correctly, you greeted me with a kiss earlier today.''

"So I did," she replied. "And you took advantage of my good nature. Besides, this place…'' She paused, looking about with a raised brow, and then continued. "This place does not lend itself to such shenanigans.''

"Shenanigans? Is that what you call it?" He grinned and approached her, arms outstretched. "Let's see if I can nudge your memory a little bit.'' He drew her into his arms, the abundant mail delivery between them.

"Kinda hard to hug you through all this," he said, looking down as if the mail had a life of its own and was purposely keeping him from his wife. "Let's just set it aside for a minute.''

"You won't want to do that when I show you what arrived for you on the morning train," she said, her voice rising, her eyes filling with quick tears.

"Sarah?" He lifted the mail from her arms and dumped it unceremoniously on his desk. "What's wrong, baby? Whatever it is, I'll fix it. Just don't cry, sweetheart.''

With nothing to clutch, her hands made their way to his shoulders and then met behind his neck, where she found the tender spot beneath his collar. "I'm not crying," she protested. "I'm just all in a dither about something that came for you. I want you to open it.''

"What? Another wanted poster? Or a note from the judge?"

She shook her head. "Neither," she said. "This is more important than any wanted poster in the world.''

He frowned. "You're serious, aren't you?" And at her nod, he bent his head to kiss her briefly. "Just find it in that assortment and dig it out," he told her. "We'll look at it together.''

She obliged him quickly, handing him the envelope addressed to Sheriff Caulfield, Benning, Texas. His eyes widened as he looked it over, and then he attempted a smile, but his lips trembled a bit, she thought. "From my father," he said quietly.

"I know," Sarah agreed, apprehension rising, coiling around her heart. What if the letter was not what she'd hoped for? A full acceptance of his son, appreciation for Brace's success and maybe a welcome into the family for his bride.

Brace tore the envelope open and drew forth a single sheet of paper, covered from top to bottom with line after line of black cursive writing. He looked at it for a moment and then handed it to Sarah. "My eyes are blurry," he told her.

And indeed they were. But that was not the only reason for his action, she knew. He feared what his father had to say. Perhaps the news, whatever it was, might come better if she read the words to him.

She skimmed the first few lines, and her heart settled down to a slow rhythm. "He says that he and your mother were happy to get your letter," she began. "And then he says, 'We are pleased with your success in Benning. Being an officer of the law is an occupation to be proud of. We are sure you are filling the position with diligence and have every hope that your success will reflect well on the family.'

"And then your mother wrote a note," Sarah told him. "She's pleased that you've found a wife, and very surprised that you were able to write a letter with no assistance."

"If she only knew," Brace said quickly, interrupting Sarah's words. "I couldn't have even considered writing to them if you hadn't believed in me, sweetheart."

"You just needed someone to get you moving," Sarah told him. "You were so ready to take the step on your own. I'm proud of you, you know."

"I do know that," he told her, and then his gaze dropped to the paper she held. "Finish it, will you?"

"Not much more," she said. "Just that they would like to see you, and if you can arrange some time from your job, they'd like you to come home for a visit. Your mother wants to brag about your success to the folks at church and maybe have a reception for us to celebrate our marriage."

"We're not going anywhere," Brace said with finality. "Not while you're in the midst of carrying a baby. We'll write them and tell them that their first grandchild is on his way and it will keep us at home for the next little while."

"Maybe they'd consider coming here," Sarah said hopefully. "I'd really like to meet them, Brace. And I want them to see you in action."

"In action?" He frowned at her. "How so?"

"You know. All dressed up in your black sheriff clothes, with your badge pinned on your chest and your gun tied to your leg."

"I thought you didn't like my gun," he said.

"Just not when it's pointing at me," she told him coolly. "I still have chills when I remember that night."

"I told you, I wouldn't have shot you, sweetheart. By the time I got a good look at your hair and the way you filled out those britches, I was ready to take you home with me." He laughed as he spoke, his eyes crinkling, his seldom-seen dimple showing in his cheek and his body relaxing against her. "And now I plan to keep you around for the rest of my life. I hope you understand that."

"Yes, sir," she said obediently, then turned from him to pick up the pile of mail he'd dumped atop the clean surface of his desk. She sorted through the contents and set aside the mail addressed to him as sheriff, piling the few remaining items to one side. "That's all of it," she said. "I'll take the rest and go home."

"What shall we do about my parents?" he asked quietly. "We can't go to them. But maybe they'd consider coming to us, like you suggested. What do you think?"

"I think you should write them another letter and tell them that. It sounds to me as though they'd accept an invitation willingly. And now that my folks are in their own place, we have room for visitors."

"Speaking of your folks," he said, smiling in a smug fashion, "when do you suppose we should tell them about the baby? I know your mother suspects, but we need to make it official. And Stephen? What about him?"

"Well," she began, "my mother is delighted with the idea. She's been counting the months already and decided that I should be in childbed sometime in March. I just hope the weather will warm up early next spring. And she'll be busy in the meantime cutting out baby clothes and helping me put them together."

She halted her words, her excitement gaining control of her thoughts, and took a deep breath. "As to Stephen, I think it would be nice if you told him about it. There isn't any hurry, you know. We have the whole fall and winter to go through."

"I don't want him to pick up on it from our conversation, though," Brace said. "He has to be included in this."

Sarah felt a melting in her chest at his words. Stephen didn't know how very fortunate he was, she decided.

And she said so in no uncertain terms. "You're a wonderful father, Brace. It makes me happy to know how much you'll love your own child, based on what I see between you and Stephen."

"He *is* my own child," Brace told her, his voice husky, his hands trembling a bit as he wiped away the tears that stained her cheeks.

"And I think you ought to be the one to verify the facts with my father," she said. "I'm sure my mama has already told him her suspicions. She can't seem to keep secrets from him, but he needs to be told by the man responsible for this whole event."

"He'll probably want a granddaughter," Brace said, pouting a bit, making Sarah laugh, as he'd obviously intended.

"And will you be pleased with a girl?" she asked.

"I'm pleased with her mama," he told her. "Girls are among my favorite people. I thought you knew that.

"Especially *this* girl," he said with a tug that drew her closer into his embrace. "You're my favorite person in the whole world, Mrs. Caulfield."

Sarah lifted her face to him, inviting his kiss with a smile. He responded, just as she'd known he would, bending to her again, his mouth moving against hers with the passion of a man totally besotted with his wife. Sarah basked in the warmth of his approval and answered his desire with a heated acceptance of his kiss, her mouth opening to him, tilting her head, the better to fit their lips together.

Brace inhaled sharply then and lifted his mouth from hers, his cheeks stained with crimson, his nostrils flaring, his mouth damp from the kiss he'd begun so casually. "Where's Stephen?" he asked after a few minutes. "Is he home alone?"

"No," Sarah said. "My father rode in and picked him up an hour or so ago. He's going to spend the day there. They took Bear along, and Daddy is planning on helping Stephen with the dog's training. He's really quite good at it, you know."

"Does that mean the house is empty?" Brace asked hopefully.

Sarah assumed a pose of innocence. "It probably is," she said. "I thought I could get things done more readily if I had the place to myself for the morning."

"I believe I'll come home for dinner right now," Brace told her. "I'll take this mail along," he said, scooping up the small pile of envelopes and circulars from his desk. "I can look at it while you put together something for us to eat, and then we'll have to rest a while. You can't be rousting around all day without taking it easy for an hour or so."

"Rest a while?" she asked. "You mean, like in bed?"

His grin was wide. "Yeah, that's what I mean."

"Alone?" she asked, her desire for him imbuing the single word with invitation.

"Not on your life, baby," he said softly. "Not on your life."

"All three of them are back in town," Brace said quietly the next evening, aware that Stephen was just down the hallway in the parlor with his grandparents. "They're at the hotel."

"What does that mean to us?" Sarah asked, aware that Brace would not have brought up the subject without good cause.

"He's entitled to have one more supervised visit with

Stephen at the jailhouse, Sarah. And he's asked for it to be day after tomorrow.''

"Are you worried about it?'' she asked.

"Not worried, exactly, but concerned. He acts like he has something up his sleeve, and I haven't any idea what it might be.''

"Would he try to take Stephen away from you?'' she asked.

"I don't think he'll try that. And we know that Stephen would never go willingly.''

"Have you told Stephen yet?''

"No, I thought I'd better let him know in the morning. If I tell him tonight, he'll worry about it, all by himself in the dark. We'll talk tomorrow.''

"Aunt Sarah?'' Stephen's voice called from the front of the house, and Sarah stepped across the kitchen doorsill.

"I'm here,'' she said, and was not surprised to see him standing in the parlor archway, a book held against his chest. "I'll be finished up in the kitchen shortly.''

"Well, are we gonna read?'' In an aggrieved voice he uttered his complaint, and Sarah laughed at his frown. "Grandpa and Grandma are getting impatient at waiting so long.''

"I know very well who's getting impatient,'' she said sternly, but her grin gave her away. "We're going to read,'' she assured him. "Just as soon as I finish hanging out my dish towel and sweeping the kitchen.''

"I don't know why you have to always sweep,'' he said dolefully. "I think the kitchen floor looks pretty clean already.''

"That's because I swept it last night,'' she told him. "I like it to be clean all the time.''

"Sweeping is a fact of life when you're a woman,''

Colleen said from the parlor, and Stephen turned to listen. "You'd might as well let your aunt do her chores, Stephen. The quicker she gets done, the sooner she'll read to all of us."

"Well, it sure seems like a waste of time to me, sweeping all the time," he said. "Then you can't even tell when you scrub it. It just always looks nice."

"Well, thank you, Stephen," Sarah said, earning a look of surprise from him. Her smile widened and she shot a look of conspiracy toward her mother, silent thanks for the support she'd given. "I'm glad you approve of my housekeeping."

Stephen walked toward her, pausing just a foot away, and then his arms circled her waist and he hugged her tightly. "I approve of everything you do, Aunt Sarah. You're just about the best thing that ever happened to me."

"Me, too, son," Brace said from the depths of the kitchen. "I'd say she's just about perfect. Don't you think so?"

Sarah turned her head and glared in his direction. "We've talked about this before," she said grimly, aggravated at Brace's words. "I'm far from perfect."

"Well, we've never gotten Stephen's opinion on the matter," Brace said with a grin. "What do you think?" he asked the boy.

"Aunt Sarah's just the best there is," Stephen said stoutly. "And I guess that's as close to perfect as you can get."

"Well, I'm glad we agree on that," Brace told him, reaching the boy's side with two long strides. "Now, find yourself a place to sit and get the footstool for your grandmother. As soon as Sarah's done, she'll be joining us. ''Cause I'm telling you, boy, there's no way she's not gonna sweep the kitchen floor first.''

The two of them went back into the parlor, leaving Sarah behind, and she simply shook her head and turned to complete her chores before the evening of reading should begin.

Chapter Thirteen

Brace found that dealing with a young man who was digging in his heels was almost more than he wanted to handle. Leaving school, Stephen had questioned the wisdom of heading back to the jailhouse to meet with Lester.

"We don't have much of a choice," Brace told him. "I know this isn't what you want to do, but we have to obey the law."

"I thought you *were* the law," the boy answered angrily.

"I represent the law in this town," Brace said, correcting him even as he sympathized with Stephen's problem. "But Lester is your legal father and as such, he has certain rights where you're concerned. Number one is his right to visit you under certain conditions."

"What if I don't want to see him?"

Brace shook his head resignedly. "That doesn't make a whole lot of difference," he said quietly. "It's called upholding the letter of the law, and it's what I promised to do the day they pinned this badge on my chest, Stephen."

The boy's feet dragged as they neared the jailhouse.

"Just remember I didn't want to do this," he muttered as Brace opened the door and they stepped inside the office. From across the room Jamie lifted a hand in welcome and Stephen grinned in his direction, then allowed a frown to take residence on his face as Lester spoke up.

"About time you got here. You know I only get a short visit, Sheriff. Seems like you could have hustled the boy along."

"You're lucky to be allowed to see him at all," Brace said sternly. "Just take what you can get and like it, Clark." He turned aside and undid the buckle of his belt and holster. Then, changing his mind, he put the weapon back in place.

"Think you'll need that?" Lester asked with a sneer "You think I'm gonna run off with the boy."

"Not while I'm wearing the gun," Brace told him. "Even a man like you wouldn't be so stupid."

"We'll see who's stupid when this whole thing is over," Lester said.

"Sit down and visit with Stephen," Brace told him. "You've got fifteen minutes to spend with him."

"Fifteen minutes? Is that all a father's rights are worth in this godforsaken town?" Lester blustered loudly as he approached the extra chair near the desk. Settling down on the hard wooden surface, he beckoned to Stephen. "Come on over here, boy, and talk to your pa."

Stephen walked unwillingly past his father to where Brace's own chair sat in solitary splendor behind the desk. "I'll sit here," he said with an inquiring look in Brace's direction. Receiving a nod of permission in return, he lowered himself into the leather depths and turned the comfortable chair on its castors to face Lester.

"How's school going for you?" the man asked, his voice cajoling, his manner causing Brace's stomach to churn. Barely able to tolerate the presence of such a creature, he walked to the window, looking out upon the street, not hearing Stephen's brief reply.

From the saloon just across from the jail gunshots broke the small-town silence and three men ran for cover behind posts before the general store. At the next volley of shots, the three of them plunged headlong through the wide doors and sought sanctuary there. The bartender plowed through the swinging doors of the saloon, leaving them opening and closing in a strange dance of their own.

A man stood in the doorway, taking aim and finally firing his pistol at the fleeing bartender. His shot went wild, breaking a window in the hardware store, the next building over from the jail. Brace headed for the door of his office and stepped out onto the porch. The gunman in the saloon retreated, apparently thinking better of his actions, perhaps deciding not to take on the lawman. He turned aside, but not before Brace had caught a good look at him.

"Looks like one of your kinfolk is makin' a ruckus out here," he said over his shoulder to the man who watched in silence. A smile of anticipation lit Lester's face as he noted Brace's moment of hesitation.

"Jamie, keep an eye on things," Brace said. "I'll be back as soon as I find out what's going on over there."

Jamie muttered agreement and drew his own gun, aiming it directly at Lester. With that, Brace ran across the street to the saloon, bending low as he watched for the gunman to reappear. The saloon doors were still swinging a bit when he got there, and the bartender was hot on his heels.

"Those men came in here the back way," he said, puffing out the words between deep breaths. "They each ordered a drink, then made a play for LuEllen. She told them off in no uncertain terms, and I backed her up. My girls don't have to take up with anyone they don't want to," he explained. "So one of them drew his gun and shot out the side window, then started on the front ones. LuEllen was long gone up the stairs, and I decided it was smart to head out the door."

Brace listened impatiently to the barkeep's words, knowing he must hear the story before he could set off in pursuit. "Where is the second man?" he asked.

"Don't know," the barkeep answered. "Probably went out the back, same way he got in."

"I'm wasting time here," Brace said, and then was alerted by shouts from across the street. Jamie staggered from the jailhouse door, waving his hand in the air, his gun nowhere to be seen.

Brace hightailed it to where his deputy stood. Jamie was obviously still shaken by a blow dealt to him, his head bleeding, his eyes glassy and dilated.

"Some guy came in from the back alley and got the drop on me," he explained. "Held a gun on Stephen," he said haltingly, "and I didn't dare fire. I was scared for the boy. Then another fella, the other one who looks most like Lester, came running in the back way and caught me broadside with his pistol butt. Hit me over the head."

"Where are they?" Brace asked, his words staccato as he scanned the street for any moving figures.

"I don't know," Jamie said. "They're all gone, Lester with them. And they got Stephen, Brace."

"We'll get some men and go after them," Brace said. "My horse is out back, but you'll need to get yours from the livery stable. I'll see if Bart Simms and Amos Montgomery can ride along."

Jamie headed for the livery stable, his gait still unstable. Brace went through the jailhouse to get his black gelding and found only an empty hitching rail. He sent a piercing whistle into the air and waited, hoping that his mount would respond.

It was just a moment before the horse appeared, dragging his reins, his mane and tail flying as he rounded the corner into the alley, then came to a stop before his owner.

"Good boy," Brace said.

Mounting and reaching for the reins, Brace rode in a half circle around the building and reached the street. Approaching from the west was a buggy driven by Nicholas Garvey, with Lin and the children by his side. Brace flagged him down, reining his horse to a halt beside the conveyance.

Nicholas was frowning, and brought his mare to a quick stop. "I just saw three fellas racin' out of town," he said. "Sure were in an awful hurry and they had your boy. You got problems? What's going on?"

"Lester and his crew made off with Stephen. Left Jamie pretty battered, but he's gone to get his horse from the livery."

"Need some help?" Nicholas asked, with no hesitation. Lin offered a look of commiseration, but did not halt Nicholas in his endeavor. "I'll pick up a mount at the livery and be right with you. Lin can take the buggy out to your place and wait for me there."

His wife nodded her agreement, and without waiting for Brace to answer one way or the other, Nicholas turned the buggy in the road and headed back to Amos Montgomery's livery stable. Once there, he leaped from the high seat and reached to grip Lin's hand.

"Get to Brace's place right now," he said roughly. "Don't linger in town. Make sure Sarah is all right and lock that house securely."

She listened and nodded, apparently willing to do as Nicholas asked.

"There are two shotguns in the parlor closet," Brace said. "The ammunition is in my desk drawer in the library. Sarah doesn't know much about shooting, but I'll warrant she can point one of those guns and look confident doing it."

"I'll bet she can," Lin agreed. "And I can shoot as good as most men."

"Better," Nicholas growled. Stepping back from the buggy, he waved Lin into action, tossing a kiss to his daughter, Amanda, as the buggy set off.

Amos Montgomery brought out a gelding for Nicholas, a gray horse with sturdy haunches and sleek lines. "This fella can catch most anything on four feet," Amos said. "I'd ride him myself, but I think the sheriff needs you to keep up with him. Jamie just flew out of here, and I'll be along right shortly. You got any idea where we're heading?"

"We'll aim for the edge of town," Brace said. "I need to be sure my wife is safe, and then we'll go on from there."

"Is the boy all right?" Amos asked, his brow furrowing as he recalled the cowering child he'd met just once.

"Seems to be," Brace said. "They took him up on one of their horses, apparently, so it'll hamper their speed a little."

With a wave at Nicholas, who was drawing the cinch tight beneath the gray's belly, he set off toward his house, knowing that Nicholas would follow inside a few minutes. All was quiet as he approached, the silence almost ominous, he decided. Riding around the back, he discovered Nicholas's buggy beneath the trees, the horse tied to a ring driven into the trunk for just that purpose. Leaving his gelding there, he hurried to the back door, catching Lin as she stumbled over the threshold.

"What's going on?" he asked. "Did you find the shotguns?"

"I was too late," she sobbed, Amanda hanging on to her skirt, her son clutched in her arms. "Sarah's folks just got in the house. They were out back working on the pasture fence and missed the whole thing, apparently."

"What do you mean? Too late for what?" Brace asked, his voice hoarse with emotion.

"She's gone. The dining-room window is broken, and I found a note on the floor, beside a big rock. Those men must have come here right off, Brace. They've got her."

As though a knife had stabbed him to his depths, Brace felt a pain in his chest that defied description. Sarah was gone, and apparently in Lester's hands. That they'd managed to accomplish the deed so rapidly told him much planning had gone into this operation. While he'd been sitting around enjoying his time as a family man, getting acquainted with his new in-laws, three men had plotted to take his wife and son from him.

"What does the note say?" he asked Lin. "Do you have it?"

She shook her head. "I must have dropped it after I

read it. I can't remember. I was so upset at the thought of Sarah being taken prisoner, I just headed for the back door. I had some crazy idea of following them, I think.''

"Show me," Brace said shortly, and Lin turned on her heel and led him to the dining room. Broken glass lay on the floor, and the large rock she'd spoken of gave mute testimony to the efforts of the Clark brothers. A crumpled piece of paper caught his eye, and he left Lin's side to retrieve it from the floor.

It was short and to the point. Lester and his brothers would give up Stephen into Sarah's care if she brought the sum of five thousand dollars to the edge of the woods that began on the west side of town. That bit of forest was thick, consisting of about fifty acres of wooded property, and was filled with all sorts of wild-life.

Brace was familiar with it, but whether Sarah knew much about it was unlikely. The depths of the wooded area held several squatters' shacks, all of them empty, but some of them still habitable.

One in particular held memories for Brace, for it was there that a dear friend, Faith Hudson, had lived for over two years, separated from her husband, alone in the world, fending for herself, until the generous friendship of Nicholas and Lin had given her a home and released her from the poverty that had dragged her into a drab existence.

Faith had moved then into the farmhouse next to Nicholas and Lin, a piece of property they owned, and had lived there for quite some time before going back to Boston, where her ties had drawn her...and where she'd found renewed happiness.

The thought of the squatters' shacks that might hold Lester's prisoners made Brace shudder. Even Faith's shack had been neglected for so long, it was no more than a shelter for wild animals.

The sound of his horse trumpeting a call caught his attention, and Brace stuffed the note into his pocket. "Does Sarah have that kind of money?" Lin asked dolefully.

"Not hardly," Brace said. "But I have."

He turned from her and headed back to the foyer, then climbed the stairs, his long legs cutting the trip in half as he took two steps as one. Their bedroom beckoned him and he crossed the threshold, noting that Sarah had made up the bed, fluffing the soft feather pillows invitingly. The trunk he'd given her for her use was open, her belongings in a state of disruption, and it was obvious that someone had scattered her belongings hither and yon.

He looked down at the bits and pieces of her past, small treasures she had hoarded to herself, mementos of her family, a picture of her sister and Stephen together, Stephen still a babe in arms. He spoke her name in a low whisper. "Sarah. Sarah, where are you, sweetheart?" As if she might answer, he lifted his head to listen for some sign of her presence. And there was none.

"Damn that man to hell," he groaned, not looking back as he left the mess behind. Lin approached down the hallway, her heels resounding on the bare boards. She watched him from the hallway expectantly as he closed the door behind him.

"She had a bit of money, but nothing like what they've demanded," Brace said. "I didn't bother searching for it. I'll almost guarantee she offered it to them for Stephen's return."

"What will we do now?" Lin asked, Amanda beside

her. The little girl clutched at her skirt, and Lin's son, held high in her arms, seemed almost too heavy for her to carry.

"I'm going to get my hands on the money in my safe and go after them," Brace said.

"Where…?" Lin asked, the single word telling him she was totally in the dark as to which direction they should seek.

"I have an idea," Brace said. "Nicholas won't want you along, Lin. You'd do well to stay here with Sarah's family and your children, I think. We can make better time without you." Hastening past her, he headed down the stairs and into his office, situated in the library. There, surrounded by countless shelves of books, sat his desk and chair, with a small safe in one corner.

He spun the knob on the front and with a steady hand chose the appropriate number that would open it. Turning the handle, he drew forth a metal box. He opened it with a quick snap and lifted a stack of bills from its depths. Sorting through them quickly, he nodded his head. "I'd thought they might have somehow gotten into this," he told Lin, "but apparently not. It all seems to be here."

"Will you offer it to them?" she asked.

"You know he will," said Joshua, standing in the doorway, looking on. "And if need be, I'll wire for money from Big Rapids. We'll do whatever it takes."

Brace shot him a look of gratitude, and then noted Colleen's tearstained face in the shadows behind her husband. "I'll do whatever I have to in order to get Sarah and Stephen back," he told her, stuffing the wad of bills into his pocket.

"I know you will," Colleen said tearfully. "Just be

careful. We'll stay here and wait. You don't need us tagging along.''

"Get me the gun and ammunition," Lin said. "I'll make a safe spot in the parlor for the children and the rest of us, and keep a weather eye on the road.''

Relieved that she had so readily acquiesced to his demand that she remain behind, Brace nodded. "That's a sensible thing to do," he said, wondering at the slow smile she cast his way.

The gun was loaded, the extra shells stuffed into Lin's voluminous pockets, and she began rearranging the parlor furniture, the better to contain her children safely. The big sofa was turned toward the fireplace, a chair at either side to offer protection, and a blanket from the sofa placed on the floor for the little boy. His sister sat beside him, watchful of his every move, and Colleen joined them on the floor. Lin took a place near the window.

"We'll be fine," she said firmly. "Just don't be too long, Brace. I'm not a patient woman.''

"So I've heard," he told her, thankful for her knowledge of handling a gun and her methodical way of protecting those who would be left behind. "I'll head out and meet Nicholas and the others. You stay safe.''

"I don't think we're in any danger here," she said. "I doubt that Stephen's father will come back. I suspect he's long gone.''

"My thoughts exactly," Brace admitted. With a small salute, he left her to her preparations, stopping just long enough to shake Joshua's hand and send an approving look in Colleen's direction. The second long gun from the parlor closet was at Joshua's side and he seemed to be comfortable with the weapon, giving Brace an additional bit of comfort at leaving Lin with the children. In moments, he'd gone through the back door, taking the key from inside the house and locking the door from the outside. He slid the key into his pocket and sought his horse.

With a wave of welcome, Nicholas rode into the backyard, his gaze searching the empty buggy, his hands drawing the gray gelding to a halt. "Where's Lin? And the children?" he asked.

"Inside," Brace told him. "I think they'll be all right. Joshua and Colleen are with her. I gave her a loaded shotgun, plus a pocketful of shells, and Joshua apparently knows how to handle a gun, too. She's got the youngsters all stashed away behind the furniture and she's keeping watch."

"All right," Nicholas said, obviously aware of his wife's capabilities. "What's our next move?"

"Finding Sarah and Stephen. Lester sent a note into the house, all wrapped around a rock, and asked for money for Stephen's safe return."

"What do you think Sarah did?" Nicholas asked. "Did she have much cash?"

Brace shook his head. "They asked for five thousand, and she probably had several hundred dollars in her things. I gave her a trunk to put her belongings in and it had been ransacked, either by her or those goons. So I took cash from my safe. Enough to wet Lester's whistle."

"You think it will work?"

Brace shrugged. "We'll give it a shot, anyway. Remember that place where Faith lived in the woods, before you let her have the farmhouse?" he asked.

"Of course," Nicholas said. "There are several of those squatters' shacks on that piece of property. Used to be a whole colony of folks living there some years back.''

''Well, it seems a likely spot for Lester to have taken Sarah and Stephen,'' Brace said. ''I doubt he'd have set off for the western side of the state till he figured he was in the clear. What do you think?''

''You may be right. Hauling a woman and child two hundred miles or so is a touchy proposition, and when the woman doesn't want to be toted along, it could mean trouble.''

''Sarah's not a willing prisoner, I'll guarantee it,'' Brace said with a shake of his head. ''She'll be giving them a hard time. And Stephen will be trying to look out for her. I'm just hoping they're not being abused. I wouldn't lay odds that Lester is feeling kindly toward either of them right now.''

''I checked on his family and looked into his claims,'' Nicholas said, riding close to Brace's side. ''He was right about having money, and the property his family owns. His pa died just yesterday, according to a wire he received last night. Apparently he and his brothers think they're going to be set for life. Another wire from a lawyer his father had put in charge of his finances came a little while ago. It seems that the whole kit and caboodle is to be left to whichever one of the old man's sons has a son of his own first.

''That puts Lester in a nice spot. Stephen is the sole grandson and seems to be Lester's ticket to the family money and a nice bit of property. He's probably made a deal with his brothers to split things three ways.''

Brace listened with no trace of surprise. ''Well, no wonder he was so set on claiming the boy. I figured there had to be some good reason for what he did. That answers several questions for me,'' Brace said. ''I knew he didn't have any great love for Stephen, but he sure enough would enjoy getting his hands on money. If he'd hold his own son hostage, he's pretty much on the bottom rung of the ladder, so far as I'm concerned. He knows he'll get his hands on Sarah this way, forcing her to bring the ransom.''

"Did she leave a note?" Nicholas asked impatiently.

Brace filled him in on the particulars, assuring him that Lin had not seen hide or hair of Sarah or any of Lester's clan, but had walked in after the fact. "I don't really think they'll come back to the house," he said. "They're on the run."

"Well, I'm determined to track them down," Nicholas said. "I heard from my friends in the bank in Big Rapids yesterday. Got a wire delivered to the house after church, and the news is good from our viewpoint. Seems that there's a warrant out for Lester for embezzlement and extortion back in Big Rapids. It sounds like Sarah's folks put the wheels in motion before they left home. I think Joshua is determined to put the man in prison, and I agree with that.''

Brace snorted, and laughed harshly. "I wish they'd been that aggressive when Sarah's sister died. Too bad they waited so long to get things straight. But they've sure tried to make amends now."

Nicholas nodded in agreement. "The best we can do now is cut to the chase and locate Sarah and the boy."

"Well, the good part is that Joshua and Colleen seem to have got their heads on straight now. Seeing Sarah and Stephen again probably made them realize what was really important."

They rode hard, and at the edge of the woods, just two miles from the town boundaries, Jamie and two other men were waiting for them. "I didn't know how much ramming around in the woods we should do without you here to direct us," he told Brace. "Amos and Mr. Simms are armed and ready to do whatever you say," he added, his face set in determined lines.

"I appreciate that," Brace said. "We have no idea if this is a consideration or not, but I'm thinking that those fellas must have set up some sort of shelter to take their prisoners to, somewhere they could hold them and wait it out till we showed up. For sure they'll be set to defend themselves. I doubt they'd take off on a long run with the probability of a posse on their tails."

"They'll want to get rid of you first," Nicholas told Brace.

"That's what I figured." His hand touched the wad of bills he'd stashed in his pocket. "I'm hoping they may be money-hungry enough to come out of hiding if I tempt them with some cash."

"Don't count on it," Nicholas told him. "With Stephen on hand, Lester figures he's got a safe bet. I think the money angle was just for traveling funds, and if Sarah had enough with her, they won't fall for a ruse."

"Let's find out," Brace said, determining his course of action. "Jamie, you and Amos ride into the woods from the north. Check out those two closest shacks first. I doubt that's where they're holed up, but we need to be certain. Nicholas, Bart and I will head in straight from here. We should find you in less than an hour if you stay on a straight path."

"We can do that," Amos said, obviously eager for the chase to begin. "That Clark fella is a nasty one. I'll be glad to see him back in jail. And if we don't show up right shortly, cut back through the woods. If we should by chance come across anything, we'll stay put till you show up."

Brace nodded his agreement and waved the two men off, then turned back to Nicholas and Bart Simms. "Let's go see what we can find."

Sarah's pleas were for Stephen's safety, and the three men laughed at her, taunting her efforts. "He's gonna be my ace in the hole," Lester told her. "You don't need to worry none. I won't let anything happen to him."

"Ace in the hole is right," one of the brothers said. "He's our ticket to prosperity, lady. And you don't want to get in the way of that. You're in over your head right now."

"Over my head?" she asked, aware of their plans for her. The thought of Brace's pain, should these men use her as they wanted and then leave her for her husband to find, was like a canker in her soul. She ached for him, for the moment forgetting about the danger she was in.

But there was Stephen to worry about right now, she decided. Would Brace be on their trail by now? Even as she sat here on the edge of a chair, was he watching from a vantage point?

If there was some way of getting Stephen to safety, she would snatch at it, but the brothers seemed to be vigilant right now. Perhaps later they might sleep. Or, if their possession of a large bottle of whiskey was an indication, they might succumb to the lure of alcohol. But neither option was guaranteed, not so long as they kept leering in her direction, their thoughts almost visible as their eyes roamed her body, seeming to peel the clothing from her.

"I'm thinking I'd like to have a talk with the lady here," one of the brothers—LeRoy—said boldly. He seemed to be the most avid of the bunch, she'd decided. "There's a perfectly good bed over there in the corner." He approached her with an outstretched hand. "We could get a little better acquainted, don't you think, lady?"

Sarah shuddered and shook her head, her distaste drawing her face into a frown.

"I don't think the lady likes you, LeRoy," Shorty said. The smallest of the three, he was stocky, and though not nearly as tall as Brace, presented a formidable presence in the room. The thought of his thick hands on her made Sarah shiver again, and Shorty laughed, a vile sound of anticipation.

"See, she likes the idea of havin' me for a friend," Shorty said, leaning close to her as she shrank back in the chair.

"Don't you hurt Aunt Sarah," Stephen said in a shrill voice. "I don't want you to touch her."

"I'm gonna do more than just touch her, boy," LeRoy told him, shoving Shorty out of his way as he approached the cowering woman. "We're gonna get to know each other right well."

"The two of you stop scarin' the boy," Lester said, not even bothering to turn his head toward the ruckus. Stationed by the window, he was intent on the woods at the side of the cabin. "If you want to be useful, take a turn at standing watch. Sarah ain't goin' nowhere. She'll still be right handy when the shootin's done."

"You see something out there?" LeRoy asked, his attention caught by Lester's words. He snatched at Sarah's hand and drew her up into his embrace. She fought him silently, her teeth clenching as he gripped her jaw and forced her face upward. Lips that knew no mercy pressed against hers and she groaned, an almost silent plea, but one that brought quick laughter resounding from LeRoy's chest.

"She's a fighter, she is," he grunted. "We'll see just how tough she is when we get her stripped."

"Not in front of the boy," Lester said sharply. "He's not ready for that kind of stuff yet."

"Huh!" Shorty snorted. "I had my first woman when I was twelve. Boy's been coddled enough in his life. He needs to know how much fun he can have in this world."

"Please, no," Sarah begged. Her mouth felt bruised, her body crushed by the man who held her. Then, with a harsh touch, she was torn from his arms and clutched close to Shorty, his hands like big hams as he pawed at her bottom through the folds of fabric that protected her from his palms.

"I'll please you, little lady," he growled, his mouth wet and disgusting against her cheek, and then she felt his teeth as he bent lower to bite at her throat. It was a brutal, bruising attack that stunned her.

"You couldn't please a sow in a pigsty," she said, hating the man with a passion that almost overwhelmed her.

"Well, we'll sure enough find out about that," Shorty said.

"Let her alone, I told you," Lester shouted from his post. "Get your butt over here and keep an eye out this window."

Shorty dropped Sarah back onto her chair and drew his gun. "If I see anything movin', I'm shootin', Les. I don't like bein' holed up like a rat in a trap."

"Just be sure you don't go wasting our ammunition on some wild critter," Lester told him sharply. And then he turned aside as Stephen nudged him impatiently.

"Pa, I gotta go outside for a minute," Stephen said, looking up at Lester with a sober look on his face. "It's kinda an emergency, Pa."

"You gotta go use the outhouse, boy?" his father asked.

"Is there one out back?" Stephen wanted to know.

"No, Stephen," Sarah told him harshly. "Stay inside. Don't make a fuss."

"I'll tell my boy what he can do and what he can't," Lester said, taking umbrage at her words of advice. He opened a smaller door at the back of the cabin, near the fireplace, and looked outside.

"See that outhouse there?" he asked Stephen. "You run out there and do your business and get yourself back in here right quick. I'll be watchin' you, so no funny stuff, you hear me?"

"Yessir," Stephen answered. "I just gotta go right now, Pa."

"He can go in here. There must be a kettle or something he can use," LeRoy yelled from across the room. "Don't be lettin' him out, Les. It just makes one more thing for us to keep an eye on."

But it was too late. Stephen was over the threshold and running like lightning for the shabby wooden structure.

"Stephen!" Sarah bolted from the chair, intent on keeping an eye on the boy, and two men clutched at her. Lester left his post by the door and slapped her an open blow across the face and she screamed, a loud cry of pain that almost halted Stephen in his tracks. He looked back for a moment, then as if something had caught his attention, he darted around the outhouse and was lost to sight.

Sarah fell to the floor, her head swimming, blackness

seeming to surround her, and barely felt the rough hands that picked her up and tossed her across the rude bed in the corner. Her dress tore, one sleeve almost ripped from the bodice, and her buttons came undone with the force of her momentum.

The lace of her chemise was exposed, along with a generous portion of a creamy, curving breast, and Shorty dropped to the floor beside the bed. One hand reached to touch her bare skin, and she pushed at him, a useless gesture, for he slapped her again, this time causing her to curl into a ball.

Her cheek flamed with the harsh treatment, and she screamed again, her head pounding as he rolled her to the edge of the bed. "You can't hide all that purty stuff from me, lady," he said, his voice low and rasping.

"Don't be greedy, brother," LeRoy said from behind him. "Save a feel for me."

"There's enough for both of us," Shorty snorted. "You'll get your turn." And then he turned to look over his shoulder, his fingers grasping with greedy strength at the tender flesh Sarah tried in vain to protect from his touch.

"Where'd Les go?"

"After the boy," Shorty told him. He ran to the back door and closed it. "If he wants to get back in, he can just damn well knock."

"That ramshackle shed must be an outhouse," Brace said, his tone barely a whisper. "Maybe I can get to it and find enough shelter there to get a good shot at the back door. If I make enough noise, they'll no doubt open it and come after me."

"Not a good idea," Nicholas said. "It'll leave you exposed."

With that, the small back door of the cabin opened and Lester appeared in the opening. "Shall I grab a quick shot?" Brace asked, already aiming his gun, only to have it shoved aside by Nicholas as the small form of a boy trotted from the cabin, aiming with purpose toward the outhouse.

A scream split the air, and Stephen paused. "Stephen," Brace breathed, and was rewarded by a quick look in his direction by the boy. "This way, son," Brace said, still in an undertone, but obviously loud enough for Stephen to hear, for he veered sharply, ran behind the outhouse and halted.

"Pa?" he called out carefully, the single syllable barely a whisper.

"Over here," Brace told him, moving just a bit, making himself visible, yet concealed from the cabin by the rude shelter Stephen hovered behind. From the cabin came another shrill cry of pain, and Brace held his tongue with difficulty.

"It's Sarah," Nicholas said quietly. "At least we know she's alive and kicking."

A shout of warning was all they had before Lester burst from the cabin and ran helter-skelter after his son. Stephen looked up at Brace and crouched low, running for all he was worth toward the man who had called him.

"Come back here, you worthless piece of—"

Whatever word the man was preparing to call Stephen died on his lips as Nicholas fired once, bringing Lester to his knees. And then with a cry of pain he fell to one side, clasping his knee to his belly.

"He won't be running off," Nicholas said with satisfaction.

* * *

The cry of a man in pain, even muffled by the walls, was enough to bring the men inside to attention. "That's Les," LeRoy said, rising to approach the back door.

"Don't open the damn thing," Shorty said. "If they got Les, they'll be watchin' for us to run out there."

"Well, you got a better idea?" LeRoy asked.

"They aren't gonna do much shootin' with the woman inside the cabin," Shorty told him. "She's still our ace in the hole."

Sarah felt less than a piece of valuable protection as she listened to the men talk, speaking of her as if she were something to be bartered.

"I've got money in my pocket," she said. "I couldn't come up with five thousand like the note said, but there's probably several hundred there."

"Not much good to us, lady," LeRoy told her. "Now, a handy roll of bills might do the trick, but I'm not risking my neck for a few paltry dollars."

"What you planning on doing?" Shorty asked, restless as Lester's cries of pain continued without ceasing.

"I'd say Les is providing good cover for us out back," LeRoy said. "I'd vote for headin' out the front door and making a run for it."

"Where are the horses?"

"Les put them in the shed next to the cabin. We can get out the cabin door and into the shed in no time flat. A couple of minutes to get mounted and we'll be on our way."

"What about her?" Shorty asked, pointing a finger at Sarah.

"She's our protection. You don't think they'll shoot if we've got her for cover, do you?"

"You're smarter than I gave you credit for," his brother said. "Now, if we can get hold of the boy, we'll be halfway home. And if we get caught between a rock and a hard place, we'll bargain for the rest of the five thousand. I'd be willing to bet that there's some money out there lining somebody's pocket right now. They didn't come after her without something to sweeten the pot."

Sarah was hauled unceremoniously from the bed, and her hands rose to hold her dress together. Slung over LeRoy's shoulder, she made a perfect target, she decided, should there be someone out in front of the building.

Chapter Fourteen

"Where are they?" Brace asked, muttering the words to himself.

"I thought sure hearing Lester howling would bring them out that door," Nicholas answered.

"Well, we managed to have one bit of success," Brace said, holding his arms wide as Stephen ran through the weeds toward him. He gathered the boy close and brought them both to the ground.

"Is Sarah all right?" he asked Stephen, his need for her superseding all else.

"She's alive, Pa. Those other two men are being mean to her, but she's madder than a wet hornet at them."

"Where is she?" Nicholas asked. "We need to figure out her position in the house, Brace," he added in an undertone.

"She's on a bed, on that side," Stephen said, pointing to the north wall of the building.

"A bed," Brace repeated, casting a look of frustration toward Nicholas. "Have they hurt her?" His arms held Stephen away for a moment, and looking down into the boy's face, he awaited an answer.

"My father slapped her once, and one of the other men hit her, too, right after he tore her dress all to pieces."

Nicholas placed a heavy hand on Brace's shoulder. "You won't do her any good if you run out there and get yourself killed," he said, his voice cold, as if icy talons of anger had gripped him. And so it seemed to be, Brace decided, looking at the stern visage offered by his friend.

Nicholas ready for battle was a sight to behold, he'd found, and today had brought all of the man's warrior instincts to the forefront. "I'd like to get around in front of the house," Nicholas said quietly. "I'd have thought that Jamie and Amos would be situated out there already, keeping an eye out for us, especially since old Lester is making so much of a fuss here."

Behind them, Bart whispered a word of warning. "Be careful, the both of you. I just took a walk around the other side, and the door of the cabin was open a little bit. I think they're considering making a run for it."

"With Sarah as a shield," Brace surmised. "You can stay here and keep an eye on Lester, Bart. I doubt he's going anywhere, but if he tries to haul his miserable body away from here, put another bullet in it. Right where it'll do the most good."

"Yeah, I can do that, Sheriff," Bart returned. "I'll just get me a good spot here, and hunker down and wait." He looked up as Brace moved to stand behind a tree. "I take it you're going out front?"

"Yeah. Nicholas and I will see what's going on."

"Me, too," Stephen said from his place on the ground.

"I want you right where you are, son," Brace told him. "Bart won't let anything happen to you. I'll guarantee it. And Nicholas and I can move faster if we don't have to worry about someone picking you off.''

''Yessir,'' the boy answered, crawling a foot closer to where Bart lay with his gun before him. ''Me and Bart will keep an eye on *him*.'' His voice was bitter as he looked in Lester's direction. Blood flowed freely from the man's knee, and he groaned aloud, with profanity interspersed amid the threats and grumblings.

From the front of the cabin a loud shout caught their attention, and Nicholas and Brace vanished into the shadows of the woods behind them, intent on circling the building and locating the cause of the alarm. Bent low, they ran as one, their clothing ripped by the branches they ignored, their hats jammed low on their heads, their guns in hand.

In sight of the door, Brace drew up short. ''Look. Over there,'' he told Nicholas, lifting his hand to point a finger toward the north. Almost entirely concealed in the heavily undergrown area were two men, and Brace breathed a sigh of relief. His backup had not failed him. Jamie and Amos were at hand.

Beside him, Nicholas growled an oath and Brace turned, his eyes questioning. ''Damn woman didn't have enough sense to stay where she was told,'' he muttered, his gaze apparently caught and captured by the sight of a wagon, and a woman who sheltered behind it.

''Where are the children?'' Brace asked. ''She surely wouldn't bring them along, would she?''

Nicholas shook his head. ''She'd die before she let anything happen to her babies. But the problem now is that there are a couple of desperate men ready to come out that door with guns firing, and no doubt using Sarah as a shield.''

Lin appeared as a dim form behind Jamie and Amos, but her body was well protected by the seat and the side of the conveyance.

From the cabin came another shout and then the door was flung wide, making a loud clatter as it struck the logs. Jamie's gun was aimed at the doorway, but something there caused him to lower the rifle and speak in a low tone to Amos.

"What is it?" Nicholas asked Brace, who had made his way far enough to catch sight of the doorway.

"One of those thugs has Sarah tossed over his shoulder and he's coming out. I think Jamie wisely decided not to take a chance on hitting her and lowered his gun."

Nicholas came closer. "They're both there now. The second one looks like he's heading for the shed door. Must be where the horses are."

The two men made a quick break for safety, and in seconds were inside the small shed, where horses could be heard milling and neighing their confusion at the sounds that had caught them unawares.

It was several minutes before the shed door opened again, and a loud voice called out. "Sheriff. I know you're out there. I just wanta know how bad you want this woman of yours. I'll bet your pockets are lined with ready cash, and you're out here to buy us off and rescue her, ain't you?"

"I've got five thousand dollars with me," Brace shouted at the open door.

Neither man could be seen, but the second one called out orders in quick succession. "Put the money on the ground right out in front, Sheriff. Drop it quick and back off. We don't want to kill nobody, but we will if any of you try to stop us."

"You can't go out there," Jamie said in a hushed tone, coming up behind the two men. "They'll shoot you, sure enough."

"Just keep your guns aimed at that door. Shoot anything that moves, so long as it isn't Sarah. If that fella heads out with her over his shoulder, aim at his legs. Getting hit in the knee sure made Lester drop in a hurry. I'll bet he's back there thinkin' about his sins."

Brace stood up and drew forth the wad of bills from his pocket. "If you shoot me, these will fly all over the place and you'll have a hell of a time finding them," he shouted.

"No, Brace, don't do it," Sarah called from inside the shed, and Brace heaved a sigh of relief. She was alive and didn't sound badly hurt. And then she appeared, one of the men hauling her up in front of him, an arm around her neck, shuffling along behind her reluctant body. His other hand gripped a gun and he aimed it at Sarah's head.

"If you want her alive, you'll drop that money and make tracks, Sheriff. And leave that gun behind."

Brace drew in a deep breath as the man and his shield stepped back inside the shed. Then, with barely a pause, the other brother appeared in the opening, bending low over the neck of a horse as he left the shelter behind. "Where's the money?" he called out.

"I've got it," Brace answered and, dropping his gun as he left the depths of the wooded area, he made an open target of himself, just twenty feet in front of the man on horseback. Holding up his hand, the money clutched tightly in his grasp, he waited.

"Don't be droppin' it, Sheriff," the man told him, riding closer and snatching the wad from Brace's hand.

Behind him, a second horseman appeared, riding double, Sarah in front of him.

Brace's heart fell at the sight of the woman he loved. She was bruised, her face swollen and already turning a deep crimson, where cruel blows had bruised her tender flesh. Her clothing was awry, her dress torn, the sleeve tattered and her arm exposed, as was the upper slope of her breast. The man holding her had a gun in one hand, waving it as a threat in Brace's direction.

And then the two men bent low and turned their mounts toward the other side of the cabin, obviously seeking shelter there. Sarah slumped against her captor, her head dropping to her chest, as if she had fainted in his arms. With a quick movement he turned her across his thighs, and Brace watched as her head lolled loosely in the bend of the man's elbow. Brace turned and slid quickly to the ground, fearful of making himself a target for the rider, yet aware that he must reach his gun in short order or lose the chance to fire.

Then a shot from a rifle split the tension-filled air and the rider who clutched Sarah tumbled from his saddle, dumping the woman to the ground. Blood poured from the man's head, and even as he ran toward his wife, Brace knew he was dead. A perfect head shot. The second man looked about the small clearing, indecision apparent on his face. Obviously deciding that defeat was at hand, he rode away, leaving his brother behind.

From Jamie's pistol another shot rang out, accompanied by a second flash from the rifle that was positioned near the wagon. The rider fell to the ground, and from the rapidly forming pool of blood beneath his body, Brace was certain he had breathed his last, as had his brother.

''Shoots like a champ, doesn't she?'' Nicholas asked,

his pride in Lin's marksmanship evident. "Got that fella square in the back of the head, and unless I miss my guess, between her and your deputy, they've nailed the other one for keeps, too."

Nicholas was fast approaching, his gun held cautiously at one side, Brace's own pistol in his other hand. "You dropped this," he said with a smile.

"Didn't have enough hands to hold it," Brace said. "I was more interested in drawing those crooks out into the open with the money. I figured being unarmed would entice them, too."

"Well, it succeeded," Nicholas said, his jaw working as he watched Lin burst through the covering of the trees, her movements bringing her to his side. Nicholas snatched her up against himself, holding her close.

"You fool woman," he said roughly. "Why didn't you stay where you belonged? You could have been killed."

"He was riding off with Sarah," Lin said, her voice breaking as she spoke. "I couldn't let him do that, Nicholas." She looked up at her husband. "I killed him, didn't I?"

"Damn right you did," Nick answered. "But you shouldn't have even been here." With another curse, he lowered his head to her, and his mouth covered hers in a possessive move that stunned Brace. The man was furious. His actions left no doubt of that, yet his first thought was to lay hands on his wife and hold her fast in his embrace.

"You just wait till I get you home," Nicholas threatened the woman he held.

"You gonna hit me?" she whispered, the words carrying to Brace as he knelt by Sarah's side. He could not suppress the laughter that bubbled from his chest as Lin's teasing reply reached his hearing.

Sarah moved then, looking up at him, her eyes wide, with no trace of pain visible on her face. Her clothing was rumpled and torn, but she'd not been the victim of a gunshot. "Stephen?"

"He's all right," Brace said quickly.

He picked her up, kneeling beside her and holding her fast. "I thought I'd lost you," he muttered against her face. And then in an unconscious manner, he did as Nicholas had done just moments before, taking Sarah's mouth with a kiss that left those watching with no doubt as to where his priorities lay. She clung to him, whispering words he could not interpret, but it made no matter, for the message was clear.

He stood and lifted her with him, holding her high above the ground. Lin tore herself from Nicholas's arms and came closer. "I aimed high so I wouldn't take a chance on hitting her," Lin said.

"You didn't even nick her," Brace said, smiling his thanks at the woman. "She's just bruised up and looks like she was handled pretty roughly."

"Did they—?"

Lin's words broke off, but Brace read accurately the thoughts that begged to be spoken.

"No, I don't think so. They hardly had time. Things were moving pretty quickly there for a few minutes."

"Where's that dirty rat, Lester?" Lin asked. "I was wishing I could get a shot at him, too."

"Missed your chance," Brace said with a grin. "Nicholas got his bullet there first."

"Is he dead?" Sarah asked, her voice faint, almost muffled against Brace's chest.

"No, he'll be alive when the judge gets here. And I think we'll be turning him over to the authorities back east. In fact, I wouldn't be surprised to find a couple of Pinkerton men in town when we get back, looking for him."

Nicholas followed behind Lin and his arm scooped her close, his mouth touching her ear as he muttered words that made her smile. "I want you to get your little fanny up on that wagon seat, and I want you to hightail it for the ranch. You got that?" he asked, his voice harsh, leaving her no option but to nod.

"Can I stop in town first and pick up the children?" she asked. "I left them at Brace's house with Sarah's folks. I couldn't think what else to do with them, in order to keep them safe."

"Probably the smartest thing you've done all day," Nicholas said gruffly. He turned her toward the wagon and then accompanied her there, lifting her with an easy motion to the seat and turning the horses in the direction of town. Standing with hands on his hips, he watched her lift the reins and crack them loudly over the horses' backs.

"Bet I beat you home," Lin taunted him, viewing him over her shoulder.

"Not on your life, lady," he called after her, and then bowed his head. With a look of resignation in Brace's direction, he shrugged. "What do you do with a woman like that?" he asked helplessly.

"Just love her," Brace told him. "Shouldn't be too difficult. I'd say you've had a little practice at it already."

"Yeah, so I have," Nicholas said, looking up as Jamie led his horse to him. "I think things are pretty well under control here, Sheriff. If you don't mind, I've got a couple of things to tend to.''

"We'll clean up the mess," Jamie answered. "I think Brace needs to take his wife home and tidy her up a little.''

"I agree with that," Brace said, full awareness of Sarah's state of dishabille hitting him squarely between the eyes. "She's a mess, isn't she?" With a grin, he looked up at Jamie and nodded his thanks. "Get Lester into a cell, and drop these other two birds off at the undertaker's place," he said. "I'll be at home."

Picking Sarah up from the ground, he made his way to his horse and lifted her into the saddle. Then, with a quick movement, he was behind her, holding her across his lap.

The house was empty when they arrived, and Sarah looked inside the back door. "Where's Stephen? Are you sure he's all right?''

"I'll guarantee he's with your folks, wherever they are," Brace answered. "Jamie was going to see to it. And now we're going to get you clean."

"Why can't I just take a bath?" Sarah asked. "It'd be a whole lot easier to just climb in the tub instead of washing up piecemeal."

"You're not going to do anything of the kind," Brace told her sternly. "You're going to sit here on this chair and let me take care of you."

"I can do it," she protested, pulling at her dress in a vain attempt to cover her nakedness. The sleeve gave up the battle and slid down her arm, and Brace viewed the bruises that had already turned a deep shade of violet.

"I haven't asked you one thing," he said quietly. "I

almost hate to bring it up, lest it make you remember things better forgotten.''

"They didn't touch me. Not that way," she said hastily, knowing his thoughts. It had no doubt been preying on his mind since the moment Lin had brought up the subject. Now she hastened to reassure him. "They would have, if there'd been time enough, but things happened so fast that they could only toss me around a bit."

"They tore your dress. And I can see bruises here," he said, one long finger tracing a mark on her breast. "I could kill them again for that."

"The marks will fade," she told him. "So long as it doesn't make you look at me any differently."

"Look at you differently?" he asked, and then he knelt before her, gathering her to him. "How could I, Sarah? You're the same woman you were before all this happened. Even if they'd violated you, hurt you beyond description, I'd feel the same way. What you are inside is what matters. Others might be able to soil your body, but they can't touch the woman you are."

She bent to kiss him, her tears blurring his face before her. "I love you so much, Brace. I was so afraid they'd hurt Stephen, but I knew you'd be there for both of us. I knew you wouldn't fail me."

"I had help," he told her. "As soon as you're clean and in bed, I'll go scout up our boy."

"Jamie will no doubt look after him for a bit," Sarah said.

"Well, when your folks show up, he'll likely be with them," Brace said. "We'd better get you washed and into clean clothes. By then they should all be home."

A pan of warm water on the table held a soft cloth, and her soap lay on a dish beside it. In moments he'd squeezed the excess water from the cloth and then wiped her skin with the warmth. With deft movements he caught up the bar of soap in his hands and formed suds against her skin, then, after depositing the soap in the dish, he rubbed her arms between his palms, cleaned the soil from between her fingers and finally rinsed her hands in the warm pan of water.

He took up the bar of soap again and washed her breasts, exposing her quickly to his sight, his fingers firm as he pushed aside her bodice and carefully, tenderly, ran his hand over the lush lines that bore bruises and marks where rough hands had clutched at her flesh.

His mouth was tight as he finished, and with the damp cloth he wiped away the residue of soap, lifted a towel from the table and dried her skin. She made no protest, simply watched his hands as he touched her, settling her gaze on his face as he looked up into her eyes. Pain drew deep lines in his forehead, his mouth was taut with anger and his eyes held a suspicious sheen of moisture.

She bent forward and kissed him, her lips touching where they would, first on his, then moving to his cheek and temple, her words a caress in themselves as she assured him of her love, thanked him unstintingly for his care of her, and finally leaned forward until his face was buried against the slopes of her breasts.

He sighed, turning his head to kiss the silken surfaces, and his hands rose to cup and lift the offering she presented. "I can't bear that someone hurt you," he murmured.

"I knew that," she said. "I thought of all the times you'd touched me and how good you've been to me, and how much I love you, and I determined that those men could not do anything that would spoil the pleasure we find together, Brace.''

"Thank you, sweetheart," he whispered. He rose and held out a hand to her. "Come on. We're going to get your clothes changed and get rid of that dress. I never want to see it again. I'll buy you six new ones to replace it."

She grinned, even though the skin pulled across her cheek and burned. "Six new dresses? I think this may turn out to be a good deal for me."

They left the kitchen and went up the stairs. In mere minutes Brace stripped her clothing off and helped her don a clean nightgown, then wrapped her robe around her and tied the sash.

"I can put another dress on," she protested, but he would not be swayed.

"I want you to rest in the parlor," he told her. "I'll find us something to eat later on, and you can spend some time with Stephen when he gets home. He'll be anxious about you." He looked her over with care. "Wherever your folks are, I'm just as glad they're not here right now. We needed some time alone."

"I'll bet they went into town. They won't have wanted to miss anything, and when Jamie brought the prisoner back, my father was probably right out in front of the jail. And I'll bet my mother took one look at Stephen and about smothered him with hugs."

Brace nodded at her words, and then bent closer to peer at the discoloring on her face. "Nothing shows except these marks on your cheek," he told her. "You'll have bruises there for a while, and there's no help for it. Stephen won't see the rest."

Together they went down the stairs again and Sarah was ensconced in the parlor, three books from a nearby table in her lap. Brace pulled the footstool close and lifted her feet to it, then covered her with a knitted throw from the back of the sofa.

"Can I get you anything?" he asked, and she smiled, shaking her head. "I'll be out in the kitchen for a while," he told her. "I thought I'd make you a cup of tea."

"That sounds good," she agreed. But on his return, he was not surprised to find her asleep, her body curved against the arm of the sofa, her feet drawn up beneath the knitted throw.

He stood in the doorway and looked at her. His heart was beating at its usual rate, his fears for her satisfied by her ability to sleep. But there was within his soul a deep sense of gratitude that would ever be a part of him. His Sarah was all right. Though her body had been bruised, her soul was intact. The flame that burned brightly within her had not been extinguished. And for that, he bowed his head and offered thanks.

The Pinkerton men, hired by the banks, had indeed made their way to Benning, Texas, armed with warrants for the arrests of the three Clark brothers. That two of them were beyond the threat of jail seemed not to matter to the distinguished-looking men, for Lester was the man they sought. His brothers were merely accessories after the fact.

The embezzlement of funds was enough to put him behind bars for a good long stretch, the men said, and the additional charge of kidnapping Sarah and Stephen assured his being held for more years than he had left to live, one of them added.

Then there was the fact of Sierra's death to be considered. Proof was not definite as yet, but the lawmen back in Big Rapids, Missouri, were pretty set on charging Lester with murder in the death of his wife. Sarah's folks had pressed the matter, once it became known to them that the evidence seemed to point to Lester as the culprit.

Now they listened as the lawmen told them the particulars of Lester's arrest. Joshua agreed to testify when the man was brought to trial, Colleen crying silently as her daughter's death was discussed.

Three days later, Jamie took Lester to the train, his leg patched up, his complaints rising above the rattle of the wagon he rode in. At the sound of Lester's belligerent carrying-on, Jamie only cast one long look of impatience at the prisoner and then ignored him for the rest of the short ride. He was cheered immensely by the thought of turning the man over to the Pinkerton agents in a few moments.

"Just shut your trap. You got nothing to complain of yet," Jamie said to his prisoner as he drew the team up to the edge of the station platform, watching as the train puffed to a halt beside them. "You're gonna be in real hot water once they get hold of you in Big Rapids."

"At least the boy ain't gonna profit from this," Lester told Jamie. "I'll bet Sarah thought she was gonna get a share if Stephen could claim my pa's property."

"I don't think Sarah cares one whit about you or your family," Jamie told him. "She's happy right where she is."

Chapter Fifteen

And where she was was very nearly heaven on earth, Sarah decided when the dust had cleared and Lester was in the hands of the authorities, on his way to Big Rapids where a judge was waiting for him. She rested for three days, pampered and cosseted beyond belief by her family. Things had progressed as Brace predicted, and tonight she felt almost like herself.

The house was quiet, Stephen asleep, the stars shining and the night breeze whispering through the curtains.

Brace held her close, his satisfaction apparent as he kissed and caressed her, his hands running with possessive measure over her silken flesh. "I didn't hurt you, did I?" he asked quietly, as if the fear of damaging her bruised flesh was foremost in his mind.

"No," she whispered. "You were so…good to me." Her pause was long, as if her mind could not conjure up the words she needed to tell him of her feelings. "You always give me so much, Brace. I can't tell you how much it means to me to have you hold me and touch me and fill me to the brim with your loving." She lifted herself from beside him and bent over to kiss him, her lips opening over his, exploring the limits of his mouth, tangling with his tongue as he drew her ever deeper into the kiss that lured him into her lair.

She was even more precious to him than he'd realized. For when the thought of harm coming to her had penetrated his conscious mind, he'd been driven to panic. For the first time in his life his body had operated automatically, his thoughts unable to achieve a sense of coherency.

"I was so afraid for you," he murmured. "I think I still can't believe that things are settled, for the most part." He watched her as she lifted her head and allowed her fingers to trace the lines of his face. She palmed his jaws, holding him there for her own benefit as she bent again to kiss the ridges of his brows, the slope of his nose, the skin on his throat where his evening whiskers had begun to form.

"I should have shaved tonight," he said, aware that her soft lips would be reddened by the stub of stiff hair against the tender skin.

"I love you just the way you are," she told him. "With a beard, without one, a neat haircut or your curls touching your collar."

"What curls?" he asked aloud, sitting upright and dislodging her from the place she'd chosen to occupy.

"These," she said, rolling to better have her hands on him, her fingertips touching the soft waves that would not be vanquished by water. They clung to her as if drawn by her soft skin, and she managed to get one halfway around her finger. "I love the little curly places back here."

"Oh, for crying out loud, Sarah," he spouted. "Why didn't you tell me before that my hair was doing that? It's not proper for a lawman to have *curls*."

"Says who?" she demanded. "Don't you dare argue with me, Brace Caulfield. If you wake up my father, you might find yourself in trouble. I'm trying to be quiet and not make any noise to disturb my folks, and you're raising a fuss over a few curls. Just remember one thing, mister. You're *my* lawman, and I love you even more with a few curls on your neck. It makes you look just a little bit vulnerable, and I like that."

"Well," he groused, "if there's anything I'm *not* supposed to be it's *vulnerable.* I'm supposed to be tough and hell-bent on catching all the bad guys. Curls over my collar certainly won't do my image any good."

"I won't say another word," she vowed. "I'll cut off your curls if you like and not even cry at the loss. Just let me enjoy them for tonight."

"Cry? *You* crying? I can't imagine you'd shed any tears over my haircuts."

"Just love me, Brace?" she asked softly. "Every bit of me, even my miserable long hair that takes such a long time to wash and dry, and causes me to fuss with it every day, in order for me to look halfway neat and tidy?"

He laughed. "I don't care if you ever look neat and tidy, sweetheart. I like you mussed and rumpled, to tell the truth. And I do love you, every bit of you, especially the curls and waves that cover your head and fall around your shoulders when you let it down at night."

"Do you, now?" she asked. "Then how can you fault my admiration of these few little wisps of hair that appeal to me so much when I stop behind your chair at the supper table, or that invite me to kiss your neck, so I can feel them tickle my mouth?"

"Really? My hair tickles you when you kiss my neck?"

She thought he looked rather pleased at the idea, a grin curving his mouth, his teeth showing white and even as his lips drew back, and his eyes glittering in the candlelight shed by the single taper he'd left by the bedside.

"There's something about you that appeals mightily to me," she told him. "Maybe it's the way you treat me, or the way you've taken to Stephen, or your kindness and generosity here in our bed. Although that sort of goes along with the first item on my list, doesn't it?"

"You'd better back up, sweet. You lost me somewhere between my ability to please you and my degree of kindness. And let me tell you, no one's ever accused me of that virtue before."

"Well, I have, several times," she said, pouting just a bit as his muscles hardened under her touch. His arms, husky and strong, held her in an embrace she could not have broken had she tried, yet she acknowledged the fact that she was his prisoner by her own choice. His chest and belly were firm, rigid beneath her as she sprawled across him. Unless she was sorely mistaken, there was another thought to be considered.

For a man who had so recently spent himself in the depths of her woman's parts, he was recovering rapidly. His virtues apparently did not include that of patience, she decided as he turned her in the bed, lying atop her, making no bones about his interest in her curves and the softness of breasts and the tender flesh of her hips and bottom.

"I thought we were going to sleep," she said, stifling a yawn for his benefit.

"Not for a while," he told her, his words sounding gruff, but softened by the glow his eyes shed upon her. He dipped his head and nuzzled between her breasts.

"You'll learn not to come to bed without being properly dressed," he muttered. "This is what you get for tempting me."

"Really?" Her voice sang with the delight he brought to her, and he laughed softly, aware of her willingness to accommodate him, her desire for him causing her to soften beneath him. Her arms rose to encircle his neck and she lifted her face to his, drawing him down to press damp kisses against his beard stubble, then on the softer skin of his cheek and ear, until he held her firmly beneath him and met her lips in a series of caresses that took her breath.

"I love you, you little tease," he muttered. "You give me such happiness, sweetheart. I promise to take better care of you from now on. You'll grow tired of me looking after you, I fear."

"You've done a good job so far," she told him. "And I don't mind you giving me attention, especially not the kind I'm getting tonight."

With a deep sigh of anticipation she opened to him, her body welcoming him in the most basic way known to womankind. He was hers, the man she had chosen to live with, to love for all time, and if loving him made him happy, if giving him all she had to offer brought him pleasure, she was more than willing to spend her affection in his direction. It was, she decided, as he sought and found the haven of warmth she extended, a no-lose situation. She was the recipient of his strength and the power of his loving. For her, there could be no better reward than to know that Brace Caulfield cherished the woman he had taken for his own.

Jamie's words proved prophetic before many days had passed. A wire arrived and the stationmaster carried it to Brace's office, his excitement visible. "Wait till you see what happened," he said loudly.

"What?" Brace asked. "Where and when?"

"Read what this here says," the man told him, holding out a page from the tablet he used to copy messages.

Brace took the paper and frowned. "Your writing leaves a lot to be desired," he said.

"Here, let me have it," the stationmaster said with a look of chagrin. "I don't have a bit of trouble readin' my writing." He perused the message and cleared his throat. "It just says that upon arrival at their destination, the authorities almost lost Lester Clark from custody. He got away and was shot for his trouble. Seems the man won't be standing trial after all."

"He's dead?" Brace asked, stunned by the news.

"That's what it says." He held out the message in Brace's direction and Brace took it, folding it and sliding it into his pocket.

"I guess that solves a couple of problems," he said slowly. "We won't have to worry about him trying to get Stephen again, anyway, will we?"

"Nope, sure won't. In fact, it sounds to me like the fella got just what he deserved, after his shenanigans, cartin' Miss Sarah and the boy off the way he did. He was just lucky neither of them got hurt bad, or he'd probably have been killed right here."

Brace nodded. "You may be right. There were some men out there that day who were out for Lester's hide. He was fortunate to get away with a bullet in his leg."

"Well, it's a sorry ending, no matter how you look at it," the stationmaster said. "The man was a crook and, from the sounds of it, an embezzler and a killer to boot."

"That he was," Brace said. "And now," he continued, "I think I'd better go home and let my family know what's happened."

He left the office and went out the back door where his horse was staked, mounting him quickly. Jamie appeared as he rounded the front of the building and Brace hailed him, sliding from his mount as Jamie approached. "Want to read something interesting?" he asked.

His deputy took the message from his hand and read it slowly, then looked up into Brace's face. "Sounds like the fella got what was coming to him, don't it?"

"I'd say so," Brace agreed. "I'm on my way home to talk to Sarah and her folks. They'll be interested to hear this."

"I'll be here," Jamie told him. "Why don't you take the rest of the day off? If I need you for anything, I'll know where to find you."

"I think I will," Brace said with a nod. "I can work on the fencing for a while. We've got it almost finished."

"Did you get Sarah's mare yet?" Jamie asked, and Brace shook his head.

"No, Nicholas is going to look for a mount for Sarah and bring it to the house. He's looking for a team for the new surrey, too."

"You'll need to add some more space to that shed of yours," Jamie said with a grin. "I think you'd might as well buy yourself a ranch."

"Don't think I haven't thought of it," Brace said. "But I'm not real big on farming. Being the lawman in Benning is enough of a job for me."

"Well, I'll be over to see how things are coming along in a few days," Jamie told him, and then waved a quick farewell as Brace turned his horse and rode toward home.

Chapter Sixteen

"We're having company, and it isn't my parents," Brace said over the supper table a week or so later. He'd written the letter inviting the elder Caulfields to visit just a couple of days before and mailed it quickly, but they certainly wouldn't have had time to receive it at this early date. "We haven't even heard back from them yet," he said.

"Well who on earth do we know who might be coming to visit?" Sarah asked, obviously perplexed by his news. "Not that it's a problem, but I just can't imagine—"

"This isn't anyone either of us knows," Brace said quickly. "And I hope it won't be a problem." He looked sharply at Stephen, who was obviously unaware of the discussion going on around him, his attention focused instead on the dog who sat patiently beside his chair.

"No feeding the dog at the table," Sarah said automatically as Stephen picked up a small bit of meat from his plate. "And please use your fork, Stephen," she said sternly. "We don't eat with our fingers."

"Bear don't mind eating from my fingers," the boy

answered with an aggrieved look at his aunt. "And it was only a little, tiny bite, Aunt Sarah."

Sarah stifled her smile, and Brace was led to support her in this. His Sarah was a softie, but she had put into place a few rules that Stephen tried to bend to his own needs on occasion. It was tough to be an enforcer, but that was what fathers did, if his memory served him right.

"You heard your aunt, Stephen," Brace said quietly. "Bear can eat when we're finished. You can feed him his meal from your fingers if you like. Just not while we're eating our supper."

Giving in with a deep sigh of forbearance, Stephen bent over his plate and consumed his meal with gusto. "Now can I be excused?" he asked politely. "I'll help clear up when y'all are finished."

"I'll call you in," Sarah said, well aware that the boy had pocketed three or four bites of meat in his trousers.

She watched with a smile as he left the table, the dog hot on his heels, his thoughts already intent on giving the pup the treats he'd pilfered from his plate.

Brace bent to her from his place across the round table. "You spoil him, you know," he said softly.

"I know," she said agreeably. "But he's such a good child, and I love him so much." She shrugged as if admitting defeat. "Spoiling Stephen is easy to do."

She picked up her own fork and filled it, then paused for a moment. "How about filling me in on our visitor?" she said. Her fork went into her mouth and she chewed on the food slowly, watching Brace with anticipation.

"I don't want you to choke when you hear this," he said. "Swallow your food first."

She did as he asked and then took a sip of her milk, a drink she had decided would be good for the baby she carried—and one in plentiful supply, given the cow in the shed. "All right, Sheriff. I'm all ears," she said dutifully, ceremoniously tucking her hair behind her ears and then smiling innocently at him.

"Don't be flip with me, lady," he told her, grinning with appreciation of her sassy mouth. "And don't forget to give me the respect due a man of the law."

"Yes, sir," she said, rising and circling the table to where he sat. "I'm all done eating. May I sit on your lap now?"

"We almost got in trouble the last time you did this," he reminded her. "Your mother came in the door and you were mighty embarrassed, as I recall."

"That's not what I remember," she told him. "You were the one who had to hide behind me while we talked to her."

"I couldn't help that," he said. "You just seem to have that effect on me. I can't seem to resist you."

"Well," she said with resignation, "I'd better not sit on your lap anymore."

He tugged her down on his thighs and his hand curled around her bottom. "I'm right fond of you sitting here, ma'am," he told her. "Makes it easy to hug you."

"Now," she said, sighing deeply, "tell me your news, Sheriff. You've fooled around long enough."

"Not nearly long enough," he said, contradicting her with a grin. "But I can wait. And in the meantime, I'll fill you in on the latest happening. I got a wire this morning from a lawyer. He's the executor of Lester's father's will, the man in charge of his estate. It seems they've been checking out the possible heirs to the property the old man left, and he wants to come here and talk to us about Stephen. He'll need proof that the boy is indeed Lester's son.''

"Possible heirs?" Her thoughts had apparently clung to that phrase, and she repeated it slowly. "They think that Stephen might inherit his grandfather's property?"

"That's what it sounds like to me," Brace said. "So I wired him back right away. I told him that Sierra's parents live here and can testify to her marriage to the man, and he can meet Stephen himself and talk to him about Lester. Not to mention you being Sierra's twin, which may be able to put the finishing touches on Stephen's identity."

"Will that upset Stephen, do you think?" Sarah asked.

"Maybe. But it will be worth it, should he inherit the ranch. And according to what Lester said, his father had quite a large holding, and family was important to the old man. I think it's in Stephen's best interests to meet with the lawyer, and in ours to provide him with anything he needs to prove Stephen's claim."

"I'll do whatever you want me to, Brace," she said. "I know this will bring Sierra's death back to my parents—not that they've forgotten it. But time has healed some of the pain, I think. I just hate to have everything dragged up again."

"I think it will be, anyway, sweet. The U.S. Marshal in Missouri is hot on the trail of Lester's connection with his wife's death, and I won't be surprised if he's found guilty and the case brought to a finish. No matter that the man himself is dead. They'll want to mark the file closed, if I have any knowledge of the thing."

"I'll feel—" she paused, and then the word she searched for came to her and she spoke it quietly "—vindicated once this is settled for all time. I was so certain that Lester had strangled Sierra, but I couldn't get anyone to listen to me. Even though my folks had suspicions, they found it more convenient to push it under the carpet, so to speak. I have a hard time forgetting that.''

"*I* believed you, Sarah." His words were quiet, but held a wealth of confidence in her judgment. "I never doubted for a moment that you were on the right track. Stephen is a lucky young man to have you as his champion. And now it's time for you to rest."

She sat quietly for long minutes, and Brace was silent, knowing that she needed to digest the latest news, needed to face the knowledge of her twin's death once more. And then she turned to him, hiding her face against his shoulder, pushing his shirt aside so that her mouth could touch the side of his throat. She whispered her love there, softly, and yet with a degree of passion that brought Brace to the edge of desire, his body responding to her with a strength she seemed to be willing to accept.

He lifted her from his lap, and she stood beside him, her fingers still clutching at his shoulders. Rising to face her, he lifted her, holding her close to his heart, and she sighed, as if it were exactly the spot she wanted to inhabit.

"Am I too heavy for you?" she asked, even though his arms were powerful and his chest was firmly muscled.

"Not nearly as heavy as you will be in a few months," he told her. "And I'll guarantee I'll still be able to carry you then. In fact, I'll make a promise. On the day you deliver our child, I'll carry you up those stairs to our bedroom and stay with you until the baby is born."

She smiled at him, and once more, tears glistened in her eyes. "I love you so much, Brace," she whispered. "I know it isn't done, but I really want you with me when the time comes."

"Well, it's going to be done in our house," he said, his tone not allowing for argument. "I was there when we started the process of having a baby, and I intend to be there at the end. I want to be the first to see our child, the second person to hold him."

"The second?" she asked.

"You'll no doubt be the first," he explained, "unless your mother is there, and then we'll have to fight for the honor."

"Well, I don't need to be carried today," she said. "I can sit or lie on the sofa in the parlor if you insist on me resting for a while. And then I have to clean up the kitchen."

"All right, you can rest in here," he said agreeably, and carried her from the kitchen, down the hallway and into the parlor, where he deposited her on the sofa and then bent to light a lamp that sat on a table near where she sat.

His look at her was stern. "I want you to stay right there and put your feet up." And then, as if she were not capable of doing it herself, he bent to slide her shoes from her feet and lifted them to the sofa cushion, covering her with the afghan that hung behind her, over the sofa's back.

"I'm feeling very pampered," she said, smiling up at him, settling her head on a soft cushion.

"I'm going to clear up in the kitchen," he said. "Then I'll call Stephen in and we can do some reading, if you're up to it. How does that sound?"

"Like heaven," she told him, making him laugh.

"Not quite," he said. "I'll give you a glimpse of that later on tonight."

They'd finished *Robinson Crusoe* many evenings ago, and were well into *A Tale of Two Cities* now. Brace had frowned when Sarah chose it for their use, but she'd explained that Stephen would be getting a history lesson, along with the pleasure of a good book. And so it had been, Stephen eagerly listening as they explored France as a family.

"I sure would like to go there sometime," he said now as they gathered together for another evening of listening to Sarah's soft tones reading the pages allotted for tonight.

"Maybe we can," Brace told him. "There are huge boats making the trip across the ocean, son, and there's no reason why we can't save our money and go ourselves in a few years."

"Do you mean it?" Sarah asked him, apparently as eager as Stephen for the experience.

"Of course, I do," Brace answered with assurance. "We'll have to get a map and maybe one of those outfits where you can put pictures on a sliding thing and look through the eyepieces at them. They look real, you know, as if you're actually there yourself."

"Stereopticons, they're called," Sarah said, providing the word he sought. "We had one at home when I was a little girl. My father gave it to Sierra and me for Christmas one year, and we traveled all over the world through pictures."

"Well, we'll get one and let Stephen have the same privilege," Brace said.

"You know what?" Sarah said thoughtfully. "I

wouldn't be surprised if my mother packed it in the things they brought from Big Rapids. Wouldn't that be fine?''

"We can ask her the next time she stops in or you go there," Brace said easily. "It would save waiting for one to be delivered from the catalog."

"I'm so glad you thought of that," she said, obviously recalling her own childhood delight with the device her father had purchased. "My folks should have a couple of boxes of pictures. I'll go over one day and help my mother look for them."

"Why don't you take Stephen along and let him do the climbing into the attic?" Brace suggested. "I'll bet he'd get a big kick out of helping his grandma, and I know Colleen would enjoy it."

"You're so smart," she said, and then tossed a glance in Stephen's direction. He was busily teaching his dog to stay down from the furniture, and Sarah wasn't sure he'd listened to the conversation going on around him, so involved was he with Bear.

"When can I go and help Grandma?" Stephen asked, setting Sarah straight in a hurry.

Sarah laughed softly. "Soon," she said. "Maybe tomorrow."

"How come you've been taking a nap every day, Aunt Sarah?" Stephen asked now. "You lie down most every afternoon. You're not sick, are you?" His boyish features were drawn into a frown of puzzlement as he looked at her over Bear's furry head. "Is that why Pa doesn't want you to climb the stairs to Grandma's attic? 'Cause you're not feeling good?"

Sarah shook her head, but Brace decided quickly to seize the opportunity to talk to the boy.

"There's something going on that you don't know

about, Stephen," he said. "And I think you're old enough to understand what's happening to your aunt Sarah."

Stephen's eyes rounded, his mouth opened a bit and he deposited the pup on the floor abruptly. Moving quickly, he went to where Sarah sat on the sofa and knelt at her feet, looking up at her with his heart in his eyes. "You're not gonna die like my mama, are you?" he asked, his tears not far from the surface.

Sarah bent to him and held his head against her own. Her fingers were lost in his wealth of dark hair—hair much like Sierra's. She bent to press kisses on the waving locks, even as she cast a look of aggravation over his head at Brace. "No, of course not," she told Stephen. "I'm not dying, and I'm not going anywhere, either, so don't worry about such things happening."

"Well, I didn't know my mama was gonna die, either—not till it happened."

He looked up, and Sarah lifted her head from his, meeting his gaze, honesty gleaming in her blue eyes. "Well, I'm as healthy as any woman can be," she said, stating the fact firmly, her words giving a promise the boy seemed to accept.

"Sarah has another reason altogether for being sleepy sometimes," Brace said, walking across the floor to where the two of them sat. He positioned himself behind Stephen on the floor and lifted the boy into his lap.

"Ain't I too old to sit on your lap, Pa?" Stephen asked, even as he cuddled close to the man who had become his father.

"Sarah sits on my lap," Brace pointed out with a grin, "and she's a lot older than you are."

Stephen looked perplexed for a moment. "I'm not sure that's the same thing," he said dubiously, "but if you say it's all right, then I don't mind."

"Stephen, your aunt and I are going to have a baby."

It was all he was able to say, for Stephen stood suddenly and wrapped his arms around Sarah tightly. He trembled against her, and Brace was concerned that the boy was unhappy with the unexpected news.

His fears were allayed as Stephen chortled with delight. "A baby? A real live baby, Aunt Sarah?" he asked, and then looked at Brace with questioning eyes. "When that happens, you'll have a baby of your own, won't you? And maybe you'll love him more than me." He stilled suddenly, as if he tried to make himself smaller.

"I couldn't love any other child in the world more than I do you, Stephen," Brace said carefully. "You are the first boy I've ever had to call me Pa, and I can't tell you how proud I am of you. You'll always be the first child in this house, and we'll love you when the baby arrives, the same as we do now. There's always enough love to go around, son. And you'll be so busy helping with things you'll soon find yourself loving the baby, too. It's going to be your little sister or brother, you know."

"Yeah." Stephen breathed the word of acquiescence and then trembled. "I think I'm gonna tell Grandma and Grandpa when I see them. Will that be all right?" He paused, and then his forehead wrinkled in thought. "I'd like to tell Nicholas and Lin, too, when we see them. Can I?"

"Of course you can," Brace said, putting his talk with Joshua on the back burner, knowing that Stephen needed to feel included in this time of waiting for their child to be born.

"Boy, oh, boy," Stephen said, wiggling excitedly. "This is gonna be fun, Pa. I've never had a brother or sister. How long does it take before babies get old enough to play?''

''A few months,'' Sarah said quickly. ''But this one won't be born for a while yet. Babies have to be about a year old before they can walk and start to talk, and it will probably be a couple of years before we can turn him or her loose outdoors with you.''

''I can play in the house with a brother, can't I?'' the boy asked hopefully. ''I mean, we can sit on the carpet and look at books and play with toys and stuff.''

''I think you're going to have a wonderful time with this baby,'' Brace told him. ''In fact, I'll bet you're going to be the best big brother ever.''

Stephen seemed to grow inches taller as he considered that prediction. ''I'll sure try to be a good brother,'' he said finally. ''I'll look after the baby real good, Aunt Sarah, and make sure he doesn't get hurt on anything and doesn't fall down the stairs.''

''I'm so proud of you,'' Sarah said. ''I knew you'd be pleased about this news.'' She hesitated, and then looked at Brace for guidance. ''Shall we talk about the other thing?'' she asked.

''I think so,'' Brace said, searching for words that would not upset the boy. He cleared his throat and then spoke in a nonchalant voice. ''Lester's father died a little while back, Stephen. He was your grandfather, you know.''

Stephen nodded, looking perplexed.

''Well, we heard from a lawyer who is handling your grandfather's will, and he wants to come here to meet you. He thinks you may have inherited some property.''

''Inherited? Does that mean that I'd have to go live somewhere else if I get some property? 'Cause I don't want to, Pa. I'm not moving anywhere away from you and Aunt Sarah.'' His mouth turned down in a determined line and his eyes narrowed defensively.

"You'll never have to go anywhere else to live," Brace told him. "Not unless you change your mind when you grow up and decide you want to have a place of your own. For now, you belong right here, and you might as well understand that fact. You're not going anywhere."

To another child, the words might have sounded harsh, like a sentence given that would make the boy a prisoner, but to Stephen they seemed to be an affirmation of his need for family. "I'm glad, Pa," he said, grinning from ear to ear. "And I don't mind if that man comes here to talk to me. I'll just tell him that I don't want to live anyplace else. Will that be all right?"

"Perfectly all right," Brace told him.

"When is he coming?" Sarah asked. "Have you contacted him?"

"Yeah. He'll be here next week."

"When do you think your folks will come?" she asked. "I'm hoping they'll make a trip to visit, and meet all of us. What do you think?"

"Will they be my grandma and grandpa, too?" Stephen asked joyously, as if the prospect of more family members converging on them was something to celebrate.

"Yes, they will," Brace told him. "You're my son, and that makes you their grandson."

"Legally?" Sarah asked.

"We'll face that when the judge shows up for his next visit," Brace said. "I've been working out a plan."

"When is he coming?" Sarah asked.

"In a couple of weeks. In fact, it sounds like we'll have our hands full for a few days by the time we have the judge in town, the lawyer coming to visit and then, if we're lucky, maybe even my folks making a trip here.'' He reached for Stephen and tugged him back to sit in his lap.

"The most important thing, though, is having the judge make a decision about Stephen. I want it all legal and aboveboard. He'll be ours, and he'll take my name. How would you like to be Stephen Caulfield?'' he asked the boy who curled against him.

"I'd like that," Stephen said, nodding firmly. "I could tell the teacher when I go back to school that I have a new name, couldn't I? And I'll have to practice writing it, so I don't forget."

"You won't forget," Sarah told him, laughing softly as she heard his plan of action. "It didn't take me long at all to get used to my name when I married Brace. I used to be Sarah Murphy, and now I'm Sarah Caulfield."

"Mrs. Brace Caulfield," her husband said quietly, correcting her with a voice that cherished the name he spoke. "I like knowing that you bear my name, Sarah. And I'll feel pleased as punch when Stephen is mine, legally and officially."

Stephen's plan to speak with his grandparents came about sooner than any of them expected. Early morning brought the older couple to the back door, and without any persuasion at all they were involved in eating breakfast.

"Aunt Sarah made biscuits and gravy," Stephen announced when his grandparents appeared at the door. "There's plenty for all of us," he said, tugging his grandmother into the kitchen.

"We don't want to intrude," Colleen said, bending

to kiss Stephen and then embracing Sarah with a new tenderness. "You all right?" she asked quietly. And at Sarah's nod, she aimed a long glance at Brace. "And how about you? Are you surviving this ordeal?"

"I'm loving it," Brace said. "We're both excited, and aside from some stomach upset and being tired, Sarah's doing fine."

"I got something to tell you, Grandma," Stephen said, so excited he could barely stand still. He tugged on his grandfather's hand and drew him into the circle, then looked at Brace. "Can I tell them now?" he asked.

"Sure, son. Go ahead," Brace told him, noting the smile Colleen and Joshua exchanged over the boy's head.

"Come sit down," Stephen said to his grandparents, leading them to the table, where he assigned chairs. "This is very important," he said, his chest seeming to expand with each word. He waited, aware that all eyes were upon him, and then spoke the words that burned to be said.

"We're gonna have a baby. Me and my new pa and Aunt Sarah are gonna have either a boy or a girl, Grandpa. But I don't care which one it is. How do you like that news, Grandma?" His eyes shone with excitement, and his face was aglow with the importance of his news.

No matter, Brace thought, that the older couple was already aware of the news—they acted appropriately surprised and stunned by Stephen's announcement. "How wonderful," Colleen said, looking up at Stephen and grasping his hand. "Won't we have a good time with a new baby in the family?"

"We sure will," Joshua said quickly, as if he would not be left out of the celebration. "And I'm with you, boy. I don't care if it's a boy or girl. I'm a little partial to both, to tell the truth. We couldn't have a grandchild we love more than you, Stephen, so another boy would fit right in. And if we have a baby girl, we'll all have to think about girly things, like fluffy dresses, petticoats and dolls and that sort of thing.''

"I'm gonna teach her how to play catch with me and Bear," Stephen said stubbornly. "It won't matter if it's a girl. She can still do stuff with me.''

"You're right, son," Brace said, quick to reassure him. "We're all willing to accept whatever kind of baby God sends our way.''

"What does He have to do with it?" Stephen asked, truly perplexed by the statement.

Sarah looked helplessly at her mother, and Colleen rose to the occasion. "Come here, Stephen," she said, and waited until the boy stood beside her before she continued.

"Your pa and aunt Sarah are the ones who will be the mother and father of the new baby, but God is the one who forms us all and allows babies to be given to parents. We'll read in the Bible if you like, where it tells how God made man in His own image.''

"Can we do that?" he asked eagerly. "And will the preacher at church know how God decides who's supposed to have babies?''

"Well, now," Colleen said, apparently at a loss for words.

"Men and women who love each other and make a home together are usually the ones who have babies," Brace said quietly, gaining Stephen's attention. "People like your aunt Sarah and me, who plan to spend the rest of their lives together, taking care of their family. Sometimes babies are born in bad situations, but it's not

God's fault when that happens. It just means that some folks aren't as good at raising children as others. Sometimes parents don't care for their children the way they should, but most of the time it all works out well.''

"Kinda like it worked out that you and Aunt Sarah got me, instead of my dad?" Stephen asked. "I think you're about the best pa anyone could have," he said earnestly, "and I'm sure glad I'm part of your family. And I'm extra glad that we'll be having an even bigger family. Wow! Just think. We'll have my grandma and grandpa and all of us. That'll be a big bunch of folks, won't it?"

"Yes, it will," Sarah said. "And if Brace's mother and father come to visit, we'll have even more in our family. They'll be so pleased that Brace has a son like you, Stephen."

"When are they comin'?" he asked, wide-eyed at the news.

"We don't know for sure," Brace said. "But I've sent a letter to them, inviting them, and we should be hearing back soon."

"Do Grandma and Grandpa know about the lawyer man?" Stephen asked. And then he turned to convey the news. "There's a man who is taking care of my other grandfather's stuff. Did you know my other grandfather died?" he asked suddenly, and watched as both Colleen and Joshua nodded, encouraging him to continue.

"Well, anyway, this man is coming to see us, and he wants to be sure I'm really who I am, so I can maybe—" He looked up at Brace as he searched for the correct word.

"Inherit," Brace told him. "So you can inherit your grandfather's estate."

"Yeah, that's what I meant," the boy said. "Inherit," he repeated, trying the word out. "Anyway, what it means is that the ranch where Lester and the other two guys were gonna take me might be mine someday."

"And how do you feel about that?" Joshua asked.

Stephen shrugged as if it were of little account. "I guess it's okay, but I'm not gonna move there. I like it here just fine."

"We'll see about hiring a manager," Brace told Joshua. "When the lawyer gets here we'll have to discuss it thoroughly."

Chapter Seventeen

"I'm Edward Lawrence," the distinguished-looking man said, holding out his hand for Brace to shake. "I hope this isn't an inconvenience to you and your family, but I think establishing young Stephen's claim is of utmost importance."

Brace nodded. "I go along with that. It seems fitting that the boy should end up with some sort of recompense for the miserable life he led with Lester Clark."

"I haven't heard much of anything good about the Clark boys, Lester in particular," Mr. Lawrence said. "The father was an old reprobate himself, and managed to get on the wrong side of the law more than once. I'm not here as his friend, you understand," he said firmly. "Only as a representative of the estate. Personally, I thought the whole clan was teetering on the very edge of trouble for years. But I'll say one thing for Lester's father. He was loyal to his family, scamps that they were. He made sure that his property would remain in the direct line of descendants. The boy, Stephen, seems to be the most likely prospect to inherit the whole she-bang."

"Well, if you'd like to take care of this today, you're

welcome to come out to the house at your convenience,'' Brace told him. ''I've reserved a room at the hotel for you, and we can take your things there first if you like.''

''I'm thinking I'd like to talk to Stephen without him knowing who I am,'' Mr. Lawrence said. ''I want to hear what his memories of his childhood are. My first job is to establish his identity, and he may be able to settle that for me without going into it any deeper.''

''Well then, I'll drop you off at the hotel and send a horse for you to use from the livery stable. They can deliver it to the hotel and you can ride out at your convenience.'' And then, as if another thought had intruded, Brace asked a pertinent question. ''You do ride, don't you?''

Mr. Lawrence laughed and nodded. ''I'm from Texas, born and bred,'' he said. ''And riding a horse was one of the first things I did as a child. Your plan is sound. Give me instructions for finding your place and I'll be there soon.''

The stop at the hotel took but a few minutes, and Brace drew a rough map directing the man to the big house on the edge of town. Then, once the lawyer was established, Brace's buggy made its way to the livery stable. ''Amos,'' he called out, waiting till the husky blacksmith came from the dimly lit barn. As his friend appeared in the open doorway, Brace got down from his buggy and approached him.

''There's a fella at the hotel, Edward Lawrence, a lawyer from the other side of the state, who'll be coming out to our place right shortly. Can you deliver a horse to him? Sure would save him a lot of walking.''

''Has he got a soft hand on the reins?'' Amos asked,

obviously unwilling to let one of his animals go to a man without finesse.

"Seems to be aboveboard to me, and he says he's been riding since he was just a little tad."

Amos nodded agreeably. "I'll take a horse over and let Simms know who it's for."

That issue settled easily, Brace stopped at the jail-house and notified Jamie as to his whereabouts. The deputy, already privy to the news of Stephen's possible inheritance, was willing to take charge of things until Brace should return.

"If there's any trouble, I'll run over and get you," the younger man said.

Once Brace arrived home, he put his buggy neatly beneath the lean-to and gave his mare her freedom in the pasture before he went into the house. "Sarah?" He called her name upon opening the back door, and was once more struck by the difference in his household with a woman in charge.

She came hastily from the front of the house and he waited for her to come to him. He was not disappointed, for she reached upward as her skirts brushed against his trousers, and she was caught up in his embrace.

"You're an easy one to snatch hold of, young lady," Brace said with a laugh. "You make it more than worthwhile for me to come in at odd hours, what with the sort of welcome I get."

"Silly man," Sarah said, swatting at his arm, laughing with the pure joy of living, Brace thought. She was confident, holding no secrets from him, keeping nothing of herself inviolate, and yet he perceived that there were mysteries buried deep inside the woman he had yet to discover.

She knew more about him and his past than any other

human being, yet loved him without any apparent reserve. He thought of the day they'd met, when she'd been so intent on shooting Lester, and his smile beamed down on her.

"What?" she asked. "What are you laughing at? Do I have dust on my nose?"

"No," he told her. "I was just thinking of you and your gun and knife and your plans to shoot Lester the first time I saw you."

"Do you think I wouldn't have done it?" she asked sharply.

He shook his head. "I don't want to get on your bad side, sweetheart. Old Lester was a fool in more ways than one, to think he could pull that kind of a stunt on you and get away with it. It's obvious that you and your sister might have been twins, but you got all the gumption in the family."

"She was nicer than I," Sarah said quietly. "And look what that got her."

She shifted in his arms. "I thought you were bringing the lawyer home with you. I've sent Stephen out to feed the animals."

Brace turned with her, looking out the window over the sink, where Stephen could be seen leaving the barn and heading for the house. The boy halted in his tracks, his gaze on something just out of Brace's line of vision, and then Stephen walked quickly toward the side of the house.

"I think our lawyer friend has arrived," Brace said. "Unless I miss my guess, Stephen is greeting him now. Probably taking a good look at the horse Amos let the fella use."

His words proved to be true, for in a few seconds a rap at the back door announced the visitor, and in the yard, Brace saw Stephen leading the livery-stable mount toward the new pasture. The boy looped the horse's reins over the top rail of the fence and busied himself taking the saddle off. It slid more rapidly than Stephen had expected, and almost took him to the ground with it.

Brace laughed, and Mr. Lawrence turned to watch the proceedings. Stephen opened the gate and ushered the animal into the pasture and then removed the bit and bridle so the animal could graze unhindered.

"Hope we can get him back into that bridle when it's time for me to leave," Mr. Lawrence said. "I doubt the animal has been faced with such an abundance of grass and a place to run free in a month of Sundays."

"He'll be fine," Brace said. "I can use a rope if we need to. In my earlier days I was quite a hand at it."

"A cowhand, were you?"

"Yeah. I came to Texas when I was barely dry behind the ears, and made my way up the ladder by roping horses and rounding up cattle."

"A self-made man, I'd say," Mr. Lawrence commented, then looked inquisitively at Sarah, who watched the two men quietly. "And this must be your wife, Sheriff. How do you do, ma'am?" he asked cordially, nodding and removing his hat.

"Won't you sit down, sir?" Sarah asked. "We always have a pot of coffee ready for visitors."

"Thank you," Mr. Lawrence said. "I'm feeling a bit dry. Breakfast on the train was nothing to write home about. And the coffee was atrocious."

After introductions were made they sat at the table, and Mr. Lawrence asked pointed questions about Stephen, his relationship to Sarah and her parents, and then he honed in on Lester's threat to the boy, given his harsh treatment and lack of concern for Stephen's well-being.

In the midst of their conversation Stephen came in the door and sidled close to Sarah, casting her a dubious look. But when the lawyer asked him several questions about Lester and Sierra, the boy answered quickly and with obvious affection for his mother. His feelings toward Lester were another matter altogether, and his voice faltered when he spoke the condemning words that told of bruises and harsh treatment delivered to Sierra and the boy himself.

"Do you know that you have family living on a ranch clear on the other side of the state?" the lawyer asked. "Your grandfather is dead, but there are still a few family members there."

"I don't care about them," Stephen said vehemently. "This is my family, right here with Aunt Sarah and my pa and Grandma and Grandpa. I'm not going anywhere else."

"Well, that settles that, I'd say," Mr. Lawrence said, leaning back in his chair and giving Stephen an approving look. "I'd say you're pretty contented with your place here, aren't you, son?"

"Yes, sir," Stephen answered. "We're gonna have a new baby next year and—"

"I don't think Mr. Lawrence is interested in that," Sarah said, cutting in sharply.

"Oh, but I am," the lawyer said quietly. "I'm interested in everything that has to do with Stephen's future." He looked at Brace, inquiry alive on his features. "Are you legally the boy's parents?"

"Not yet," Brace admitted. "We're going to ask the circuit judge to do something about that a few days from now when he next comes to town."

"Do you have any paperwork set up to state your intentions? Or a lawyer here in town to represent you?"

"No, we haven't," Brace told him. "We're hoping the judge will decide in our favor. He's very familiar with Stephen and his problems in the past."

"I think you could use some legal advice," Mr. Lawrence said firmly. "I propose to remain here in town until the judge shows up, and in the meantime, I'll be spending time with Stephen's grandparents and you and Mrs. Caulfield. We need to get this thing settled as soon as we can."

"You'll represent us in court?" Sarah asked in surprise.

"I'm prepared to do that very thing," Mr. Lawrence said. "I think the boy really fell into a bed of roses here. Seems to me you folks have offered him a wonderful home, and he's obviously happy with both of you."

"Brace is my new pa, you know," Stephen said in an undertone to the lawyer. "And Aunt Sarah has always taken care of me, especially after my mama died. My real father wasn't very nice, you know."

"I know," Mr. Lawrence said. "And I'd like to work out things so you'll have a secure place in life, Stephen." He looked up at Brace and smiled. "Let's talk about your claim to the boy and see what we can come up with. I'll need to see the grandparents, too, to get their opinion on the matter. They actually have first rights, you know, as blood relatives—as the mother's parents."

"There won't be a problem there," Sarah said quietly. "They'll always be a big part of Stephen's life, but they are in agreement that he should be with us."

"Well, let's get rolling on this, then," Mr. Lawrence

said. "Do you think we can get that bridle back on my horse, son?" he asked Stephen.

"Yes, sir, we can," the boy assured him, grinning widely, obviously aware that his future was settled as far as Mr. Lawrence was concerned.

The judge was impressed with the appeal handed him as he sat behind the impromptu bench a few days later. "You've got everything covered, I'd say," he told Edward Lawrence, and then looked to where Brace stood with Stephen.

"Do you know what this means, Stephen?" he asked, pointing at the paperwork he held in one hand.

"Yes, sir, I do," Stephen answered politely. "It means that if you say so, I'll really belong to Aunt Sarah and my new pa. For the rest of my life."

"Well, you can't be a belonging, as such, for you're a human being with rights of your own, but you can claim them as your mother and father," the judge told him. "And if you are agreeable to that, I see no reason to deny the petition drawn up by your lawyer, Sheriff Caulfield."

Sarah released her breath, her anxiety turning to appreciation as she heard the judge's ruling. Joshua and Colleen sat behind her, and she felt her father's warm hand on her shoulder as the judge stood and looked her way.

"Will you step up here?" he asked her, and then waited as she made her way to where Brace and Stephen stood and took her place beside her nephew. He looked up at her and his grin held a wealth of happiness.

"I'm gonna really be yours, Aunt Sarah. Just like you were always my mother."

"But we won't forget your first mother," Sarah told

him. "Sierra was my sister, my twin, as close to me as another person could ever be. It seems only right that I take her place in your life. She was a wonderful mother and a good woman, Stephen. Don't ever forget that."

"Yes, ma'am," he said dutifully, almost unable to stand still, his excitement apparent. "Now do I get my new name?" he asked eagerly.

Mr. Lawrence spoke then. "I've petitioned the court to legally change the boy's name to Caulfield, Your Honor. Is there any objection to that?" He waited, standing behind Stephen, one hand on the boy's shoulder, and it seemed a long minute before the judge nodded with finality.

"I proclaim here and now that the boy known as Stephen Clark be henceforth given the name of his adoptive parents, and from this day on he will be known as Stephen Caulfield. Does that meet with the approval of all the parties?"

Colleen and Joshua stood and made their way forward, Colleen reaching for her daughter and the boy beside her. Joshua shook Brace's hand and then took the hand of the lawyer who had befriended them all.

Stephen was almost smothered in hugs from his grandmother and Sarah, but seemed not to mind, for his smile was visible for all to see.

"I think we can close the books on this," the judge said. "And now I'll need to speak with Edward Lawrence for a few minutes."

Brace marshaled his family outside the building and together they awaited the lawyer's presence. When he reappeared, it was to greet them effusively.

"Things are pretty much settled," he told them. "I'm satisfied as to the boy's identity, and the judge and I have come up with a plan for the inheritance, if it meets with your approval, Sheriff and Mrs. Caulfield.''

Sarah had tears in her eyes, but her smile was brilliant. ''I'm sure you'll be fair to Stephen,'' she said.

''I will,'' the lawyer assured her. ''There's no family left and our plan is to find a man capable of running the ranch for the next fifteen years or so, at which time Stephen should be old enough to fend for himself. We can keep the ranch hands on for now. I'd expect Sheriff Caulfield and Joshua Murphy to keep a close check on the financial picture and perhaps make their way across the state once a year to look things over. As for my part, I'll be in close contact with the estate, and the man you choose as manager of the ranch will be answerable to me to some degree.''

''I think you've done well for our boy,'' Joshua said. ''I couldn't have asked for more. Our sole concern was that Stephen be given to Sarah and Brace to raise as their own child, and that the boy's inheritance be kept intact for him.''

''Well, we've settled all that,'' Mr. Lawrence told them. ''And now I'm going to gather my belongings and find out when the next train heads west. I plan to be on it.''

''Tomorrow morning is my guess,'' Brace told him.

''That sounds fine to me,'' the lawyer said. ''I'll get a haircut and shave and then a good night's sleep tonight before I leave town.''

''I'll take care of returning your horse to the livery stable,'' Brace offered. ''And I'll be there in the morning to be certain you catch the train.''

''How is the riding coming along?'' Lin asked Sarah. She'd come to spend the afternoon, and together they sat beneath a tree near the meadow. Stephen was leading his horse toward the barn, a rope tied to his halter, and Sarah was silently hoping Brace would arrive from work before Stephen took it into his head to show off his newfound prowess with saddle and bridle.

"Brace is pleased with his progress, but he won't let Stephen loose on his own yet. He makes a point of riding with him. The mare is becoming a pet, I fear. Stephen and Bear spend long hours with her, and the dog and horse have taken a real liking to each other. Bear seems torn between sleeping next to Stephen's bed and settling down in the shed with Sugarfoot."

"My bet's on Stephen," Lin said. "Dogs are faithful creatures, and Bear seems very attached to your son. On the other hand, it's not unusual for a pair of animals, such as a dog and horse, to form close bonds."

"Well, I've told Stephen he can get out his saddle and be ready to ride when Brace gets home." She looked up to where the sun was shining brightly in the western sky. "I'd say they have time to ride before supper."

"How are you feeling?" Lin asked Sarah. "Stephen thought he was so smart, stealing a march on you and Brace when he told us about the baby."

"We told him he could spread the news, and he didn't lose any time doing just that," Sarah said with a loving glance in the boy's direction.

"He's really excited about it, isn't he?" Lin asked. "We had somewhat the same situation when our boy was born. Amanda is Nicholas's niece, you know, and I'm the woman who was her nanny before Nicholas and I were married. We feared she might feel left out when we had a child, but she considers him her private property. There's never been a problem."

"I didn't know that," Sarah said. "Brace has always spoken of your children as if they were both naturally born to you and Nick."

"Well, it feels that way," Lin said, watching as her toddler son made his way to the pasture fence. Hot on his heels, Amanda reached for him, clutching his hand and bending to speak to him.

"She's very good with him," Sarah said. "And I can see where having a boy might be just the ticket for me. Not to mention that it would give Jonathan someone to play with down the road a ways."

"It's a girl," Lin said bluntly. "I can tell from the way you're carrying it. Besides, I'm planning on a girl myself, and I'd like her to have a playmate. It feels like we've become family, Sarah. I hope our children can spend time together on a regular basis."

Sarah's mind worked rapidly and she turned to Lin sharply. "Did you just tell me that you're going to have another baby?"

"Something like that," Lin said, laughing aloud.

"When is it due?" Sarah asked.

"Almost the same time as yours," Lin told her. "Early in March."

"Why didn't you tell me before?" Sarah asked. "I'm so thrilled for you and excited that we'll be sharing babies together."

"Well, you get to tell Brace, although I'm quite sure that he suspects already. He's given me that measuring look of his several times lately."

Sarah looked at the other woman, gauging her waistline, comparing it to her own. "I'd say we're of a size, all right," she said. "I'm having trouble getting my dresses together at the waist, and Brace just bought me some new things to wear."

"I heard about that, from Mr. Metcalfe at the general store," Lin said. "He was pretty smug about the whole thing, said he figured you were going to add to the family, if Brace's purchases were anything to go by. Did you know that your husband ordered a bolt of white outing flannel and several yards each of blue and pink from the Sears catalog?"

"No," Sarah said with surprise. "We talked about it, but I thought he was waiting till Mama and I decided how much we needed."

"He's apparently not taking any chances on the wrong colors," Lin said lightly. "He's covering everything with his blue and pink fabric." She smiled widely and then asked a favor. "Do you think your mother would lend a hand one day making a quilt out at our place? I want a new one for Amanda so we can turn hers over to the new baby. We could make one for you, too," she said, her gaze dreamy as she watched her children. "Katie is good at piecing quilts, and every new baby needs one, you know."

"Mama would love it," Sarah said. "And I'm anxious to begin cutting and sewing all the stuff I'll need."

Lin reached for her and hugged her tightly. "We'll have such fun," she said brightly.

"Fun doing what?" From behind them, Brace's voice cut short Lin's words.

Sarah turned quickly and smiled at her husband. "We're talking baby stuff," she said.

"And what's Lin's interest in this?" he asked, his smile broadening.

"As if you didn't know," Nicholas said, walking up to join the group.

"I had some suspicions," Brace admitted, "but I wasn't certain."

"Metcalfe at the store told half the town that you'd bought your wife a new wardrobe a couple of weeks ago," Nicholas said, grinning at Sarah. "He said you seemed to be gaining weight."

"The dirty rat," Sarah grumbled.

"Oh, well. Misery loves company," Lin told her. "We'll face this together."

"Want to see my new dresses?" Sarah asked, and at Lin's nod, she rose and lent a hand, helping Lin to her feet. "You two," she said, including Nicholas in her instructions, "need to go out and get Stephen up on that horse before he loses patience. I'm not at all sure the cinch is tight, and I don't want him to try mounting without you checking it out, Brace."

The two men watched their wives walk to the house and Brace gave Nicholas a commiserating look. "Do you think we'll survive?"

"I don't know about you, but I intend to enjoy every minute of it," Nick told him. "Women take on a special glow when they're carrying a child, and Lin has already taken to snuggling with me with no urging whatsoever."

Brace felt his face flush. "I wondered if Sarah was the only woman affected that way by pregnancy. And don't you dare let her know I said that, Nick. I don't want to lose my happy home."

Nicholas laughed and headed for the pasture where Stephen waited impatiently with his horse. "Not much chance of that, I'd say," he told Brace. "You've got a family that depends on you and a woman who loves you, and I'm possessed of the same situation. What more can any man ask?"

Chapter Eighteen

Benning, Texas
March 1902

"Lin's had a girl," Brace said without any pretense at ceremony. Coming home midmorning should have told her something was up, Sarah thought, but this news was well worth the trip Brace had made in the midst of his busy day. His cells were occupied by cowhands, whose celebration on Saturday night had terminated in a grand fight of epic proportions, according to Jamie. A third man having been put in a sickbed for the foreseeable future, the two roustabouts were awaiting the outcome.

But Brace had taken to dropping by the house at odd moments over the past couple of weeks, and so Sarah had not been surprised to see him at the back door as she readied the churn for her weekly chore.

"A girl?" she asked excitedly. "When? How big is she? Is Lin all right?"

"Yes, a girl, sweetheart. I don't know exactly how

big she is, but Lin is fine, so I'm assuming that all went well.''

"How did you find out?" she asked.

"Nicholas asked the doctor to stop by when he came back to town, so he walked into my office as big as life and made his announcement. You'd think it was all his doing, he was so pleased.''

"I am, too," Sarah said. "She was sure she was going to have a girl this time, and she's predicted one for us, too.''

"Well, if you don't have it pretty soon, I'd say you're going to burst," Brace told her. "I didn't know a woman's body could stretch so much.''

Sarah grimaced. "Well, obviously it can. And for your information, Mama was here a bit ago and she's coming back. She has a notion that I'll be having this baby a little early.''

"Early? How does she figure that? I'd say you've been pregnant forever already," Brace said with a grin of admiration as he beheld his wife. Well-rounded, possessed of a constantly aching back and swollen feet, she was still the most beautiful sight he'd ever had the honor to behold. He told her so in short order and she smiled and blushed at his words.

"I mean it, Sarah. You're a rare being. A woman with love to spend on all those around her, a wife any man would be proud of.'' He held her close, a small hand or foot nudging him as the baby protested the pressure of Brace's big body against Sarah's enormous bulk.

"Mama thinks I'm ready," Sarah told him as she cuddled close to his warmth. It was a beautiful spring day, and the thought of her child sharing a birthday with Lin's new baby made her smile happily.

Brace looked to be making plans, she decided, his

face a brown study, his eyes narrowed as he looked at her. And then his words confirmed her thoughts.

"I'm going to let Jamie know that you're a little under the weather and then I'll stop by the school and leave word with his teacher for Stephen to come right home when the bell rings. And I might even let the doctor know he might be on call today. If I let him know now, it'll give him a chance to rest up before you need him."

"You've got it all organized, haven't you?" she asked. "I'm surprised you're not making plans to do the delivering of your child yourself."

"Not on your life, sweetheart," he said with emphasis. "I'll be more than willing to let the doctor and your mother have that privilege."

And they did. For just before midnight, a baby's squeal of anger was heard throughout the house, and Joshua settled back with a snifter of fine brandy, toasting his new grandchild. Beside him on the sofa, Stephen slept undisturbed.

In the room upstairs, Brace knelt by the bed and leaned over Sarah. "It's a girl, honey," he told her. "A beautiful little girl. Want to see her?"

"In a minute," Sarah told him. "I still feel like I need to push, Brace." She began to cry, her mouth quivering, her body trembling as she cried silent tears. "I'm so cold," she said, shivering.

He rose and found a quilt to pull over her body, covering her shoulders and arms. "It's not cold out," he told her, and then was set straight by the doctor, who seemed to be very pleased about the proceedings.

"I'd say your missus is about to present you with another young'un," he said. "I wondered last time I saw her if she wasn't carrying two little ones in there, and I'll be doggoned if she hasn't surprised us all.''

"Sarah, do you hear him?" Brace asked eagerly.

"I'm not deaf," she said, "just pregnant." And with that she inhaled deeply and obeyed the doctor as he worked with her, delivering a second child in less than a minute.

"Another girl," he said. "And here comes the afterbirth. Just one, Mrs. Caulfield. It looks like your twins are identical."

"I kind of suspected," Colleen said happily. "But I wasn't sure, and I didn't want Sarah to be disappointed if she only had the one child."

"Disappointed?" Sarah asked. "How could I be?" She held out her arms for the babe her mother held. "Let me have Brenna.''

"Brenna?" Colleen asked. "What about the second twin?"

"Brianna," Sarah said softly. "We'll call her Bree."

"You had two names ready," Brace said, his eyes asking a question Sarah seemed to understand as she held the first baby at her side, her hand firmly clutched in that of her husband.

"I knew," she said. "For the past few weeks I knew there were two of them. And somehow I felt like Sierra was with me today. We were so close and loved each other so much. I just hope my girls will have as wonderful a childhood as Sierra and I did."

"They will," Brace vowed. "We'll see to it. All of us. Your folks and mine and all of our friends."

"Your folks?" Sarah asked, realizing what he'd said.

"My folks. I got a letter in the morning mail. They're on their way here, sweetheart. I was so excited about the baby coming today, I forgot to tell you. Forgive me, honey.''

"After what you've given me today, I'll put up with you for the rest of my life," she told him. "Thank you, Brace...for my babies...for my life with you...for loving me." She lifted his hand from her breast where she'd held it close, where it had given her such comfort over the past hours, and kissed it, a lingering caress that was more eloquent than the words she spoke.

"I do love you, Sarah, wife of mine," he said softly. "You've filled me with joy—not just tonight, with the babies, but over the past months, ever since we spoke our vows."

"Well," Colleen said, walking to Brace and depositing his second daughter in his arms. Both babes, wrapped in lengths of flannel, washed quickly and inspected by the doctor, were quiet, almost as if they felt the love that surrounded them. "Here's your Brianna," she told Brace. "One for each of you."

"Both of them for each of us," Brace said quietly. "We'll raise them together, and with Stephen's help we'll give them all they need to have a good life."

Sarah looked up at him, aware of the tears that flowed from his dark eyes, matching those that she'd given up trying to control. It was worth all the waiting, she decided, worth all the pain, for there had been an abundant amount of that. Just to see Brace with his child, his face wreathed in smiles even as his joy took the form of tears, was enough to cement this memory for all time in her heart.

"I think your father will want to know what's going on," Colleen said. "I suspect he's aware that we've been busy up here, what with the babies announcing themselves. I'll just go down and tell him it's time to come up and meet his new grandchildren.''

''And don't forget Stephen. Wake him if you have to,'' Brace said. ''I want him to be part of this tonight. He needs to share in our happiness.''

And then he bent to Sarah. ''Are you truly all right?'' he asked. His mouth touched hers softly as if he could not bear to leave her side. ''Can I sleep with you tonight?'' he whispered.

She laughed aloud, and he frowned. ''You aren't supposed to laugh at me,'' he said. ''I just want to be in here with you and the babies.''

''Doggone right you're going to be in here. You'll be an expert at changing diapers by morning. I'll guarantee it,'' she told him. ''And yes,'' she whispered in return, ''you can sleep with me, and hold me and tell me how wonderful I am.'' Her smile was wide as she teased him. Teased and tempted him, with her grace and beauty, with the love she bestowed on him.

''You can sleep in my bed,'' she told him tenderly, her eyes holding happiness and desire and the passion of a woman who loved deeply and well. ''Not just for tonight, you understand, Sheriff Caulfield, but for the rest of your life.''

She whispered the words again, as if she would impress them on him for eternity.

''For the rest of your life.''

* * * * *

HHH Harlequin Historicals®
Historical Romantic Adventure!

TRAVEL BACK TO THE FUTURE
FOR ROMANCE—WESTERN-STYLE!
ONLY WITH HARLEQUIN HISTORICALS.

ON SALE JANUARY 2005

TEXAS LAWMAN by Carolyn Davidson

Sarah Murphy will do whatever it takes to save her nephew
from dangerous fortune seekers—including marrying lawman
Blake Caulfield. Can the Lone Star lawman keep them
safe—without losing his heart to the feisty lady?

WHIRLWIND GROOM by Debra Cowan

Desperate to avenge the murder of her parents, all trails lead
Josie Webster to Whirlwind, Texas, much to the chagrin of
charming sheriff Davis Lee Holt. Let the games begin as
Davis Lee tries to ignore the beautiful seamstress who stirs
both his suspicions and his desires....

ON SALE FEBRUARY 2005

PRAIRIE WIFE by Cheryl St.John

Jesse and Amy Shelby find themselves drifting apart after
the devastating death of their young son. Can they put
their grief behind them and renew their deep and abiding
love—before it's too late?

THE UNLIKELY GROOM by Wendy Douglas

Stranded by her brother in a rough-and-rugged Alaskan
gold town, Ashlynne Mackenzie is forced to rely on the
kindness of saloon owner Lucas Templeton. But kindness
has nothing to do with Lucas's urges to both protect the
innocent woman and to claim her for his own.

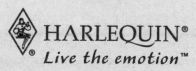